FORBIDDEN PASSION

"It's not the years between us that cause the distance, Alexandra," Burke said.

"I will not think about it," Alexandra said. "We have this moment, this time, and while we're here I will not think about anything else." She put her arms around his neck and drew him down to her.

"Oh, Alex," he whispered, "you are so lovely. I think now I have lived only to see you, to be with you again."

Harper
Monogram

The Highwayman

Doreen Owens Malek

HarperPaperbacks
A Division of HarperCollinsPublishers

This is a work of fiction. The characters, incidents, and dialogues are products of the author's imagination and are not to be construed as real. Any resemblance to actual events or persons, living or dead, is entirely coincidental.

HarperPaperbacks   *A Division of* HarperCollins*Publishers*
               10 East 53rd Street, New York, N.Y. 10022

Cover illustration by Diane Sivavec

First printing: April 1993

Printed in the United States of America

HarperPaperbacks, HarperMonogram, and colophon are trademarks of HarperCollins*Publishers*

❖ 10 9 8 7 6 5 4 3 2 1

1

An obedient woman is like a jewel unto her family...
—Walsh,
Elizabethan Commentaries

London, England
March, 1599

The young woman burst into the silent study, breathless and unable to speak.

Her uncle looked up from his writing, quill in hand, and his complexion reddened in the candle-light when he saw her dishabille. "Alexandra, what is the meaning of this?" he demanded. "You look like a charwoman with your hair about your face and your garments in disarray. Compose yourself!"

"Uncle," Alex gasped, "is it true?"

He sat back in his chair and folded his arms across his doublet. She saw from his resolute expression that it was.

"Annie says that you will send me to the sisters at St. Mary's whilst you journey to Ireland with my lord of Essex," Alex said with a wail.

"Annie's wagging tongue will lose her her situation," Philip Cummings said. "One less lady's maid matters little to me."

"But you said I might abide here at Stockton House while you were about the queen's business," Alex said, overlooking Annie's fate in concern for her own.

"I have remembered me on that subject," Philip replied. "I cannot leave my brother's only child unsupervised and in the care of servants."

"Then take me with you," Alex said. "I've heard talk of your destination, Inverary Castle near Dublin where my lord of Carberry resides. It is thought a fair place, set in a green countryside and suitable for gentlefolk."

Her uncle snorted. "Don't be foolish, child. An expedition to suppress an armed rebellion is no place for a woman. A simpleton would not consider it."

"Just take me on the ship," Alex said. "I will eat little, sleep in a small space. I will be good and quiet. Once there I will stay within the castle walls and make myself useful. . . ."

"You will go to the nuns," her uncle said. "Annie will pack for you this evening and Luke will see you to the convent gates in the morning." He looked back down at his desk. "That is all," he said, dismissing her.

Alex's eyes filled with tears of frustration. "I will not go to the convent! Uncle, it is insupportable!"

"You'll do as you're told, miss," he snapped, raising his eyes to hers again, "or instead of stopping there whilst I'm away you'll take the veil for good!"

Alex gulped, fear tightening the muscles in her dry throat. He could do it. He was her only living relative, and women without means or protectors frequently wound up in nunneries, dedicating their lives to God when no one else would have them. Philip would hand a bag of sovereigns through the grille to the mother superior, and Alex would disappear inside, swallowed up by a religious community as corrupt as the late King Henry who had "reformed" it.

Alex bit her lip, stifling a sob. Oh, why had her parents died and left her at the mercy of a testy bachelor who disdained her? He lived only to advance himself in Queen Elizabeth's eyes. This Irish venture, commanded by her favorite, Essex, the stepson of her lost love, Robert Dudley, was Philip's best chance of currying favor. He was not going to let a little thing like an unmarried ward interfere with his plans. So Alex was to be shut up with the nuns while Philip danced attendance on the aging queen's cavalier. She was to scrub floors and recite matins while he was trudging through the peat bogs and shooting rebels out of trees.

"Well?" Philip said, interrupting her reverie.

Alex pressed her lips together firmly, making a decision.

"I'll ready my things at once." She dropped a half curtsy to placate him while her mind raced.

"I thought you might agree," her uncle said as he returned his attention to his correspondence.

Alex withdrew to the hall and then stopped short, closing her eyes. She had no more intention of obeying her uncle than she had of turning spy for the Spanish ambassador. But a pretense of acquiescence would give her time to formulate a plan. She lifted her skirts and hurried back to her chamber.

Annie was waiting there, pacing and crying. Alex dismissed her. She didn't want to implicate the servant in whatever she might do. She sat down to think.

Two hours later Alex rose and stole into the hall. All was quiet. She slipped down through the darkened house and out onto the lawn, which was flooded with spring moonlight. She hurried to the stables and past the groom's boy, Luke, who was sleeping in the tack room. The horses whinnied and stirred at her approach, but she managed without waking Luke to remove a set of his clothes from the chest where he kept them. She took a leather jerkin, homespun breeches, shoes, and a leather cap. Then she ran back to her room, her heart pounding all the way.

Once there, she changed into the horsey-smelling clothes and tried in vain to tuck her heavy hair under the cap. She quickly decided the hair had to go and hacked away at her thick auburn tresses with Annie's sewing shears, glancing down sorrowfully as the shorn locks gathered at her feet. When she was done she jammed the cap on her head and stared at herself in the silvered looking glass.

She had done well. She was slim enough to pass for a boy, and the haircut gave her the look of a ragged adolescent, a page or a court messenger. She gathered up a few necessary items and tossed them into a bag, which she slung over her shoulder.

The *Silver Swan* set sail at dawn for Ireland. Her uncle would be on the ship, and so would she. By the time she was discovered, it would be too late to turn back.

Philip wouldn't check to see if she was leaving for the convent. He regarded her as an annoyance, but it would never occur to him that she would do something so outrageous. Her problem now was to get to the ship and stay on it until it was well out of the harbor. Anything was preferable to being buried alive in a cloister.

Alex sighed. She realized that her task would be a lot more difficult than it had seemed at first.

The London streets at night were not safe for any foot traveler. They were thick with cutpurses and criminals of every type. The quays where the boat was docked were the worst of all. Taverns spilled roistering, drunken patrons into the offal-strewn streets, and sailors, many of them impressed into service from prisons, were hardly better than the thieves who preyed upon them. Alex would have to negotiate this battlefield to reach the ship, and once there, she would have to find a way to get on board and remain there.

She had an idea that might facilitate her passage. She left her room once more and went down to Philip's study. He had retired, but she knew he left the door unlocked to enable the servants to start a fire the next morning. She slipped inside and lit a candle from the hall sconce, hoping no one would see the light.

She knew where her uncle kept his letters. She opened a drawer in his desk and shoved aside quills and folded missives until she saw one with the queen's seal, the scripted *E* and *R* entwined in the wax. The seal was split, since Philip had read the note. Alex seized the letter and held the wax to the burning candle, melting it enough to reseal the note as if it were new but leaving Elizabeth's insignia intact. Satisfied with her handiwork, she shut the drawer quietly and fled with her prize held away from her body, to let the wax cool and harden.

On the way out of the house she stopped in the kitchens and took a leg of mutton and a round of bread from the larder, wrapped them in a napkin, and stashed them in her pack. The she slipped out through the pantry and headed once more to the stables.

Sunbeam was her favorite roan mare and Alex rode her almost daily. The horse nickered when she drew near. Alex shushed her and led her out of her stall through the paddock door at the back so she would not have to pass Luke again.

The ride to London from Stockton House was about two miles along the Thames. The night was warm for early spring and the moonlight bright enough to see by; she passed no one on the road. As she neared the town she could see the distant outline of Essex House, the riverside estate that Lord Essex had inherited from his stepfather, Leicester. It was below Fleet Street along the Strand, within view of Whitehall, and its wide lawns sloped down to the water where boat taxis dislodged passengers at a private gate. After going through a warren of cottages and inns, she reached her destination, the town home of Ronald Feeley, a solicitor friend of her uncle's. Feeley had a daughter Alex's age, Caroline, and the two girls often rode together. Caroline would recognize Sunbeam and return the horse to Stockton.

By then, everyone would know what Alex had done.

Alex kissed the blaze on the horse's nose and tied her to the post bordering Feeley's garden. She left her contentedly munching grass while, inside the house, everyone slept.

Alex took a deep breath and stepped out of the sheltering darkness. It was only a mile more to the docks, but it was through the part of town she feared most. Shoreditch, where actors and other disreputables abounded, disgorged people into the shadow of London Bridge nightly, and Cheapside, where they patronized many taverns, loomed as an obstacle in her path. She put her head down and walked rapidly down the cobbled streets toward the water. Prostitutes whispered to her from doorways as she passed, and she took care to avoid the traffic from the alehouses. She made her way as unobtrusively as she could while proceeding at top speed. She tried not to inhale too deeply, as tenants had tossed garbage from windows into the alleys and the gutters ran with refuse of all kinds. The warrens got narrower as she neared the river, the wooden buildings crowding the passage so closely that three men could hardly stand shoulder to shoulder across the road. It was here that villainous creatures sprang from shadows. Twice, hands reached out for Alex, but she was nimble enough to escape. She sprinted the last few yards to the ship, which she identified from its fluttering flag, and then paused to plan her next move.

The *Silver Swan* was still being loaded for the journey, and as she'd expected, there was a guard at the plank, watching everyone who came and went. Essex had been dispatched for his trip that very day by cheering London crowds, but he might not yet be on board. Alex couldn't tell if the guard was a sailor or someone from the earl's retinue, but either way she had to take her chances.

She marched up to him and said, lowering her voice several octaves to a shaky tenor, "Message from Her Majesty the Queen for my lord of Essex."

The guard, looking bored with the proceedings, extended his hand for the letter.

Alex slapped it into his palm with all the authority she could muster.

He examined the seal by the light of a torch fixed to the ship's hull and then tucked it under his arm.

"I'll see His Lordship gets it," he said.

Alex's heart sank. For a moment her mind went blank, and then she added hastily, "My sovereign lady requests the favor of a reply immediately. I am instructed to return with it."

The guard sighed, handed the letter back to her, and waved her past him. Alex almost ran up onto the deck, past sailors carting bales and boxes. Then she darted down the companionway and into a cabin.

She had no idea where she was; she only knew that she was alone.

She leaned her head against the rough planks of the hull and forced her breathing to return to normal. Below her in the hold she could hear the thud and thump of the supplies being stored. When she felt calmer, she took stock of her situation.

It was almost time for the shifts to change. It was likely that the guard would stumble off the ship and into the Mermaid Tavern in Bread Street or some other hole, leaving his successor to deal with the messenger he'd permitted on board.

In the meantime, she had to find a place to hide.

The cabin was bare of convenient cubby-holes. When she was sure the coast was clear she tried another, in which she found an empty arrow chest. She was small enough to fit inside along with her pack. She made herself as tiny as possible and lowered the lid, putting her nose and mouth to the chinks between the slats for air.

Alex was sure she wouldn't be able to sleep, but the trip and her anxiety had exhausted her. The muffled cries of the seamen calling to one another and the gentle rocking of the boat at anchor soon lulled her to into slumber.

When she awoke again, the swaying of the floor and the roiling of her stomach told her she was at sea.

Kevin Burke shifted his position in the elm tree and peered more intently down at Inverary Castle in the distance. Something was up with the English. Carberry's men had been bustling about for the last ten days; the bustle suggested that some new reinforcements from London were expected.

Burke climbed to a higher branch and twisted impatiently, wishing that he could take action. He had sent an urgent message to Tyrone, his chieftain, but was still awaiting a response. Communication among the rebels was poor because of the difficulty of the Irish terrain and the necessity for secrecy. He was loath to act without instructions, but inactivity was making him restless. If he didn't hear from Tyrone soon, he would be strongly tempted to take his men and try to rescue his brother Aidan on his own.

Aidan Burke had been in English hands at the castle for a week now, and every time Kevin thought of his younger sibling languishing in the Inverary dungeon, he wanted to kick the walls down single-handedly. Years of fighting the British had taught him the virtues of caution, however. The English weren't stupid, but they were regimented, and the rebels' strongest weapon had always been surprise. They would be expecting him now, so he must wait.

He swung to the lower branches of the tree and then to the ground, moving with the peculiar grace common to big men. He was a prime target for the enemy because he was easy to spot, standing a head taller than most of his band and with shoulders so wide that his hips seemed nonexistent. His glossy, sandy hair fell over his deep-set blue eyes. He was clean-shaven, defying current fashion, and had a long jaw and high cheekbones, which gave his face a fierce, almost primitive aspect. When he frowned, as he did now, he was truly a frightening prospect. The smile, which displayed splendid teeth and an alluring light in his pale eyes, came far less often. For an Irish patriot in the waning years of Queen Elizabeth's reign there was little enough to smile about.

Burke walked to his horse and leapt onto it bareback, checking the knife sheathed at his waist. Brigands were known to fall out of trees onto the backs of hapless riders, and being ready for anything was a matter of habit. His woolen tunic was spattered with raindrops from the overhanging leaves as he rode back toward his camp, and even at midday the forest was dense enough to shelter pockets of mist, which rose to envelop him. He kicked the horse gently with his skin boots, picking up speed as he went along trails he could have followed blindfolded. He had learned to ride almost before he could walk, and these woods were as familiar to him as his brother's voice—which he might never hear again if he didn't take some action soon.

Aidan Burke had been captured on a scouting mission, when he'd ventured too close to the castle. Now it looked as if Lord Carberry was preparing to lay in more English troops, which made the prospect of rescuing Aidan even dimmer than when he had been taken. Kevin scowled and prodded the horse for more speed.

His mood was grim as he entered the camp and headed for his tent. The men standing about the cookfires, all young and fit and restless, turned their heads to follow his progress. Burke ignored them, sliding from his horse while it was still moving. He handed the reins to a boy who led the horse away as he motioned for Rory Dunne, his lieutenant, to join him inside.

Rory waited for Burke to speak, watching his leader with the eager attention of a recently elevated second in command.

"They're expecting new arrivals at the castle," Burke said in Gaelic. Rory nodded.

"Set up a watch, eight-hour shifts. I want somebody overlooking the castle every minute of the day," Burke ordered. "Any change that takes place might help us, and we have to know what's going on in order to take advantage of it."

"Right." Rory turned to go.

"And Rory?"

Dunne turned back to him.

"Take the first shift yourself."

"I will," Rory said. He disappeared through the flap.

Burke followed him out with his eyes. Rory was a good lad, but Kevin missed his brother.

Alex lay perfectly still in the trunk, afraid to move. Her fear was her undoing, because while she was still trying to work up her nerve, one of the seamen entered the cabin and attempted to shift the chest. She froze as he grunted with the effort and then, muttering to himself at the unexpected weight, hauled up the lid of her hiding place.

Alex cringed as he stared in shock at the stowaway. He remained speechless as she unfolded herself from the trunk, standing unsteadily before him.

"Cor, blimey!" he finally exclaimed, staring at her clothes, her hair. "Wot's this?"

Alex was trying to think of something intelligent to say when her uncle strode through the door. Right behind him was Robert Devereaux, second earl of Essex.

Alex closed her eyes. She was in for it now, and no mistake.

The sailor jumped back in the presence of his superiors, unsure of what he should do and fearful that he would be blamed for this unexpected development.

Philip's eyes widened as he took in the sight of his niece, hair shorn and dressed as a boy, standing before him on the deck of the ship when she was supposed to be devoting herself to prayer in a cloister. His face turned purple and seemed to swell as Alex contemplated throwing herself into the waves at the earliest opportunity.

"Well, well," Essex said, stepping around Cummings and examining Alex from head to toe. He waved the sailor toward the door, and the boy fled gratefully.

"A most imaginative costume, I daresay," Essex said. "I take it you know this young person, Stockton?"

Alex's uncle found his voice and said in a hideously controlled tone, "My niece, Alexandra, my lord."

"Your niece indeed!" Essex said, highly amused.

He moved closer and tipped up Alex's chin with his hand. "Look at me, girl."

Alex complied, forcing her eyes to meet his.

She could see immediately why Queen Elizabeth had forgiven Devereaux his parentage in light of his charms. He was the son of the queen's cousin and former romantic rival, Lettice Knollys, the lady who had married Elizabeth's one true love. But the old woman had overlooked the youthful transgressions of the mother and made the son her chosen cavalier, giving him command of this Irish expedition over others more experienced and qualified for it. Alex met his penetrating gaze, feeling his power entrance her as it had entranced their sovereign.

He was imperially tall, with gleaming russet hair and fine dark eyes. His whole being bespoke swagger and arrogance; it was said that he alone in the kingdom could refute the queen and live to tell the tale. His black velvet doublet was slashed with purple silk, his hose shot through with silver thread, and on his head he wore a hat trimmed with a jeweled band and topped with an ostrich feather. Like the queen's pirate, Francis Drake, he wore a small gold hoop in his ear.

"Where have you been hiding this choice cub, Stockton?" he asked. With light fingers on her chin, he turned Alex's head slightly and examined her face. "Why, even with her hair butchered, 'tis plain she'll soon be a beauty."

Philip, furious but stymied by Devereaux's admiration of his niece, said nothing.

"How old are you, lass?" Essex asked.

Alex looked at a point beyond his shoulder. "Seventeen," she said.

"And what are you doing here, pray tell?" Essex inquired, obviously entertained.

Alex glanced at Philip, who glared back at her stonily.

"My uncle was going to leave me with the nuns at St. Mary's whilst he was gone, and I . . ." She stopped.

"Could not bear the thought of it?" Essex suggested.

She nodded. "Yes, m'lord."

"Quite right, too. To smother such a flower in a convent, even for a short time, 'twould be a pity. How did you get on board?"

Alex swallowed.

"Speak up, lass."

She might as well tell the truth. Nothing could make her position much worse at this point.

"I rode to London dressed as a boy and went down to the quay with a letter of mine uncle's from the queen," she said rapidly. "I had resealed it and I used it to get past the guard."

"As clever as you are bonnie, I'll warrant," Essex said. "Proceed."

"Then I hid in this empty arrow chest until I was discovered this morning."

Essex burst out laughing. "God's teeth, you have

spirit! I like to see a woman with mettle. Your cub is to be admired, Stockton."

Cummings' expression conveyed that he disagreed heartily. "I will deal with her, my lord, in my own way," he said. "You have my word on it."

"Oh, no," Essex said. "No punishment for this pretty child, I forbid it. We can ill afford to quell such courage when we find it." He raised Alex's hand to his lips and kissed the back of it, then turned it over and kissed the palm. Alex jumped as she felt the hot tip of his tongue sear her flesh.

"I am your servant, lass. Be mindful of it," he said, and favored her with the devastating smile that had turned the most powerful woman in the world into a jealous harridan. He turned and walked to the low cabin door, then wheeled and faced her uncle.

"Heed me, Stockton. No hard duties for this filly. If I hear of it, I will be most displeased." He strode out into the companionway, and the sound of his footsteps faded away.

Alex glanced at her uncle and, for the first time in her life, felt almost sorry for him. He was so clearly torn between his desire to retaliate for what she had done and his powerful need to ingratiate himself with the queen's favorite. The latter impulse won, as she had known it would.

"I do not wish to see your face again for the rest

of the voyage," Philip said in a tense, modulated tone, careful to keep his voice down. "Stay in this cabin and out of the way of the sailors on the vessel. Meals will be brought to you, and I will see that you are supplied with tasks to be done. Everyone else on board has to work, and so shall you. Obey me in this or I will not be responsible for the consequences."

He turned on his heel and stalked from the cabin. Alex waited until she was sure he was gone before sagging against the hull, grateful that she had survived the encounter.

Cummings was as good as his word. For the remainder of the journey, Alex did not encounter him. Mounds of needlework, sailors' clothing and stockings, and even a rent sail, were deposited outside her door in the morning and picked up again at night. She sewed relentlessly in between bouts of seasickness that left her spent and shaken. By the time they docked, at dawn on the sixth day, no one was happier to make landfall than she was.

She sat in the cabin and listened to everyone else disembark, wondering if she was to be left on board while the rest of the travelers went to the castle. Then her uncle finally appeared, gesturing wordlessly for her to follow him. She picked up her small bundle and followed him up to the deck and then off the ship.

She would never forget her first sight of Ireland. It was early morning, and the mist was rising from the water, burning off to reveal a landscape so lush and flowery that it caused her to stop short and catch her breath. She had many times witnessed the astonishing miracle of an English spring, but this was new to her experience, a picture of Eden as Eve must have seen it. No wonder the natives clung to this place so tenaciously, she thought. It was truly lovely.

"Don't tarry, Alexandra," her uncle said. "My patience is not to be tested."

A procession wound through the distance ahead of them. She didn't know how far it was to the castle and decided it was wiser not to ask.

To her surprise, she was led to a horse, which she mounted in silence. She cantered along in the rear of the caravan next to her uncle's sorrel for several miles, until they topped a slight rise and she saw the castle nestled in the valley spread out at their feet.

"Inverary," her uncle said briefly, as if it needed explanation. "We shall arrive before noon."

Alex relaxed just a bit. This was practically the first remark he'd addressed to her since he had discovered her on the ship.

"There's a woman at the castle," Rory announced.

Burke stared at him doubtfully. It was midafternoon, and Rory had just arrived back from his watch.

"I'm sure of it," Rory insisted. "We saw about

fifty people come off the ship. They were met by Carberry's detachment with horses and taken to Inverary. A couple of hours later a woman was out walking on the leads."

"How do you know it was a woman?" Burke asked.

"She was wearing a skirt," Rory said, gesturing in a circle around his hips to indicate hoops. "And a headdress, you know, with a veil. Unless the English are even stranger than we think they are, one of the new arrivals is female."

Burke absorbed this information in silence. Since the death of Carberry's wife two years before, the castle had been populated solely by men.

"Do you think the old fool got remarried?" Burke asked.

Rory shrugged. "Anything's possible. I just thought you should know about it."

"Watch her movements. Find out when we can snatch her."

"Snatch her?"

"Think, man," Burke said impatiently. "She's got to be a wife, daughter, some kind of relative, or else what is she doing here in the back of the beyond, carted all the way from England? She'd be valuable as a hostage."

Rory said nothing, watching Burke as he concluded, "It might just be we've found a way to get Aidan back."

* * *

Alex lifted the stiff linen coif off her neck and stared out through the castle window across the rolling Irish countryside. Her uncle had insisted that she be properly dressed as soon as they arrived, so Lord Carberry had given her his dead wife's wardrobe, which had been folded into trunks for months. It was in the Spanish style, very much the vogue, with wide farthingales and high ruff collars. Despite having been packed with scented pomanders and pressed between silken covers, all of the clothes smelled musty. But Alex had done the best she could, not wishing to irritate her uncle further by prancing about in Luke's leggings. Carberry had not commented on her presence or her ill-conceived hairdo. He acted as if she'd been expected and took command of the situation graciously, as only an English gentleman could do. Alex was content to fade into the background and to let her uncle attend to business. But the gorgeous countryside beckoned. After the close quarters of the ship, she yearned for a long, leisurely walk. The men, preoccupied with their plans for the Irish, seemed to have forgotten completely that she was in residence.

She would bide her time and escape the castle walls as soon as she could.

Alex's opportunity came several days later, when the guard assigned to her was at dinner and dusk was falling over the Inverary valley. Essex, her uncle, and Lord Carberry had ridden off at dawn and weren't expected back until the morrow. Chafing at the bonds of her uncle's orders, which restricted her to the keep, Alex changed into Luke's clothes again and waited for her chance. When some local horsemen left the castle to return to the neighboring village of Carberry's retainers, Alex quietly fell in with them and walked across the drawbridge. She was assumed to be one of the grooms and passed out of the gates unmolested.

Delighted with her success, she broke into a run, flinging her arms wide to embrace the soft mist and the falling night.

Her happiness was extremely short-lived. She had not come a quarter mile from the castle when she was seized roughly from behind and dragged into a thicket. She was bound and gagged as she struggled wildly, unable to make a sound loud enough to attract attention. A rough woven blindfold was tied round her eyes as she kicked helplessly. Her assailant then lifted her and tossed her across a horse as if she were a sack of meal. He climbed up behind her, taking off at a breakneck speed that set the animal's hooves pounding beneath her.

The ride was short but wild and desperately fast. Alex barely had time to realize she'd been kidnapped before the rider stopped abruptly and hauled her off the horse. She stumbled and fell to her knees. She was trying to get her bearings when strong hands lifted her as if she were a straw puppet and set her on her feet.

The blindfold was removed, and she was staring up at a shaggy-haired giant dressed in a homespun tunic with a dagger thrust into his belt. He looked about thirty years in age, with wide shoulders and long, slim legs clad to the knee in hand-sewn boots. The top of her head barely reached his chest.

Alex almost fainted with fear. Why hadn't she obeyed her uncle?

He might not be very kind to her, but at least he was of normal size and didn't look as though he skinned his enemies with his bare hands. She had heard that the Irish painted themselves blue and went into battle naked; this one was dressed but otherwise looked capable of almost anything.

Burke examined Rory's prize and then turned to his lieutenant.

"What the devil ails you, Rory?" he said in Gaelic, not bothering to conceal his disgust. "This is a *boy*!"

2

Almost all (Celts) are of tall stature, fair and ruddy, terrible for the fierceness of their eyes, fond of quarreling and of overbearing insolence . . .

—Ammianus Marcellinus,
Historae

  The rebel band gathered around to view the spectacle, and Alex stared at the ground, afraid to meet their eyes. They weren't as big as the one who had spoken, but they were all rough hewn and similarly clad. The younger man, who was evidently her kidnapper, replied in the same coarse language, which Alex decided must be what her uncle called Erse. It sounded to her like fits of coughing.

  "It's the woman I told you about," Rory said. "I've been watching her for five days straight, I ought to know. She's just dressed like a boy, Burke."

Rory reached for the neckline of Alex's tunic to prove it, but a harsh command from the leader stopped him in his tracks. Rory's hand fell away, and he looked chagrined.

Burke moved closer to Alex and stared down at her, his muscular arms crossed upon his massive chest. His eyes moved over her face, then her figure, and Alex felt her face grow hot as he determined her sex for himself. He didn't touch her, but he didn't have to; she felt his gaze burning through her clothes.

"Who are you?" he finally said in English.

Alex was startled at the sound of her native language, but she didn't know how to reply.

Burke seized her roughly under her arms and lifted her off the ground, holding her up to his eye level. "I'll ask you once more," he said in his slightly accented English. "Who are you?"

His blue eyes blazed into hers. She noticed that his lashes were long and thick, an absurdly feminine touch in a man who fairly exuded masculinity. She was terrified, but she knew instinctively that, like his enemy Essex, this towering rebel would respect a show of courage.

"I don't have to tell you anything," she replied defiantly, her voice sounding a lot stronger than she felt.

Burke set her down abruptly. "Right enough,"

he said, circling her as a wolf would a felled deer. "But I don't have to let you live, either."

"You kidnapped me, didn't you?" Alex said. "If you want to use me as a hostage, I'm not much good to you dead."

"You're not much good to me alive if I don't know who the hell you are!"

"Then perhaps you should have determined that before your minion here trussed me up like a prize goose and carried me off !"

The large man's expression darkened, and Alex wished instantly that she had held her tongue. When he bent from the waist to put his eyes on a level with hers, it was plain that he was furious. Alex shrank from him, conscious that he could snap her neck in two with a twist of his hands.

"Now you listen to me, Miss Fine English Lady," he said. His accent was strangely like hers, that of the upper classes, but with a lilt that made it sound almost musical.

Alex stared back at him, willing her knees to stop shaking.

"I'll not believe that the first female to arrive at the castle in two years is a charwoman, dressed up like the Spanish infanta and moving about the grounds with a guard. You have one second to answer my question!"

Alex hesitated an instant too long, and Burke turned from her sharply, barking an order in Gaelic to her kidnapper. The younger man advanced on her with his rope at the ready, and she realized she had to take her chances with the giant.

"Wait! I'll tell you."

The leader looked back at her expectantly.

"I'm Lady Alexandra Cummings, niece of Sir Philip Cummings, scion of Stockton House and my lord Essex's man, special envoy from the queen to Lord Carberry," she recited proudly.

The Irishmen exchanged glances.

"A pretty speech," Burke said after a moment, "but what does it mean? Is your uncle kinsman to the queen?"

Alex nodded.

Rory looked at Burke hopefully. "Her hair is the same color as the English queen's," Rory said in English.

"Her hair is the same color as the queen's wigs," Burke said. "The old hag is as bald as an egg."

Under other circumstances, Alex might have found this comment amusing. It was widely known that Elizabeth's luxuriant red mane was a thing of the past.

"How are you kin to the queen?" Burke demanded.

"By marriage. My aunt, sister to my uncle and my late father, is wed to Henry Howard, the queen's cousin."

Burke considered this. It was close enough. He was well versed in English politics, and the queen was known to be solicitous of her Howard relations. In any event, this Cummings would certainly want his niece back.

"What are you doing in Eire?" Burke demanded.

Alex sighed. "My uncle is my guardian and did not wish to leave me behind in England."

Burke looked skeptical but didn't pursue it. "What are the English plans here?"

"I have no idea," Alex said.

"Did you hear anything of a prisoner at the castle?"

"I myself was a prisoner at the castle," she replied. "They didn't talk to me. I stayed in my room and ate alone. The only person I saw regularly was my guard, and he didn't talk to me either."

Burke studied her, and Alex wondered where he had learned to speak such good English. With the exception of the one called Rory, it was clear that the rest of the men didn't understand her.

"What befell your hair?" Burke asked suddenly.

"It was burned in a fire."

"Why were you outside the castle walls dressed like this?"

"My uncle didn't want me to leave the grounds, and I felt like going for a walk."

"And you just happened to have a set of boy's clothes at hand?" Burke said sarcastically. "Something is not right about you, English miss, and I mean to know what it is." He moved away.

"What are you going to do with me?"

He ignored her as he said something in a low tone to Rory. The leader turned his back, and Rory headed toward her. With her hands still bound behind her there was little she could do to resist, but she struggled futilely.

"Don't you touch me!" she gasped.

Dodging her kicks, Rory scooped her up, strode into a nearby tent, and deposited her on a bundle of skins. A single candle burned on an upturned crate inside, giving feeble illumination to her primitive surroundings.

"Wait!" Alex yelled as Rory walked away, but he gave no indication that he'd heard her.

Time passed, and nothing happened. The rope was cutting into Alex's wrists, her legs were cramped, and fear of the unknown overcame her. She was trying hard not to cry when Burke suddenly appeared, unbuckling his belt and pulling his tunic over his head. Alex looked on in horror as she realized that this was his tent and he was about to undress for the night.

He glanced over at her and read her expression.

"Never fear, my lady," he said. "When I take a fancy to twelve-year-old boys you'll be in danger, not before. All you are to me is a chess piece to trade."

"For what?" she whispered, finally finding her voice.

He didn't answer. Alex watched as he stripped to his leggings. The long ropy muscles in his arms stood out beneath his skin as he reached overhead to drop the tent flap.

"Are you just going to leave me here like this?" Alex demanded.

"Oh, and what would Her Ladyship like?" Burke asked.

The light brown hair on his chest fanned out to cover his flat nipples and then narrowed to a line that disappeared below the waistband of his leggings. The trousers were tight enough to reveal the lean, powerful muscles underneath. Alex swallowed uneasily and looked away.

"I'd like a bath," she said.

"Would you now?" He put his huge hands, twice the size of hers, on his narrow hips and surveyed her with detachment. He seemed bemused.

"Yes, I would. That ruffian who kidnapped me tossed me about on the ground, and I've got dirt in my hair and under my nails and my clothes are filthy."

"Ah, shall we call one of the maids to wait upon you, then?" Burke said.

Alex gave him a black look. "All I need is some hot water and soap, and well you know it."

"That will have to do, since we're sorely lacking in servants here," Burke replied. He left the tent and returned some minutes later with a length of rough linen and a gray shapeless lump, both of which he dumped in her lap.

"What's that?" Alex said, looking down at the greasy ball with distaste.

"Lye and tallow soap," Burke replied. "We don't have fine-milled beauty soap here. Rory will be in with a tub and hot water in a bit." He turned away.

"Aren't you going to untie my hands?"

He returned to her and slashed through her bonds with his knife. Then he held the blade under her nose.

"No tricks, my lady fair, or you'll be making a closer acquaintance with this, I'm thinking."

Alex closed her eyes to block the sight of it, and by the time she opened them again, he was gone.

Rory entered shortly thereafter with a wooden tub and a pail of hot water. He carried in two more buckets of cold water to make a tepid mixture. "Don't be long. The tub is needed." He handed her a clean linen shift, his face expressionless. It was clear that he disapproved of providing this comfort for their captive, but Burke was giving the orders.

Alex waited until he was gone and then stripped off Luke's clothes, which were by now almost in tatters. She sank gratefully into the soothing water, which was just deep enough to cover her thighs. The homemade soap did not provide much lather, but it cleansed well and had a clean, piny fragrance. She lost herself in the pure pleasure of bathing, momentarily forgetting her circumstances.

* * *

Burke walked around the silent camp, giving the woman time to complete her bath. Rory had balked at supplying luxuries for her, but Burke intended to see that she was well treated. If the English knew that she was not being abused, they would be more likely to surrender Aidan in exchange for her. In the morning he would send word to her uncle.

Burke had no reason to suspect that she was lying about her identity, and her arrival at the castle had provided him with a useful pawn. His major task right now was to keep her safe from his own men, some of whom hated the British so indiscriminately that they might vent their feelings on her. It was a testy situation, but he was confident that he could handle it. His hold over his men was a strong one, and one of long standing. He watched the clouds drift past the moon for a while longer, and then went back to his tent.

He pulled back the flap and then froze in his tracks. The woman was not finished, as he'd expected, but just rising to rinse herself off. Bathed in flickering candlelight, she was silhouetted against the canvas backdrop of the tent in all her naked loveliness.

Burke could not tear his eyes away. She bore very little resemblance to the twelve-year-old boy of his earlier reference. Her pale skin was glowing, stained pink from the heat of the bathwater, which was running down her slender arms as she lifted them to douse her hair. Her small, perfectly formed breasts were as round as apples, the tan nipples puckering in the cold air. She had a narrow waist that tapered to a dark red tangle of hair at the apex of her thighs and the delicate, stripling legs of a fawn. When she turned he saw the damp curls clinging to the back of her neck, and his eyes traced the line of her narrow, graceful back down to the dimple at the base of her spine.

Burke stepped back abruptly, swallowing hard. His heart was beating painfully, and he felt a familiar tightening in his groin. It had been a while since he'd had a woman—they were all back at the main camp, deep in the countryside—and he knew he was vulnerable. But she'd stirred more than just a basic need in him; he felt shaken and disturbed, unsettled by the sight of her.

Lord, she was beautiful. He wished fervently that he had not seen her, as he would need objectivity in his future dealings with her.

He had just lost it.

When Alex awoke in the morning, she was alone and tied up again, a slipknot fixed firmly around her ankle and secured to a peg hammered into the dirt floor. She could hear the murmur of voices outside the tent and smell breakfast cooking, which made her realize how hungry she was.

Her stomach rumbled and her mouth watered, but when Rory appeared with a clay pot filled with some sort of stew, she turned her face away resolutely.

Rory set the pot on the floor within her reach. When Alex saw that he was about to leave without a word, she called after him, "Where's your leader?"

Rory looked over his shoulder briefly, favored her with a stare, and left the tent.

So much for that, Alex thought.

Several hours passed, during which Alex could glimpse the men striding past the tent purposefully, none paying the slightest attention to their unwilling guest. It did not improve her spirits to realize that she seemed to be the only woman in the camp. When the warmth of the sun beating down on the tent told her that it was about noon, Burke suddenly appeared in its entrance, blocking the light like a stormcloud and filling the space with his unmistakable presence.

"Starving, is it?" he said to her, his alert gaze taking in the cold portion of stew, now congealed under a layer of fat.

"What are you going to do with me?" Alex demanded.

"Cannot you say anything else?" He squatted next to her and picked up the bowl of stew.

Alex eyed him warily, afraid of what she knew was coming next. In the bright daylight, his amber hair was shot through with golden sunstreaks, and his eyes were the warm blue of an August sky. When he dipped his fingers into the pot and extracted a large lump of cold meat, she clamped her lips shut and glared at him defiantly.

He responded by pinching her nose closed with the thumb and forefinger of his free hand and waiting. When she finally gasped, unable to hold her breath any longer, he shoved the meat into her open mouth.

She coughed and spat it out.

Burke retrieved the meat, now covered with dirt, and held it to her lips again.

"Please," she moaned, her eyes filling with tears. "Please don't force me."

"Will you eat, then?" He riveted her with his stare.

"Yes, damn you," she replied, looking away from him in defeat.

"I'll see that this is heated." He rose and tossed the scrap he held through the flap of the tent. Alex saw one of the dogs that hung around the camp run over and scoop it up avidly.

"I hope my lord of Essex comes with a hundred men and quarters all of you!" she yelled as he disappeared through the flap of the tent.

Alex sat miserably, nursing her injured pride, until Burke returned with a steaming bowl and a slice of seeded bread. He handed them to her and sat crosslegged on the floor while she ate grudgingly, taking small bites and chewing as slowly as possible.

"What is this meat?" she asked, unable to identify it.

"Coinin."

"Coinin?"

"Rabbit."

The mixture didn't taste like rabbit stew, but she didn't argue the point.

He studied her without expression as she got it all down and then proffered a flask from the depths of his homespun tunic.

"What's that?" she asked suspiciously.

"Have a nip. It will settle you."

"What is it?"

"Uisce beatha," he said. "The water of life," he added, translating from the Gaelic.

Thirsty enough for nearly anything, she took the flask from him and downed a healthy slug. Then she sputtered helplessly, spraying him with a fine mist of fluid.

"That's brandywine!"

"Whiskey," he corrected, taking a belt himself.

"You tricked me."

"Not at all," he said as he put it away. "I said it would soothe your stomach, and so it will."

"I don't need a nostrum, I need an explanation of exactly what I'm doing here!"

He stood and took her empty bowl with him.

"You made me eat because I'm no good as a hostage if I starve to death. You think you've won, don't you? But this isn't over yet!"

He started to walk away.

"Where did you learn to speak English?" she called after him.

"Where did you learn to be such a *soigh*?" he said, using a Gaelic word she didn't understand.

"What does that mean?" she demanded, suspecting the worst.

"I thought Englishwomen were quiet and ladified."

"Like their queen?" Alex asked, smiling thinly.

He sighed.

"Maybe you picked the wrong Englishwoman."

"Any one would do. They are as alike as pebbles on the shore to me."

"Have you told my uncle that I'm here?"

"Have you not noticed that you're talking to yourself? If you don't let up with that yammering I'll have to gag you, so have a care and be still." He left.

If Alex could have found anything to throw, she would have thrown it, but the floor around her was as empty as her hopes.

That evening there was some sort of meeting among the rebels. Alex could hear them all talking in their incomprehensible language as they sat around the campfire, the flames casting shadows on the tent. She wondered if the leader—Burke, he was called— had presented his ransom demand to her uncle. The thought did not exactly cheer her, though, as she had reason to suspect that Philip Cummings might not be all that eager to get her back.

She knew that she must conceal that doubt from her captors. To insure her safety, it was essential they continue to believe she was valuable. What puzzled her more was why she had been taken. The Irish had been battling the English for a long time; why this kidnapping now? What did Carberry or Essex have that Burke wanted? He had mentioned chess, so he must be thinking of a trade.

Alex tugged on the knot encircling her leg, and it gave a fraction of an inch. She had been working on it all day, but it felt as if it had been tied by Hercules. What she really needed was a wedge, something to insert between the coils and loosen them.

When Rory appeared with the evening meal she watched him put the bowl on the floor and then fold his arms.

"Don't worry, I'll eat it," she said to him wearily. "I don't want another feeding session with your chief."

He stood watching her until she picked up the bowl and began to consume its contents, which tasted quite similar to her earlier repast. Alex bided her time, eating steadily, until Rory walked idly over to the tent opening and looked out of it. While his gaze was occupied elsewhere, she held the clay bowl over her head and hurled it to the floor, where it exploded loudly. Rory turned at the sound and then glared at her, disgusted by her apparent clumsiness and the resultant mess.

"I'm sorry," Alex said, doing her best to appear meek as she glanced down at the bond that prevented her from moving to clear away the debris.

Rory stalked out of the tent, and as soon as he was gone Alex scooped up the biggest, sharpest shard of crockery within her reach and concealed it behind her back. Rory returned quickly with another portion of food, handed it to her grudgingly, and then proceeded to clean up the floor while she consumed the stew. By the time she was finished he was done also, and he left without a word.

Alex's heart was beating so loudly she was sure it would be heard and draw attention to her. Rory couldn't have noticed that one of the pieces of the destroyed pot was missing, but she was afraid to take the shard out and use it, since any of the men could walk back into the tent without warning and discover her sawing away at the rope. As anxious as she was to get started, it was more prudent to wait until everyone was asleep.

It seemed an eternity before Burke entered the tent and began to disrobe, removing his tunic and glancing over at her. Again she was struck by the massiveness of his shoulders and torso, the sheer brute strength of his arms and hands. She shivered inwardly but forced herself to hold his gaze steadily.

"Is there something your ladyship requires?" he asked sarcastically, raising his thick brows. He was as fair-skinned as the rest of his followers, but so tanned that he looked dark, which made his eyes all the paler by contrast.

"I require that you let me go," Alex replied.

"You are a tedious talker, my lady," he replied, tossing his pelt of skins onto the floor and stretching out on it, clad only in his tight woven leggings and skin boots. His pantherlike grace in movement did nothing to dispel her fears. If she twitched the wrong way, he would be on her in an instant, and she knew it. "You want a bit of variety in speech, it livens up a dull day." He crossed his arms under his head and closed his eyes.

"You won't get away with this."

"You'd never ken what I plan to get away with, and more," he said, without opening his eyes.

"A savage like you will never outsmart my uncle."

"Savage, am I?" he countered. "As compared to who, the civilized English with their civilized royalty? Old King Henry, too busy murdering his wives to run the country? The boy Edward, whose ministers persecuted the Catholics; his sister Mary, who purged the new religion from her realm by burning so many heretics her own people called her Bloody Mary? And now Elizabeth, who beheads any who disagree with her and plants their heads on Tower Bridge to rot as an example? If that's civilized, I'll be savage, and grateful."

This was the most Alex had heard out of him since she'd met him, and she was momentarily stunned into silence. She found her voice only after a long moment.

"When Carberry's men finally find you, they won't miss," she said.

"Carberry's men have been missing me for years," he replied, unperturbed.

"My uncle is very fond of me."

"I don't see him pelting after you."

"He's . . . he's probably planning an attack, that takes time. And when he finds out what's been done to me . . ."

Burke opened one eye and turned his head toward her slightly. "And what's been done to you? Are you hungry or cold? Have you been ravished or beaten, mistreated in any way?"

"I'm tied up like a dog!" Alex wailed.

"My dogs are much better behaved. Go to sleep."

Further attempts to elicit information failed, and Alex watched him fall asleep with remarkable ease. She waited until his chest was rising and falling in an even cadence. Then she took out the piece of pottery and began to fray the rope on her leg with the ragged edge, working until her wrists ached from the repetitive motion. She kept it up relentlessly, her fingers going numb, until finally the unraveling hemp snapped and fell away, leaving her leg free and the tether still attached to the peg.

As her gaze fixed on Burke, she was afraid to move. He slept on, not stirring, and eventually she found the courage to creep past him soundlessly, too terrified to breathe. Once she had made it to the flap of the tent she looked back anxiously, but Burke was still in the same position.

She glanced out into the clearing, which was empty except for several smoldering campfires, doused but still sending thin trails of gray smoke skyward. She was sure there were guards around, but she couldn't see anybody. The sky was the sapphire blue of pit water, moonlit, and the chilly spring night was filled with the faint sound of birds and nocturnal animals.

Alex took a deep breath and bolted across the camp and out into the woods on the other side. She ran for her life, not sure where she was going but seeking only to put distance between herself and the rebel camp. She ran until her lungs were on fire and there was a violent stitch in her left side, until she could not remain on her feet an instant longer. Then she collapsed under a tree, falling onto a bed of crushed ferns and mossy twigs that received her yieldingly. Too spent for any further effort, she dozed and then drifted into slumber.

Alex did not know it, but Burke never slept straight through the night. Years of insurgence against the British had trained him to take short, refreshing naps. Alex had only been gone a brief time when he stirred and glanced over at her corner. Finding it empty, he leaped to his feet, muttering profanities when he saw the frayed rope and the pottery shard lying on the ground. He dashed out of the tent.

Curse the woman, she was clever. He didn't waste time wondering how she had managed her escape or chastising his guards. Instead, he glanced up at the moon and realized he'd been asleep barely an hour. He shrugged into his tunic and checked the placement of the knife at his hip as he ran. He must not lose the English girl, as she was essential to his plan for getting his brother back.

Tracking through the woods was second nature to Burke. He found her trail easily and smiled to himself when he saw that she had gone the wrong way, toward the sea and away from the castle. All guts, no skill. Still, he had to admire her. Not one captive in ten would have even tried to escape.

Burke tracked her to where she had fallen, almost tripping over the prone figure. She lay limp, as if dead. Her short hair was plastered to her head with perspiration, her linen shift stained by dirt and grass, and her bare feet abraded from running through the underbrush. He knelt down next to her and shook her roughly.

Alex opened her eyes and looked around helplessly. When she focused on his face, she tensed visibly, and he could see the pulse pounding in her neck.

"I've a mind to tie you to a tree and leave you here for the animals to gnaw," he said grimly.

Her body went rigid as a drawn bow, and she fell back into his arms in a dead faint.

Burke sighed wearily. Scaring her to death was

not part of his plan. He scooped her up and carried her to a softer bed of long grass. Then he went to a nearby brook and wet a strip torn off from his tunic. He returned to Alex and wiped her face with the damp cloth briskly.

Her eyelids fluttered, and she looked up at him fearfully, swallowing with difficulty. "Don't," she whispered.

"Don't what?"

"Hurt me."

"I'll not hurt you," he replied gruffly, "but you must stop scampering away."

"You can't expect me to stay with you and accept it," she said, her eyes glistening.

Burke considered the situation. Maybe if he told her why she had been taken, she would see reason and cooperate. Otherwise this chase scene might be repeated, and if she kept running, it would waste valuable time, and she might injure herself doing it.

"It won't be for long," he said finally. "I took you to exchange for my brother, who's being held at the castle. I sent a message this morning to Carberry, and I expect a reply in a short time."

Alex stared up at him, and he could see her turning over the information in her mind.

"So you see, I have no plans to keep you as a slave, or throw you to the wolves, or whatever else you've been thinking. Calm yourself. Your uncle will soon buy you back with my brother's freedom, · and all will be well with you."

There was a timbre in his voice she had not heard before, not gentleness exactly, but an appeal to logic that convinced her he meant what he said.

"Do we have to go back now?" she asked wearily, her lower lip trembling.

"And why not?"

"I'm so tired," she said, brushing the auburn fringe back from her forehead.

"We can wait for the light. It's only two hours 'til dawn. Rest now, go back to sleep."

Alex lay back and tried, but the dim outline of his large, lean form propped against a tree kept her awake, and the cold air didn't help. The night was raw and misty, with a penetrating damp that seeped into her bones and made her shiver visibly.

"What's amiss?" he asked, his voice a deep basso in the encompassing darkness.

"I'm cold."

There was a long pause. "Come here to me," he finally said.

Alex hesitated.

"Do you want to shake yourself to cinders, my lady?" he asked.

Alex climbed unsteadily to her feet and went to his side.

He reached up and took her hand, settling her in next to him and draping his arm around her shoulders.

"Better?" he said.

"Yes," she murmured. It *was* better; he felt so

large and solid and warm, and he smelled like the homemade soap he had given her to use, not like a savage at all. It was difficult to remember that not long ago she had been running away from him.

Burke held her loosely, wide awake. He was careful not to arouse any feelings beyond the desire to keep her safe so he could surrender her to the English when the time came.

His body heat slowly melded with hers, and as Alex drifted into sleep she snuggled closer.

When the sun finally rose and penetrated the thick canopy of leaves above their heads, its light shone on two people entwined on the ground like lovers.

3

A device fit for the Irish and other such savages . . .
—Queen Elizabeth I, on the installation
of a water closet in Richmond Palace

Burke awoke at first light, as he usually did, and studied the still figure asleep in his arms, clutching his tunic in one fist like a child. Her skin was poreless, with the faint blush poets associated with an English rose. The chopping job she had done on her hair could not disguise its vibrant color or fine texture, and he was restraining himself from touching it when her eyes opened and she looked directly at him. His hand fell away.

Alex gave a start when she realized where she was. She sat abruptly and pulled back from him hastily, arranging her clothes. She drew her legs up and hugged her knees, avoiding Burke's eyes.

Burke stood in one smooth motion and held out his hand to help her up. She ignored it and got to her feet herself, wincing when her lacerated soles took the weight of her body.

"Can you walk or shall I carry you?" he asked.

"Of course I can walk," she snapped as she stumbled.

Burke took a step toward her. "Put your arms around my neck," he instructed.

Alex hesitated.

"Do as I say or on my oath I'll leave you here where you stand," he said. "I must get back to my men, I've wasted enough time on you already."

Alex hooked her arms around his neck, and he hoisted her into the air as if she weighed no more than the morning mist that surrounded them. He set off through the trees without another word, taking them back the way they had come the night before, his deliberate pace covering the ground quickly. Alex tried not to think about the solid feel of his shoulder under her cheek or the strong grip of his hands as he held her. She closed her eyes and drifted into a dreamless somnolence, which ended abruptly when his arm dropped and he set her once again on the ground.

They had reached the camp in less time than Alex would have believed possible. It had seemed so far when she was fleeing the night before. Burke sent her back to his tent and instructed Rory to tie her up again and, in the future, to serve her food in a napkin.

Alex didn't see Burke for the rest of the day. She was almost asleep that night when a commotion at the entrance to the tent disturbed her. She looked up to see Burke gesturing for two other men to carry a prone figure inside and put it on his pallet.

Alex sat up straight when she saw that what they were carrying was an injured man. His wound, obviously long festering, was badly inflamed and draining from his side. Burke didn't even glance in her direction as the men laid the invalid on Burke's bed and then stepped back, making room for Burke to crouch by the sick man's side.

Alex looked on as he spoke soothingly in Gaelic to the feverish man, who sweated and rambled incoherently, seeming to fix on Burke's face in rational moments and then descend into delirium again. Alex sucked in her breath when she saw Rory coming through the tent flap with a white-hot knife, recently withdrawn from the flames of a campfire.

Burke gripped the mumbling man's shoulders and spoke a sentence clearly, holding his gaze. The man's eyes widened as he realized what was about to happen to him, and a second later Rory plunged the knife into the festering wound.

The man screamed and Alex looked away, unable to watch as Rory cleaned and cauterized the wound, making several trips out to the fire to reheat the knife. By the time she looked back, the injured man's moans had subsided, but he was still gripping Burke's hand with enough strength to whiten his knuckles.

Burke never stopped talking to him, keeping up a line of reassuring commentary while signaling with his eyes to the other men, directing them what to do. He didn't let go of the invalid's hand until the man had subsided into blessed unconsciousness. Then Burke stood watch while Rory washed and bound the wound, not moving until Rory had drawn the rough woolen blanket up to the man's chin and left the tent.

"What were you saying to him?" Alex asked.

Burke glanced at her as if he had forgotten she was there. He didn't answer.

"Will he be all right?"

"I know not. If not, one less savage for your queen to worry about," he replied shortly, and left the tent.

Rory came in a while later to offer water to the sick man, but he was too weak to drink.

"May I have some?" Alex asked.

Rory looked at her sourly but came to her side with the flask.

"What was Burke saying to him? When you were cleaning his wound?"

Rory took the flask back and replaced the stopper in silence.

"Please, I want to know."

"Why?" Rory asked, examining her with the first hint of curiosity he'd shown since she was captured.

"It seemed to comfort the man so much. I would love to have that consoling effect on another person, especially someone so sick."

Rory considered for a moment, and then said, "Burke was telling him how brave he was, that he had never seen another man take such an injury so well."

"And was that the truth?"

Rory shrugged. "I've never seen a man take a wound as well as Burke, and I've seen a lot of English weapons gouge into Irish flesh," he said meaningfully, turning his back and disappearing through the flap of the tent.

Alex watched the injured man, who was very still, until she fell asleep.

The sick man died during the night. His body was gone when Alex woke up in the morning.

Rory said nothing to her all day as he brought her meals, and when Burke finally arrived, well after nightfall, he looked exhausted and dispirited.

"I'm sorry about your friend," Alex said in a small voice.

"Oh, indeed you are," Burke replied.

"It's true. I hate to see anyone suffer."

"Do you now? Isn't that a charming sentiment? On this island we've been suffering at English hands for generations, and I've never seen any fine ladies like yourself weeping buckets about it." He tore off his tunic and tossed it in a corner.

"I would have helped him if I could."

"My fault," he said as if talking to himself. "I waited too long to open him up, and by that time he was too weak from the fever to fight."

"How was he hurt?"

"He was on a survey mission around the castle and he was picked off by an English sentry." Burke looked at her narrowly. "You should be celebrating, shouldn't you? Another glorious victory for the Crown, to be sure."

He unfolded a clean tunic from a pile in the corner and yanked it over his head.

Alex glanced down at her bound hands, unable to answer.

"Why don't you bloody people get the hell out of my country?" he said as he stalked back out of the tent.

Alex's monthly flux started during the night. By morning she felt sticky and uncomfortable, and paralyzed with embarrassment about her situation. There was little she could do about it without confiding in her captors.

She didn't consider talking to Rory; he would just think it was another ploy to get loose and probably ignore her. She knew instinctively that Burke would listen to her, but even the prospect of discussing her problem with him made her flush crimson.

When Rory brought her breakfast she said,

"Will you tell Burke that I crave the favor of a talk with him?"

Rory glanced at her but did not reply.

"Please. It's important."

Rory left, and she began to calculate miserably how long she could last in her current position before her dilemma became obvious.

Fortunately, Burke appeared shortly thereafter, his blue gaze impassive as he stood before her.

"What is it now?"

"Have you had any message at all from my uncle?" she asked, delaying.

"If so, you would be long gone from this place, my lady," he said, turning to leave.

"Wait. I . . . I have a problem."

He turned and faced her, his arms folded.

"I'm bleeding," she blurted out, her cheeks burning.

He scanned her figure, looking for an injury. "What are you saying?"

"As a woman bleeds with the change of the moon," Alex mumbled, staring at his boots. She could feel more hot color flooding into her face.

There was a long pause, and she sneaked a glance at him. From his expression it was clear that he was as discomfited as she was.

"What is it you need?" he asked gruffly.

"Some clean strips of nappy cloth for folding." She paused. "Aren't there any women in the camp?"

She hadn't seen any since she came.

"They're all inland. I'll see that Rory brings you the linens. Anything more?"

"I would cherish another bath, and I've been tied up for long days now without exercise. Can't you turn me loose for just an hour to wash and walk about a little? I am galled with cramps, and I can feel that my legs are weakening."

Burke studied her suspiciously.

"I have no plot to run again," she said quietly. "'Twould be folly, when I'm surely close to safe and happy reunion with my kinsman."

"Would that it were nigh at hand," Burke said dryly.

"Amen," Alex responded. She could have sworn she saw a trace of a smile on his lips.

"There's a stream on the other side of the camp, in a different direction from the one you took when you ran. Rory will bring you there tonight and you can bathe and have exercise, see to your needs."

"Oh, can't you bring me yourself? Rory makes me so nervy. He . . . hates me."

Burke shot her a glance that implied that he was not exactly fond of her, either.

"If you would escort me, I shall not forget it when I'm restored to my uncle. I will report to him that I was treated fairly, as befits a gentlewoman of my station. No doubt it will influence him in future dealings with you."

He studied her in silence and then left the tent.

* * *

That evening, Alex waited anxiously as the camp settled down for the night. It was a long time before all the voices had ceased and the sound of the sentry's pacing had become as monotonous as a musician's metronome. Finally, Rory appeared at the opening of the tent and regarded her without enthusiasm.

Alex's heart sank. She didn't realize how much she had been counting on going with Burke, until she saw his lieutenant.

Rory had a bundle of clean rags and clothing under his arm. "Come along, then," he said in his accented English as he cut her bonds. "I have my orders." His dull manner made it clear what he thought of this duty. "And no tricks," he added, fixing a length of rope to her wrist and leading her by it. "You ken what will happen if you try to get away."

Alex stumbled along in his wake, noting the smoldering fires and the stillness of the sleeping camp. She knew that Burke kept her close confined when most of the men were around to see her. The timing of this excursion was not accidental.

Rory set a quick pace, and Alex was trotting to keep up when she crashed into him as he suddenly stopped short.

Burke had stepped out of the shadow of the trees, appearing like a phantom. He said something in Gaelic to Rory, who stared at him for a long moment, and then glanced quickly at Alex. He handed her the bundle of linens and dropped her rope. Then he set off through the trees, surefooted as a deer, without looking back.

Burke picked up the length of rope and cut it swiftly, leaving a circlet of hemp around Alex's wrist. Still stunned by his unexpected appearance, Alex stared up at him.

"Well, don't take root there," Burke said, returning his knife to the sheath at his waist. "I call to mind that this excursion was Your Ladyship's idea."

He started off along the path, and Alex hurried after him. She kept silent until they reached a clearing where she could hear, but not see, the splashing of a brook.

"Why did you let me think Rory was taking me out here at first?" she asked.

He looked at her but didn't answer. Alex sighed. She didn't know why she wasted her breath asking him questions, as he bothered to respond only when it suited him.

Burke sat on the ground, propping his back against a tree and stretching his long legs before him.

"The brook is just through the brush that way," he said pointing. "And take warning . . ."

"I've already had the text from Rory." She hesitated, then sat at Burke's feet. He watched her warily, not objecting, but merely observing her movements closely.

"You speak such fine English, like a gentleman. How came you by that knowledge?" Alex asked.

"Does it offend your ears to hear a savage speak like an English gentleman?" The bitterness in his tone was unmistakable.

"I was merely . . . surprised. How did you learn?"

Burke leaned his head back against the tree trunk and closed his eyes. He knew it was a mistake to talk to her, to treat her as a person, as anything other than an object to be traded for his brother. But he was tired of the soldier's life—the brutish conversation of the men, the crude meals gobbled over open fires, the single-minded pursuit of the enemy. It allowed for little else. Surely a small respite from all that would not be harmful.

"My mother worked in the kitchens at the castle when I was a boy," he said. "Carberry's lady, now dead, took a fancy to her and had her as a maid for years. I learned your language in her chambers."

This explained his upper-class accent and vocabulary, most peculiar to his situation.

"And Rory?"

"Rory is my cousin; his mother was my mother's sister. She worked at the castle, too. He and I practice the language and speak it to each other when we can."

"So Lord Carberry knows you."

A satisfied smile touched his lips. "Aye. He

knows me, and all of mine. He'll know more of us in time."

The manner in which he spoke sent a chill down her spine.

"Why can't you give it up, this fighting?" she asked softly.

"Would you, if it were your own country in the hands of a foreign power?"

Alex shook her head. "I know little of such things. Politics and government were not thought fit subjects for my study. I've learned naught but needlework and homely duties, a little music, some Spanish and French for conversation, the preparation of medicines and recipes . . ."

"Hadn't you cooks in your uncle's house?"

"Yes, but I learned to make fancy dishes, such as would please a man and adorn his table for fine occasions."

"And what are they?"

She smiled. "Do you think I dissemble? Are you demanding examples?"

"I am."

"Very well. I can prepare a dressed partridge stuffed with grouse and served with a sauce of leeks and Madeira wine, a custard-and-whey posset with pressed currants, a cream comfit of cherries and quince pears, venison pasty. . . ."

Burke made a disgusted face. "Fancy fare. I'd rather a boiled fowl and a glass of stout. What else did you study?"

"Latin to read the classics and for church service. Prayers. My uncle is a devotee of the new learning."

Burke snorted. "Religion. An excuse to be a coward."

"You have no religion?"

He gestured to the woods around them. "In the old days we worshiped the trees and the stones."

Alex laughed. "You worshiped objects?"

"In the time of the Druids, Celtic people felt the power of nature in the natural things around them. It's no more foolish than worshiping a God you never see."

"They do say that in the Welsh Marches there are people with speckled skins and webbed feet who worship a goddess who demands human sacrifice."

"Who says such things?" Burke asked, amazed at such ignorance. "Your uncle?"

Alex nodded. "All his retainers believe it. And my maid, Annie, told me that the Irish rebels boil captured English children and serve them, carved like suckling pigs, to English prisoners."

Burke waved his hand. "The English think that anyone who doesn't live forninst the London Bridge and change religions with the Tudors must be swinging from the trees."

"You're not a Christian, then?" Alex said. The idea was foreign to her, as she had never in her life met a heathen. "I thought that Ireland was converted centuries ago."

He shrugged. "I'm an Irishman, that is my only loyalty. All religion is the same to me. It seems clear there is a power above us; as for the rest, I leave that to the scholars and the priests to debate."

"'So if there is one God . . . all the rest is a dispute over trifles.'"

"Just so. Who said that?"

"My queen, whom you profess to hate," Alex said, smiling.

He made a face, but conceded the point. "I have heard that she has great wisdom. She must, to remain so long on the throne in your contentious country."

"My uncle says that history will deem her the greatest ruler of the century."

"But she is old, and I am young," Burke said. "Time is her enemy and my friend. I can wait."

"How long?"

"As long as need be. Your queen can send an Essex, she can send ten of him and a hundred of him, and as long as I have breath in my body I will fight."

"But Lord Essex is a nobleman acting on an express commission from the queen's lawful majesty—"

"Nobleman!" Burke exploded, cutting her off in midsentence. "'Noble' is who curries favor best, who buys the richest title with the richest purse."

Alex was silent.

"Well? Is this not true?" he challenged her.

"'Twould be treason to say so," Alex murmured, avoiding his heated gaze.

"Your Lord Essex's stepfather was party to a secret marriage which quite enraged your queen, I think. Her Royal Majesty tossed him into the Tower when she heard of his indiscreet union, did she not?"

"Yes." Alex wondered how he got so much information, tucked away as he was in the middle of this forest. "The queen was advised to release Dudley because no one should be imprisoned for partaking of a lawful marriage."

"And was not Dudley called 'the Gypsy'?"

"Yes. He was dark-complected, it was a familiar name. 'Beware the Gypsy, he will betray you.'"

"Who said that?" Burke asked, furrowing his brow.

"Cecil, the queen's oldest and most trusted adviser, now dead."

"And did the Gypsy betray your queen?"

"No, he never did," Alex replied softly. "In their younger days he wanted very much to marry her, but she would have no one on the throne but herself." She paused. "From what I've heard, I think he did truly love her."

"But she loved her crown more," Burke said.

"Yes. Her royal station."

"Bah! They're all very royal, I'm sure. In King Henry's time any scoundrel with a pretty daughter could climb his way into lands and livings by parading her at court in hope of catching the old lecher's eye. Don't talk to me of 'royal,' madam, the word sticks in my craw."

Alex was silent, taken aback by the vehemence she had provoked in him. She hoped he wouldn't remember that her uncle was the fawning minion of the people Burke was so roundly denouncing.

"Oh, go and have your bath," he said, as if vexed at the sight of her.

She obeyed, fearful of continuing the conversation. She had been wishing he would talk to her, but now she was sorry he had. This man would not be deterred from his goals, and she was worried about the silence from the castle. What if her uncle had received Burke's message but didn't want her back? In that event, she had little doubt what her final fate would be.

Alex washed quickly in the brook around the bend, and donned the clean shift she had been given. She suspected it was Rory's as he was the smallest of the men she'd seen. The leather belt was much too large; she fitted it as closely as she could and then let it slip down to her hips. She added the pair of short boots, which made her look like an elf, and smoothed back her hair with her hands. When she rejoined Burke, he looked her over from head to foot and then shook his head.

"My lady fair, you are a cautioning sight."

"This apparel was not my choice, sir," she said.

"Give that belt to me," he commanded.

Alex undid the strip of hide and handed it to him. He unsheathed his knife, cut two extra holes in it, and gestured for her to come nearer to him.

She stood stock still as he slipped it around her and tightened it properly. When it was fastened, she looked up and met his eyes.

They blazed a brilliant blue in the dark, and their expression carved a hollow in her stomach. Why was he looking at her like that? He was too close, his breath fanning her cheek, his powerful masculine scent of wool and leather and soap overwhelming her. She found that her chest was constricted and she could barely breathe.

He set his hands on either side of her waist. His fingers almost met across her back.

"I could snap you like a twig," he said.

"Do you want to do that, Burke?" she replied. They were both whispering.

He swallowed with difficulty. "Oftentimes I do. And other times . . ." he stopped.

"Other times?" she persisted, leaning into him.

"You play at games you don't understand, girl," he said quietly, his grip tightening.

"Then explain," she murmured, inching closer to him.

He bent his head, at the same time lifting her up to meet him. Alex felt her eyes drifting closed.

Then he released her abruptly.

"Be off with you," he said huskily, stepping back and breaking the spell.

"Where?" she said, looking around at the encroaching trees.

Burke sighed. "Follow me."

* * *

Two weeks passed, during which Alex waited every day for some sign that her uncle had responded to Burke's message. Rory brought her food and took her out to the brook and occasionally released her for exercise.

She didn't see Burke at all. He had moved out of the tent and was apparently bunking elsewhere.

Alex had grown used to sleeping in her bound position, so she was surprised when she was awakened in the early hours at the end of the fortnight, not sure what had alerted her.

The first thing she noticed was that Rory was missing from his position by the opening of the tent. Since Burke's departure he had slept just outside it, guarding her. She peered into the darkness beyond the guttering candle set on the crate to her left. She could make out nothing but the shapeless pile of his cloak on the ground.

Alex was just sitting up when a large hand clamped over her mouth from behind. Jesu, please, not again! she thought wildly as her bonds were sliced swiftly and she was dragged through a slit cut in the back of the tent. She knew instinctively that none of Burke's men would be doing this; he controlled them far too closely. She kicked and struggled uselessly, terrified.

A rag was stuffed in her mouth, taking the place of the hand that had gagged her. She was dragged a distance, unable to see her captor, and then thrown unceremoniously to the ground. Hardly a second passed before her body was covered by a larger, foul-smelling one. She stared up into a fierce-looking, bearded face with piggish eyes and a leering, red-lipped mouth. Her scream of horror emerged as a muffled shriek.

The hooligan pinning her to the ground levered himself off her far enough to reach for her shift and rend it from neck to waist. He pulled aside the flaps, leaving her torso bare, and yanked at the garment impatiently, trying to separate the rest of it from her body. Alex closed her eyes, and at that instant her attacker's weight was lifted from her abruptly.

Her eyes flew open again to see Burke, naked except for a linen breechclout, holding her attacker by his shaggy dark hair, his arm around the ruffian's neck and his knife to the man's throat. The blade dug in just enough to draw blood and then Burke tossed the other man aside, kicking him solidly in the backside.

The dark man scrambled to his feet and drew his own blade as the two men faced off, yelling in Gaelic. Alex scurried out of the way, sobbing, trying in vain to hold the pieces of her tunic together. She crouched on the ground with her arms across her chest, ignored by the crowd of men from the camp who had gathered, torches in hand, to watch the combat.

Burke and the other man circled and lunged

over and over again until finally Burke slashed Alex's attacker on the bicep and then tripped him as he staggered. The man fell heavily to the ground, and Burke stood over him, his foot on the prone man's neck. He pronounced a sentence in Gaelic, looking around at the onlookers to confirm the finality of his victory. He signaled Rory and another man to carry off the defeated man, and then snatched a cloak from one of the bystanders.

Alex was weeping, incapable of speech, as Burke draped the borrowed cloak around her and gathered her up in his arms. He carried her back to the tent, shouting orders over his shoulder all the while. Once inside, he set her on the ground, folded the cloak about her, and then shouted an order to Rory.

Alex's teeth were chattering so loudly they sounded like the castanets used by the Spanish in their folk dances. Rory pushed his way into the tent and handed Burke a woolen blanket. He said something that caused Burke's expression to darken. Burke responded tersely.

Rory looked at Alex disdainfully. "I told you something like this would happen if you kept her here," he said, speaking English deliberately so that Alex would understand.

"That'll do," Burke said to him.

Rory shrugged and left the tent.

Burke wrapped Alex in the blanket, but she was still shivering. He finally picked her up and sat down on the floor with her in his lap. He held her quietly, stroking her back as if comforting a child, and after a while she stopped crying and gave a shuddering sigh.

"Better now?" he said quietly.

"Yes," she said.

"Warm enough?"

"Yes." Alex stirred and pushed aside the blanket. She was suddenly acutely conscious of the fact that she was lying with her head against Burke's bare shoulder, and that neither of them was wearing much clothing.

Alex nuzzled him, marveling at the softness of his skin. He looked so masculine and hard, but the satiny surface beneath her lips was as smooth and flawless as a baby's cheek.

His arm tightened around her.

"Hold me," she whispered.

"I am," he replied.

"Closer."

"I'll break your ribs," he answered, but he obeyed, pulling her more securely into the curve of his body and smoothing her hair back from her face.

"I was so frightened," she said. She moved her head and kissed his bicep, which flexed involuntarily.

"You're fine. I'll not let anything harm you."

Alex slipped her arms around his neck and pressed herself against him. She felt him stiffen in response.

"Don't . . ." she began, but it was already too late. He moved away from her as she tried futilely to cling to him.

Burke set her aside and stood. In the flickering candlelight, he was revealed in his almost naked splendor, his long muscled limbs and broad chest covered with a fine mat of light brown hair. Alex swallowed and looked away.

As if aware of her scrutiny, he draped the blanket around him like a cloak and tied it at his shoulder.

"Burke?" Alex said tentatively.

"Aye?"

"Why did that man attack me?"

Burke was silent.

"What did Rory mean by what he said?"

Burke sighed. "Pay no mind to Rory, he sometimes speaks too freely, like a strumpet at the town pump."

"I think I deserve to know," she persisted, her strength returning.

"Do you now?" he said.

"He wasn't one of your men."

Burke squatted next to her and thumbed his hair back from his face.

"No."

"Then who?"

"There's another faction of the rebels, split off from the O'Neill, and Scanlon, the one who . . ."

"Brutalized me," Alex supplied.

Burke nodded. "He wants my place," he said

simply. "He thought to make trouble for me by spoiling my plan to get Aidan back."

"How did he know I was here?"

"Informers are everywhere."

"So you're fighting each other as well as the English."

"That's always been the way of it," he said, rising. "We could drive your people from these shores forever if only we'd stand together."

"Why did you leave the tent and let Rory guard me? If you had stayed, this wouldn't have happened!"

"There was good reason."

"What reason?"

"I'll say no more." He paused. "And don't be laying the blame at Rory's door. His relief was responsible and not himself."

"No, not your precious Rory. I'm sure he's in grief that I'm not cut to ribbons, or worse—" she broke off, starting to cry again.

"Leave off that wailing now, you're safe," Burke said quickly, afraid that she would start another fit.

"Oh, you don't care, nobody cares, not even my uncle!" She stopped short, swallowing her words.

"What's that?"

Alex gave way to despair and blurted out, "You haven't heard from my uncle, have you?"

Burke didn't answer.

"How many messages have you sent?"

He looked away.

She leapt to her feet. "I see that in spite of your exalted position as the leader of this fine band of fighting men, you still do not understand your situation."

"Perhaps then you will clarify it," he replied testily.

"Your prize is valueless, Mr. Burke, your hostage is no hostage at all. My uncle doesn't want me back. He thinks himself well rid of me."

Burke stared at her. Clearly this possibility had not occurred to him.

"You don't know how I really came to be here," Alex went on. "My uncle did not bring me with him; he wished to leave me behind in England with an order of nuns. I cut my hair and dressed as a boy and stowed away aboard his ship."

Burke absorbed this in silence, and then closed his eyes.

"He doesn't intend to trade your brother for me because he doesn't give a brass shilling what happens to me. I embarrassed him in front of Lord Essex and I'll be a bother and an expense in the future. Your kidnapping scheme has solved a problem for him. If I disappear in the wilds of Ireland, he need do nothing further, his responsibility is discharged. Do you understand now?"

Burke was staring at the floor in contemplation. "Say nothing of this to Rory, or anyone else," he said, finally looking up.

"Why? Because they might decide to kill me when they learn I can't be used to get Aidan back?"

"I make the decisions here," he said gruffly.

"And how long before you get tired of feeding a worthless wench, the daughter of your enemies? How long can you keep your men away from me once they know, or guess, the truth? Oh, why don't you just let me go? I'm of no use to you, nothing but a burden."

"Quiet," he said, a warning tone in his voice.

"Nothing could be worse than this waiting, or what would happen to me if I fell into the hands of ruffians like that man Scanlon."

"Forget him, he'll not bother you again."

"Oh, it's hopeless, don't you see? Let me go, please. I won't tell a soul where I've been." She lunged for his dagger and he caught her in his arms.

"Be still," he said, shaking her.

Alex kicked him and twisted her head to bite the hand clamped on her shoulder.

"Tuatha da dann!" Burke exclaimed, reverting to his native language and releasing her with an oath, lifting his injured thumb to his mouth.

"You're no better than Scanlon!" Alex cried. "Do you think I don't know what's going to happen to me? I'm being driven mad, tied up all day, with nothing to think about but when and how I'm going to die. But I will thwart you! If you don't let me go, I'll kill myself first and take away your triumph! I'll find a way, make no mistake. My mother didn't birth a weakling to sit and wait for execution like a criminal!"

Burke should have been angry, but instead he calmly allowed her ravings. He knew only too well how near she had come to being raped by Scanlon.

He took her by the shoulders again, holding her steady. "Alexandra, listen to me. No harm will come to you here, on my word. Haven't I shown that to you this night?"

"Maybe . . . you just wanted to save me for your-self," she gasped.

If she had been in control, she would have seen his face change. "What do you mean?" he asked quietly.

"To keep me for a drudge, or for a last resort in case my uncle does decide to answer you. How am I to know? You always have a plan for everything you do."

She could not guess it, but when Burke had been roused from sleep by Scanlon's raid, his only thought had been to save her. Not because she was a hostage, but because he wished to keep her from harm.

"You're dithering and making no sense at all," he said. "Calm yourself, now."

Her legs gave way suddenly and she would have fallen if he hadn't caught her. He pulled her into his arms and took her weight, holding her up and waiting for the storm of her tears to pass again.

Alex sobbed helplessly, too witless from her earlier terror to make sense, and too drained to care if she did. She clung to Burke as if he were the only stable object in a spinning world. She had nothing, no home, no family. Her uncle's silence was proof that he didn't care about her, and she was miles across the sea from her native land. Her only connection to safety and sanity was this looming barbarian who held her so tightly in his embrace. Since her capture, whether or not she wished it, he had become the center of her universe.

Burke laid his cheek against her head, his lips in her hair. With his breath warm in her ear, he shushed her and then began to caress her delicate shoulders through the thin garment. It was a while before he became conscious of what he was doing, and then he released Alex so abruptly that she reeled backward.

"Why did you tell me about your uncle?" he demanded, partly to cover his own confused emotions. "You might have hung on for some time to come, pretending to think that he would redeem you."

"I did think, that is, I hoped . . ." Her voice trailed off. "I wasn't sure. Somehow, today, I just knew. He will do nothing. He's probably told Lord Essex that he sent me away somewhere, to explain my absence."

"Where?"

She smiled faintly, wiping her streaming cheeks.

"He seems to favor convents. There are many such places in Ireland, I think."

Burke was pacing about the tent, absorbed.

"What do you plan to do?" Alex asked, sniffling.

Burke held up his hand. "You'll not wind up in a convent or any such place shut away from the world. You leave the rest to me."

He strode through the flap in the tent, and seconds later she heard him shouting orders in Gaelic.

Burke got no sleep for the rest of that night. He sat up next to the campfire, his thoughts in turmoil, until dawn streaked the sky.

Much good he had accomplished by leaving her tent. He had thought to remove himself from temptation, to stop thinking of her as a woman instead of a mere prisoner. If he hadn't seen her attacked as a woman, he might have been able to do it.

It would not be long before his men realized that the English weren't interested in exchanging Alex for Aidan or anyone else. Then he would have to keep her safe, as he had promised.

He could see no way around it. He had to take action. Now.

Burke sighed heavily and stood up just as the sun topped the trees.

* * *

When Alex awoke the next morning there was an eerie stillness about the camp. It did not take her long to realize that everyone was gone.

But not quite everyone. Rory appeared with her breakfast as usual shortly after she stirred.

"Where is everybody?" she asked him.

He shot her an inscrutable glance but said nothing as he set the food before her and left her alone.

Alex's mind was racing. She couldn't help but think that the men were off on an excursion, perhaps as a result of what she had told Burke the previous night. Had he decided to raid the castle to get his brother, once he realized that there would be no trade?

She didn't have long to wait for an answer. That night, the sound of horses' hooves drummed through the camp, and a few minutes later Burke himself strode into her tent, followed closely by Rory. Burke wore a rough woolen cloak of heavy tweed draped over his tunic, fastened at the shoulder by a brooch of hammered metal. Both articles of clothing were stained with dirt and grass, and the left shoulder was soaked with blood. Without looking at her he tore off the cloak and the tunic, exposing the wound, which was raw and purple, and oozing freshly from the motion. He dropped himself on the upturned crate and set the candle on the dirt floor.

Alex gasped and stared at his haggard face.

"Get me some water," Burke said to Rory in English.

"Boiled water," Alex called after him. To Burke, she said, "Cut me loose and I'll help."

"I think you've done enough," Rory retorted as he left the tent.

"Is it very bad?"

"I've had worse," Burke replied, glancing down at the wound in annoyance.

His appearance belied his casual words. His skin was ashen, and beads of sweat stood out on his forehead. He had obviously lost a good deal of blood.

"Please cut me loose. I am trained in the healing arts. I can help you."

"Alex, leave off that babbling," he said in a tired voice. "Your domestic skills are of no use here."

"Truly, I did charity work in a hospice near my uncle's estate and was taught by the nuns. I can be of service."

"How shall we know you won't dirty the wound and make him worse?" Rory asked as he returned with a cauldron of steaming water. He set it on the floor.

Alex looked at Burke. "Do *you* think I would do such a thing?" she asked him.

The look that passed between them disturbed Rory. He had been around Burke too long not to know what it meant. He was about to protest when Burke said, "Turn her loose."

Rory's mouth fell open in astonishment.

"Do it," Burke said, closing his eyes, his tone brooking no argument.

Rory's glance shot sparks as he looked at Alex, but he obeyed grudgingly.

Alex sprang up from the floor, rubbing her wrists, her eyes intent on Burke's pale and haggard face. "Is the arrowhead still in the wound?"

"It is," Burke replied. "I tried to gouge it loose in the field, but I hadn't the leverage." He sighed deeply and bowed his head, on the verge of losing consciousness.

"Rory, you'll have to help me."

Burke's cousin stood at her elbow and whispered into her ear, "Have a care for his health if you care for your own."

Alex stiffened.

"I think you can guess what will happen to you if he's not alive to stand between you and his men," Rory added. He nodded toward the shadows playing on the surface of the tent, backlit by the campfires. The men were gathered outside, anxious about their leader.

"Do you want him to die of a poisoned wound, like the man you brought to my tent?" Alex countered.

"What's that you say?" Burke asked, lifting his head, his eyes flying open and fixing on them.

"Nothing at all," Alex said. "Rory, get his pallet from the tent where he's been sleeping. It will be better if we lie him down flat for this."

"For what?" Burke said as Rory left.

"You know that the arrowhead, if still in, must now come out."

"Rory can do it."

"I know more about this than Rory does. I saw several such wounds in London during the late rebellion against the queen's majesty. I learned then a procedure that saved many lives."

Burke examined her. Was this calm, confident nurse the same wild woman who'd been hysterical in his arms less than twenty-four hours earlier?

"You have often asked me to trust you, have you not?" Alex said quietly.

He inclined his head in agreement.

"Then trust me. I know very well what I am doing."

When Rory returned Burke said to him, "Go out and speak to the men. Tell them I am well and disperse them. Then come back in here and do as she says."

Rory stood stock still.

"Did you not hear me?" Burke said in a stronger voice.

Rory turned on his heel and left. Seconds later they heard him speaking in Gaelic to the men assembled outside the tent. This was followed by a shuffling of feet.

"How were you hurt?" Alex asked, using the edge of his discarded tunic to wipe the gathering perspiration from his forehead. "What happened?"

"They were waiting for us," Burke murmured as if speaking to himself. "They knew. When I saw it was a trap I sent the men back, but not before they got me and a few others."

"How could Carberry have known that you were coming? Who could have told him?"

Burke raised his weary eyes to hers.

"Rory thinks you did."

4

*It becomes not a female to speak in public on so
desolate a subject as her own marriage.*
——Mary Tudor to the
Spanish ambassador,1554

Alex gaped at him. "He thinks *I* did? I've
been trussed up in a tent right here under your
nose for the last four weeks! How could I have
done anything?"

"Rory thinks that you're a spy . . . that you were
planted here . . . that you talk to confederates in
the woods when you take your exercise." He was
gasping, the words obviously costing him tremen-
dous effort.

"I'm always supervised when I'm turned loose.
And how could I be a spy when I was kidnapped?
Had I consulted an astrolabe to determine the future?

The idea is preposterous! You know it's not true."

Burke looked past her shoulder, and did not answer.

"I see," Alex said quietly. "It doesn't matter if it's true, or even possible. He's spreading rumors, laying the groundwork to eliminate me if anything happens to you."

"I can curb Rory's tongue."

"You're not with him every minute! The others hate my countrymen so much they'll use any pretext to fall on me just like that man Scanlon. That's the way of it, isn't it?" Alex suddenly noticed that she was even beginning to talk like these people.

"Nothing will happen to me," Burke said, looking as if he might faint momentarily. "So nothing will happen to you."

"Don't talk any more," Alex said, kneeling next to him. "You must conserve your strength."

"Stay close by me," he said in a low tone as Rory rejoined them. He would have said more, but that was enough to make his message clear.

So, he was afraid for her. As strong as his hold was on his men, he knew he was injured now, not capable of walking among them and exerting control over them. Without his influence, the subversive forces among them would have a chance to do their worst. It had to be more than Rory making disgruntled remarks or Burke would not be so concerned.

"Set the pallet on the floor over there," Alex

said, indicating the corner by the light. She had to dismiss such disturbing thoughts, with the more pressing problem of Burke's health at hand. "And I'll need to gather some herbs, so you must take me out to the woods."

"Herbs?" Rory said doubtfully.

"I must make a clay poultice to draw the wound. And I'll need St. John's wort and marjoram to reduce the swelling, lady's mantle to help to close the wound, purple foxglove for the pain, and marigold to aid the scab in forming."

"I know not if such things grow here," Rory said, looking concerned and glancing at Burke.

"They do, I have seen them all on my walks," Alex said. "I will show you where they may be found. There's a full moon and plenty of light to see."

"Take a basket and go with her," Burke said, shifting his weight to the skins on the pallet, favoring his injured shoulder.

"Let me wash your wound first." Alex picked up his cloak and draped it around his legs.

He shook his head. "Go and get what you need. I'll be ready for you to remove the arrowhead when you return."

He was reaching for the cauldron of water when they left.

Alex gathered the plants as quickly as possible, but by the time they got back to the tent, Burke was failing noticeably. His complexion was gray, he was shivering, and his eyes were glassy and unfocused.

Rory glanced at Alex nervously. "What's amiss? He looks worse."

"It's to be expected."

Burke gazed at them as if from a distance, his tweed cloak tossed aside on the floor. He said nothing.

"Are you certain we should do this now?" Rory asked, still eyeing their patient. The cauldron of bloody water stood abandoned in the middle of the floor.

"It cannot wait. That piece of stone imbedded in the wound must come out," Alex insisted, drawing the cloak over Burke again.

She set about making the poultice immediately, crushing the leaves to release the green sap and then mixing them with clay. It adhered badly, but she plastered it on, murmuring snatches of prayers under her breath and bathing Burke's face intermittently.

"How long will it take for that mess of pottage to draw the stone?" Rory asked, hovering nearby.

"It should take several hours. I will watch it. In the meantime he'll need something for the pain." She got up and selected two dark blue blossoms from her basket and snapped off the pistils, mashing them in a cup with water to extract the yellow powder.

"What is that noxious potion?" Rory asked. "It smells ill."

"It will kill the sting of the wound and help him to sleep," Alex said.

"Too much of it will stop the heart."

"So then you do know something of this art," Alex said, glancing up at him.

"I know that plant well enough. A bit of it on the tip of a dart will numb the flesh."

"Yes, it stops the course of feeling, which can only help him." Alex lifted Burke's head and held the cup to his lips.

He was almost insensible, and getting him to drink was a chore. About half of it went down his neck, but he swallowed enough to calm the fire of his wound in time.

"And now?" Rory asked.

"We keep him quiet and wait. When the tip of the stone appears, we take it out."

"And if it does not appear? Is it not best to go in right away and search for it? That is what we always do."

"That adds to the risk of inflammation. Isn't that how your friend died, the one you brought to this tent?"

Rory's silence was confirmation.

"I'm doing all that I can," Alex said looking him in the eye, noticing not for the first time his vague resemblance to his larger, more handsome cousin. "I give you my oath on it."

"It puzzles me greatly that you should want to help him," Rory said.

"He rescued me from Scanlon, he's kept me safe during all my time here."

"It was he who gave the order for you to be taken in the first place."

"I understand now why he did that," Alex said as she wiped Burke's brow.

Rory stared at her. "That's a powerful leap of understanding for an English lady."

"He wants his brother back again. It's not a difficult concept to grasp."

"Blood calls to blood?" Rory said sarcastically. "As yours calls to your uncle? He's a bit tardy about his familial obligations, it seems to me."

"My uncle and I are a different case."

"Are you not relations? Are you merely his ward?"

"We are relations, but there is little bond of affection," Alex said, careful not to reveal too much. Telling Burke the unhappy facts was one thing; telling Rory was quite another. "As I child I never knew him, and I was visited on him like an unwelcome guest when my parents died. He was an old bachelor unused to children. . . ." She stopped. "Suffice it to say that Burke feels more for any of his men here, brother or not, than my uncle feels for me."

"Then why should he redeem you?"

"He has always been most careful to maintain appearances. He would not want it said in his circles that he neglected his care of me. Lord Essex would most certainly not approve, and he is an intimate of the queen, who is watchful of the Howard branch of her family." Would to God that it were true, Alex added to herself.

Burke stirred, and they both looked at him.

"He should be more peaceful soon," Alex said.

They settled in for the vigil.

The sun had just risen when Alex scraped off the poultice and saw the gray, ragged tip of the arrow-head protruding from Burke's wound. She leaped up and threw her arms around Rory, forgetting his enmity for her, forgetting everything except her hope for Burke's recovery.

Rory prised her arms loose from his torso and said gruffly, "Now?"

"Yes, yes! Pull back the flaps of the tent, I'll need as much light as possible, and I want to give him another dose of the sleeping potion so he'll not feel the probing of the wound much."

"He'll feel it."

"The worse danger is in the poisoning that might come after," Alex said, crossing herself to ward off the bad luck.

Rory made a corresponding sign with his hand. Whether it was a supplication to one of his old gods or a confirmation of Alex's offering to her own, she had no idea.

Alex knelt next to Burke and washed his wound as well as she could, hesitating as his eyelids fluttered but did not open. Rory heated a pair of tongs in one of the campfires until it glowed white, and Alex used the instrument to remove the arrowhead. Its exit was followed by a rush of blood and pus, which Alex wiped away, and even in his drugged state Burke bucked when she pressed the dressing against the tender edges of the reopened flesh.

She signaled to Rory to hold his cousin down while she worked.

"Which herbs are in that mixture?" Rory asked, watching her.

"A blend of those you gathered with me last night."

Rory shook his head. "It seems like witchery to me."

"Not witchery, but medicine. The priests in the monasteries recorded their homely cures before the dissolution, and their books came into the hands of the queen's physicians. The remedies I'm using are well known in court circles."

"An English cure for his tough Irish hide. There's some humor in that, isn't there?"

"I'll laugh when he's well. Until then I intend to pray." She sat back on her heels and stroked Burke's forehead.

"What do you think?" Rory asked.

"He's hot," she said, frowning. "Go and get some cold water from that brook where you took me to bathe. The coldest water, where it runs on the rocks."

Rory obeyed without question, taking up the

cauldron from the floor and dumping its contents outside the tent. Alex fixed her gaze on her patient.

True to her word, she began to pray.

Despite Alex's best efforts, Burke's temperature began to climb, and he was delirious for two full days. During that time she hardly slept, constantly bathing his face and changing his dressing when needed. When he thrashed and tossed she tried to hold him, but even in his illness he was fearfully strong, and sometimes she called Rory to help her. Rory kept the rest of the men away. Alex couldn't imagine what he was telling them, but she didn't care. She needed time and quiet, and he made sure that she got both.

Burke seemed to exist in a state of suspension, no worse but no better, until his fever finally broke on the morning of the third day. Alex came alert suddenly from her dozing and noticed that his entire body had broken out in a cool sweat and he was no longer restless. She was watching his face when he opened his eyes and looked at her. She could tell by his expression that he knew who she was.

"Are you feeling better?" she whispered.

He raised his hand slowly and touched her cheek. Alex covered it with her own much smaller one. She didn't realize that she was crying until her tears fell on his fingers and ran into her mouth.

His parched lips moved.

"Don't try to talk," she said.

"Alex," he croaked.

"Yes, I'm Alex. Do you want a drink?"

He closed his eyes and nodded.

Alex got him the water and helped him to drink, holding his head and tipping the cup to his lips. "Not too much now," she said when he tried to gulp it. "You can have more later."

He sighed as she eased him back onto the pallet. "How . . . long?" he gasped.

"Just a few days. Everything is fine. Rory's been in charge, and he's kept the men in hand."

"You?"

"I've been right here, with you."

He closed his eyes again.

"Go back to sleep, you need to rest."

He didn't stir, and she thought that he had obeyed until she moved to get up and he caught her hand. She paused, and he pressed it tightly.

"What is it?" she asked.

"Thank you," he murmured, and then fell asleep.

Alex released his hand and pushed through the flap of the tent into the early morning sunshine. She blinked and wiped her damp cheeks with the back of her hand.

Rory turned from the cookpot where he was preparing breakfast and met her gaze.

"He's not . . ." he said, alarmed by her wet eyes.

"No, no, he's better. He came out of it and spoke to me."

Rory rushed past her to see for himself. When he rejoined her, he was grinning. "He is better. Even I can see it."

Alex smiled and nodded.

"All thanks to you," Rory added. "You saved him."

"Oh, Rory, he saved himself. You know how strong-willed he is, and very hale. He just needed time—"

"You saved him," Rory repeated, interrupting her. "And from now on, you'll have no more trouble from me or mine. I'll stand with you against any who would harm you."

For some reason, this moved her as much as Burke's recovery had. Sullen, childish Rory, loyal only to Burke and their mutual cause, was pledging his fealty to her like a knight kneeling before the queen. She began to get teary again.

"Come along inside," Rory said, clamping his hand on her shoulder. It was the first time he had ever touched her voluntarily. "Maybe in a while we can feed him some broth from the pot."

As soon as Burke began to feel better, he behaved like a child and wanted to be on his feet at once. This attitude persisted in spite of the fact that he almost fell the first time he tried to stand; Rory caught him and set him back down on his pallet. Burke thereafter grumbled that he was being treated "like a puking babe," which was accurate since the first thing he ate came back up again. Alex was reduced to standing guard to make sure he stayed horizontal and inventing amusements to distract him from his desire to get up and take charge again.

Although she saw as little of the men in the camp as she had before, she could tell that their opinion of her had changed from controlled hatred to grudging respect. Rory must have told them of her role in Burke's recovery, and the aura of veiled threat she had sensed before was entirely gone.

The atmosphere in the camp was not the only thing that had changed; Alex herself was different somehow. The man upon whom she'd depended for her very survival had almost died, and she'd saved him. When Burke finally came to after days of fever and looked at her and touched her face, she knew then that she loved him, and was certain that he felt the same.

Her conclusion was unshakable, even though she'd had little experience of any kind of love. Her uncle had always spoken of "romance" in sneering terms, as if it were an affliction of the weak, but Alex didn't feel weak; she felt strong. Nothing and no one could keep her from Burke. Suddenly all the stories and songs made sense, the books she'd read since childhood and the lays of the minstrels sung at banquets and on feast days. Love had once seemed a distant dream, wonderful if ephemeral, but the reality was even more powerful. She would do anything to preserve it.

Alex didn't even question that her love was reciprocated. She could read Burke's every expression and gesture, and she knew he had been fighting his feelings for her for some time. He'd give in to them, she would see to that. It wouldn't be long before he recognized and admitted their mutual desire.

It had to be love, what else could make her feel this way? It was difficult now to remember how she'd felt in the beginning other than mortally afraid of Burke and desperate to get away from him. Now, the thought of their being parted filled her with panic. She wanted to stay with him, even if it meant living in camps like this one, going deep into the Irish countryside, never seeing England again. All her previous experience of life was muted—her time in her parents' house and later with her uncle—as if it had never been.

"No more of that gruel," Burke announced to her as she entered the tent with a bowl of marrow and curds on the fourth day of his recovery. "I'll have meat or naught at all. I'm being fed like a nursling. And leave off with that flower potion, too; it keeps me in a fog."

"You seem the better for both," Alex said, setting the bowl on the floor and postponing that argument for later.

"And I want a glass to shave. I feel like a beggar at the manor gates. All I lack is a stump."

"Why don't you grow a beard? I've taken note that everyone else in camp has one."

"I had one. It itched."

"Liar. You're vain."

He gave her a disgusted look.

"Vanity is a great sin," Alex said. "You want to look out for your soul and compose yourself in modesty."

"And I need to cut my hair. I'll be mistaken for a maid."

"Some hopes with that beard. And that size. The woman never lived to come near your shoulder."

"Tell Rory I'll go to the brook and have a wash," he said.

"I will do no such thing. You'll rest for two days more before you go anywhere."

"You're a tyrant, and I vow you'll pay for it once I'm back to myself again."

"Until then, you'll do as I say. I'll cut your hair and shave you when you're up and about." She smiled. "I'll crop that mane and give you curls like Alexander."

"Who's that? Your father?"

"No, but my father named me after him. He was the greatest leader of ancient times, in Greece, more than three hundred years before the birth of Christ."

"And what did he do?"

"He conquered the entire world, as much of it as was known to him, all the way to Persia."

"Persia?" he said doubtfully. "Where is that?"

"A long way from here," Alex replied, at a loss to describe the immense distance she had once seen on her tutor's cartograph. "Many times the distance from England to Ireland."

"And were the Persians, whoever they might be, difficult to conquer?"

Alex nodded. "They fought him from their elephants."

"Elephant? Is that a sort of fortress?"

Alex giggled. "An elephant is an animal, as high off the ground as one man standing on another's shoulders, with a long nose like a pig's snout that reaches all the way to the earth."

"From that height?"

"Yes."

He snorted. "You mock me. There is no such creature."

"But there is. I've seen drawings of them."

"You must think me dull-witted," he said, hitching his shoulder in irritation.

"Certainly not. But since I've seen the pictures, you might forgive me for believing."

"I've seen drawings of the green men said to come out on the lawn on midsummer eve at midnight and grant the beholder three wishes. That doesn't mean I believe in them. Why am I talking to you at all? A woman who thinks the people in the Welsh Marches have webbed feet!"

"I was telling you of Alexander," she said, dropping the subject of elephants.

"So you were."

"He reached the limits of the world before the age of thirty. He died at thirty-three, weakened by old wounds and poisoned, it is often said, by tainted water. My father was a student of history and a great admirer of his."

"For his victories?"

"For more than that. My father thought he was very forward looking, a man out of his time. He told me stories of him when I was a child. But after he died and my uncle took charge of my care, my new tutor instructed me in wifely duties only. I heard no more then of Alexander," she ended sadly.

"Why do you remember all this so well?" Burke asked. "You must have been very young when you heard about him."

"I was young but often left alone to think, and I was captivated by what I'd heard. I looked up his image on the bookplates in my father's library, before his books were sold with his entailed estate when he died. There were copies of Alexander's likeness. He was fair, like you, with the same brown-gold hair."

Burke stared at her, listening.

"He was clean-shaven also, in a time, like now, when the fashion was for beards." She smiled. "Perhaps he was vain, too."

"And?"

"Not so big as you, not above middle height, but very comely. The story goes that his games master believed in a strict regimen of sparse diet and little sleep for children, and this kept him small. He blamed his childhood for his size, which he felt was a failing. His greatest friend, Hephaestion, was described as taller and better looking, in which case he was certainly handsome. Alexander went near to mad when Hephaestion died, of physician's neglect, so he thought. He gave orders immediately to hang the doctor."

"That was not wise," said Burke. "So your hero had a flaw."

"Yes. I remember it because it seemed such a lack of judgment, as if he must have been quite driven from his senses."

"Great fondness followed by a loss can do that."

"True. He seemed to think he and his friend were twin souls, almost the same person. How you feel about Rory, I imagine. Or your brother."

Burke rubbed his shoulder, lost in thought.

"Don't touch that," Alex said.

"This bloody thing is putting me in hopes of an asylum," he complained.

"It almost put you in your grave," Alex said. "And I must take issue with Rory. He once told me you stood wounds very well."

"He stands the wounds well," Rory said, entering the tent. "It's the mending he can't bear."

"I'll take a walk," Burke announced.

Alex rose as she and Rory exchanged glances.

"Tomorrow," Alex said. "And now you must

rest. You've been listening to me babbling all this time when you should have been napping."

"She treats me like a stripling," Burke said to Rory.

"You're behaving like an infant," Rory replied.

Alex sighed. "It's time for you to sleep."

"Tell me some more interesting stories about your namesake."

"Stories?" Rory said, arching his brows. "Are we in an English nursery now, pestering the governess for bedtime stories?" He rolled his eyes and left the tent.

Burke looked at her expectantly.

Alex resumed her place on the dirt floor. She told him what else she could remember about the man who had changed history, back when Burke's distant ancestors were still migrating from the banks of the Danube, to keep him quiet until he fell asleep.

Burke awoke in the middle of the night, sweating and parched, and reached for the deerskin flask Alex had left at his elbow, wincing as the movement stung his shoulder. He drank deeply and then considered his nurse, sleeping a short distance away, curled up on his tweed cloak.

This must stop, he thought. He must get some exercise, find some way to relieve the pressure of her constant presence. He was not so injured after all, despite the protestations of his attendant. He was at least well enough to spend every waking moment when he wasn't talking to her indulging in fantasies of making love to her.

And sleeping was worse. Each night, like this one, he awoke, perspiring and dizzy with desire, from dreams in which he caressed her creamy skin and kissed her budding lips and the languid, heavy lids of her emerald eyes. He told himself that it was hopeless, that their situation made it so, but logic did not avail him. He told himself that sooner or later she would surely be restored to the English so his feelings were a waste of time. Lastly, he told himself that she was a child—which he knew was a lie.

She was a woman fully grown, and she wanted him as much as he wanted her. He knew it from her furtive looks, the longing glances she had not the cunning to disguise, the way she trembled when they touched. But she was young and sheltered, and aside from all other considerations, this presented another problem.

Burke had never taken a virgin in his life. From his fifteenth year he'd had ready access to the easy women who hung around the inland camps and asked no questions. His current favorite was Deirdre, an attractive hybrid with the ebony hair of the Spanish invaders, who bedded him well and regularly. He did not deceive himself that it was a sentimental attachment; she liked the honor of being chosen by the local chieftain and the considerable pleasure of coupling with his strong, healthy body. She milked him dry and then left him, satisfied, with no conscience about it whatsoever.

Such would not be the case with Alexandra. She was no Deirdre to take her pleasure where she found it. And it was different for him, too. He wanted to be with her all the time. He found himself, in weaker moments, wishing heartily that he'd never sent a message to the castle that he had her.

There was a hole in his shoulder, his brother was still an English prisoner, and he was in love with his hostage. It was a mess all around, but Burke resolved that he would save something from it and not touch her. He may have misused her in this instance, but he did not have to ruin her entire future. The one thing he could decently do was return Alex to her uncle intact, not despoiled for a wealthy husband, the political marriage Cummings must certainly have in mind for her.

Burke closed his eyes. He must get back on his feet quickly. His dependence on Alex was only worsening the situation. In the morning he would walk.

And in the morning he did. Rory went out to the woods with him, and he felt stronger, but when he got back he was glad of his bed. He squinted down at his shoulder as Alex changed his dressing and said, "It should be left to the open air."

"Tomorrow. After your bath we'll leave it uncovered."

"Tomorrow, tomorrow. Is there nothing at all that can be done today?"

Alex sighed. The wound had puckered shut but was still oozing slightly. She had to keep him occupied one more day. She'd run out of Alexander stories. "I wish I had some books. You have none here?"

There was a long pause, and then Burke said, "Who would read them?"

Alex looked at him. "You cannot read and write?"

"Most people cannot read and write."

Alex knew that this was true. The general population, even in England, was largely illiterate.

"But I thought . . ."

"You thought what? You thought I had a private tutor come to my father's study and teach me letters and tell me stories?"

Alex was silent.

"I speak your language because I listened to others speaking it for a long time, as I told you," he said. "No one gave me lessons."

"Then I shall do so."

"What?"

"Let's begin with your name," she said, picking up a stick and drawing a line on the dirt floor. "What's your first name? No one ever calls you anything but Burke."

"Burke will do."

"You have no first name?"

"Kevin," he said reluctantly.

"What does it mean in your language?"

He thought for a moment. "Strength."

"Your parents chose well." She carefully spelled out *Cayvin* on the floor, for that's the way it sounded when he said it.

"Doesn't look like much."

"This is English, of course." She added *Berk* for good measure. "There. I wonder what it would look like in Gaelic."

"Not like that," he said. "I've seen some books, the figures are very different."

"A different alphabet," she said.

"What?"

"The letters used to make up the words. In any case, one language at a time is enough."

"Show me your name," he said.

She wrote it for him on the floor.

"It's longer than mine."

"Yes, it is."

"I'll need to know more than names."

"Let's start with the letters. Once you learn them you can form them into words."

And so she began the task of teaching Burke to read.

The next day, as promised, Burke went to the brook with Rory and bathed. Alex stood at a discreet distance until she was summoned to cut Burke's hair.

No one thought any longer that she would run away.

"I leave you to it, and welcome," Rory said sourly. "He's the worst patient I ever saw, and I've seen a few."

Burke called after him in Gaelic, and Rory glanced over his shoulder as he left and threw his cousin a black look.

"What did you say to him?" Alex asked.

"It doesn't bear repeating."

"Give me your knife."

Burke, freshly shaved, was stripped to the waist and seated on a rock. His damp hair was pushed back off his face, his shoulder disfigured by the swollen purple weal left by his wound, adding to a gallery of other, faded scars. It was late morning, and the thin sunshine was just strong enough to warm the skin. He handed her the weapon.

"Do you usually just slice it off yourself?" she asked, picking up a lock of his hair.

"What other could I do?" he replied as she stood behind him.

Alex made a tentative slash, his thick, coarse hair like raw silk against her fingers. It came away in her hand like a sheaf of wheat. She thought it was almost a shame to cut it.

He sat up straight as she gained confidence while she worked and the hair fell about their feet like a shower of burnt gold. After a time she walked around to face him and said, "Just a bit more."

"Oh, hack it off and get it done," he said impatiently.

Alex finished as quickly as she could, admiring the effect, and then began to brush the loose hair from his shoulders. He stiffened when she touched him.

"What are you doing?" he asked.

"Just cleaning you up. Be still."

She trailed her fingers slowly, tentatively, down the back of his neck, and he jerked away.

"Stop," he said, trying to rise. Still weak, he put a hand back to steady himself on the stone.

"We're not finished yet," she said, moving to face him.

"Yes, we are."

Alex knelt in front of him, putting a restraining hand on his arm. "Why don't you want me to touch you? I've been touching you every day that you've been ill."

He looked away.

Alex let the knife fall to the grass and inched closer to him. She moved as one hypnotized; she knew what she was doing but was powerless to stop herself.

"Answer me," she said softly.

He closed his eyes.

Alex seized the opportunity, leaning in to grip his shoulders, the skin smooth and taut under her hands. She kissed his collarbone a few inches from his wound.

"I was so afraid when you were brought so fearfully low by this injury," she whispered, her mouth still against his skin.

He pushed her away from him, grabbed her wrists, and held them up before her face.

"Go back to the camp," he said, clenching his jaw.

"Don't put me off. I've been days waiting and working up the courage to try."

"You don't need courage, girl, that's never something you could lack," Burke said, releasing her. "Go along ahead of me, I'll be just fine on my own."

But she stood her ground and faced him. She was looking down at him from a slight advantage, a strange perspective, since he normally dwarfed her. How could she make him admit what she felt so strongly to be true?

He waited, looking intensely uncomfortable, and almost afraid, if that were possible. Alex had seen Burke display many emotions, but never fear.

"Can you imagine," she began slowly, "what it was like for me to stand by and watch you so ill, thinking that you might die, that I might never have the chance to show you . . ."

"Show me what?"

"How I feel," she said, losing her nerve at last and looking at the ground.

"I know how you feel," he said, deliberately misunderstanding her. "You have discharged yourself on that subject many times in my hearing."

Alex knew instinctively that talking was not the way to break through his armor, but she was almost too intimidated to try again. Almost.

She took a step closer and hooked her arms around his neck. He sat rigidly, staring straight ahead, not resisting but not inclining toward her touch.

"I love you," she blurted out, edging closer to him.

"You do not," he replied as if he'd been expecting her to say it. His voice sounded strained.

She drew back to look at him. "Why not?"

"You've been sheltered, Alexandra. Too much so for your good, I think. Carberry had a daughter who was sent to live in England and died there of the plague. We were of an age. She lived at the castle when young, and I saw how an English girl of the moneyed class is raised. You've never been away from your home or close confined with a man before, and you're confusing that with . . ."

He stopped at Alex's entreating look, her eyes wider than ever. "Once back with your uncle you'll forget me in a fortnight," he concluded. The whole speech sounded rehearsed.

"Never," she said.

"You will marry a suitable man chosen for you by him."

"Never," she repeated. "I will marry where my heart lies, and nowhere else."

He sighed. "Heed me well, Alex. I know you saved my life, and I'm grateful. But . . ."

Just then, Alex bent and pressed her lips to his.

He turned his head abruptly. "Alex, leave off this or I'll not be responsible . . ."

"Don't be responsible," she said against his mouth. "Don't be. Forget how we came together. I have." She licked his lips, her movements inexperienced but urgent, her lack of sophistication conveying a raw longing that only made her more difficult for him to resist. With a low, helpless sound, almost a groan, he leaned forward and scooped her into his lap.

His full strength had nearly returned, and for just a moment Alex was frightened of him, as she had been in the beginning. Then she forgot her fear in the delicious sensation of being enclosed in his arms, being engulfed by his warm mouth.

He *does* want me, she thought in triumph. He does!

He certainly did. He kissed her deeply, his mouth soft and vulnerable, his lean body hard. She clung to him, winding her arms around his waist, feeling the muscles there contract beneath her fingers. He bent his head, and she arched her back as his lips trailed over the tender skin of her throat. She pulled aside the neck of her tunic to bare the way for him. She could feel the overwhelming need building in him, a need reflected in her own reckless desire to do whatever he wanted.

The next instant she was on her feet, dumped from Burke's lap like a fractious child. She looked up into his flushed face and saw that he was staring intently over her shoulder.

She followed his gaze to Rory, who was standing in the clearing, watching them.

5

*Her hips were white as foam, long, slender, soft
as wool . . . he desired her as he had no other.*
—The Competition for Etain,
fifth-century Irish saga

Burke greeted Rory in Gaelic, and his
tone was not friendly. Alex wasn't exactly sure
what they were saying, but she had picked up
enough of the language through daily exposure to
know that they were discussing her.

Burke said something that sounded like the end of
the conversation. Rory, refusing to be dismissed, stood
glaring at him. Burke repeated the phrase, and Rory,
with a final, mutinous look, turned abruptly and went
back into the woods from which he had emerged.

Burke stood up, a little bit unsteadily, but when
Alex rushed to his side he shook her off.

"I can walk on my own," he said gruffly, not looking at her.

She stood staring after him as he set off in the direction Rory had taken, leaving her no choice but to follow.

It was a grim, silent trip back to the camp. Alex felt like a chastised child who had been caught stealing honeycomb from the kitchens. Was it so wrong to demonstrate her love? And was it not reciprocated? Burke was acting as if she had forced herself on him.

"Go along inside," he told her when they reached his tent. It was the first thing he'd said to her since they'd left the glade.

"Aren't you going to tie me up again?" she said, unable to resist taunting him. "If left unbound, I might throw myself at Rory or some other poor fellow unable to defend himself."

Burke had the good grace to flush at that, and his eyes met hers briefly. Then he stalked off, leaving her quite alone.

Rory saw his opportunity and followed Burke to the edge of the camp. The other men glanced at them curiously but gave them privacy.

"Well?" Burke said, turning to face him, resigned to completing their aborted conversation.

"You have to ask?"

"Stay well out of it, Rory."

"Kevin, I mean to have my say. You know what we have at stake here. What in the name of old King Conchubor are you doing?"

Their conversation, conducted in the ancient language, proceeded in staccato bursts.

"This is an English girl!" Rory said. "A rich, privileged English girl whose uncle is a counselor to the queen, *and* her kinsman! Kevin, are you mad? This is no lay-up in the long grass with Deirdre or her like; you risk more than a by-blow if you bed this one."

"I know all that!" Burke said impatiently. "You tell me nothing I've not told myself a hundred times. But I have a care for her."

Rory sighed. "Cousin, listen to me," he said. "I know I was wrong about her. I don't want her treated badly either, she's a good girl."He used the encompassing phrase, *pastheen finn*, to indicate a young woman held in affectionate regard.

Burke nodded slowly.

"Then what's amiss?"

"Tha miannaich mi," Burke said simply. I want her.

Rory was flabbergasted. "You want her! What do you mean, you want her?"

Burke merely looked at him. He thought his meaning was clear enough.

"Then perhaps for once in your life you should not get what you want."

Burke shook his head impatiently. "You mistake me. I want to keep her with me."

"Keep her longer than we had planned?" Rory asked him, puzzled. "Why?"

"Keep her," Burke repeated. There was no mis-understanding the note of finality in his voice.

Rory stared at him, comprehending at last. "You *are* mad," he said. "And what about your brother?"

"We've had no response at all from the uncle. He doesn't want a trade."

"So we just let Aidan rot in the Inverary dungeon while you go bathing with the niece?" Rory demanded, incredulous.

"I did not say that."

"Then what's your plan?"

"I have no plan," Burke admitted. "I know nothing for to do," he added in English, reverting to the Gaelic construction as he sometimes did when troubled.

Rory surveyed his cousin, more worried than he would have admitted. He had never seen Burke indecisive; until now, that trait had not seemed part of his nature. "Will you really go to war over this woman?" he finally asked, straining for a calm tone.

"We're at war now," Burke replied. "This respite cannot last." He rubbed his sore shoulder absently, his expression distant. "I've had a summons from Tyrone. I go north tonight to the border, to settle up with Scanlon and discuss future plans. Word is that the Essex campaign goes badly, and Tyrone thinks the time to strike will be soon."

Rory listened intently, his heart beating faster.

"How long have you known this?"

"The rider came last night, while you slept."

Rory waited.

"Will you have a care for her while I am gone?"

"As you wish."

"I mean only, handle her gently. Nothing more should be required. She's in no danger now from the men, and she won't run. . . ."

"Because she wants to be with you," Rory finished for him. "She'll wait for your return."

Burke looked past him at the line of trees. "At times I wish to all the Druids who once ruled this isle I'd never seen her face," he said quietly, and then walked away.

The spring rains began the day Burke left. It was usually raining in Ireland, drifting mists and sudden showers alternating with bright intervals, but this was a drumming downpour that turned the camp into a mud wallow and drove everyone inside the tents.

Alex waited tensely, bored and restless, her spirits as damp as the weather. Rory would say only that Burke had gone to Ulster for a conference and should return in ten days.

Time passed so slowly that it seemed an eternity before a runner came into the camp to announce Burke's arrival. It had finally stopped raining an hour earlier, but the ground was spotted with puddles, and the trees dripped so steadily that it still seemed to be drizzling. Alex was waiting just inside the open flap of the tent when she saw Burke's sorrel horse. Her pulses began to pound. She was about to run out to greet him when she noticed that he was not alone.

A man and two women were riding behind him. They dismounted as he did, and Alex saw that one of the women was young. When she drew back the shawl she'd worn over her head to keep off the rain, her shining black hair cascaded to her waist.

Alex watched as the girl walked to Burke's side and put her head on his shoulder. When he turned away, she trailed her hand along his neck and then walked on alone.

Alex stared at her, unseen, as the woman passed. She was wearing an ankle-length dress of plain muslin, cut low at the neck to expose swelling breasts above a tiny waist cinched by a belt of linked metal circlets. Alex touched her own cropped hair ruefully as the girl lifted her heavy mane off her neck and then let it fall again.

Alex turned away and went deeper inside the tent, her thoughts in turmoil. She had her back turned when Burke swept inside and stopped short at the sight of her.

She whirled to look at him. "Who is that woman?"

They eyed one another, both restraining the urge to run forward. Was it possible that he had forgotten how pretty she was? The impact of her presence was like a blow: the pale skin tinged pink now with emotion, the tendrils of her cropped hair curling around her face in the dampness, making her look like a Flemish doll.

"A friend," he said.

"A friend!" She threw the word back in his face. "I'm not a simpleton. I saw the way she touched you." The way I long to touch you now, she cried inwardly.

Burke said nothing.

"What is she doing here?"

"She travels to the coastal village of her brother and his wife and will put up here a few days."

"How convenient. Is her presence your defense against me?" Alex inquired.

Burke saw how this conversation was likely to go and stepped outside, calling for Rory to close the flap of the tent and stand guard next to it.

"You assume I need a defense against you," he replied coolly when they were alone again.

This comment stung, as he knew it would. "Is she your mistress, then?" Alex demanded.

"She was."

"And have you had her many times?" Alex asked, her lower lip trembling.

"Many times," he confirmed, wondering why he was doing this when all he wanted in the world was to take her in his arms and kiss her until they were both breathless.

"And is she very skilled?" Alex asked, keeping up the farce, her voice shaking.

"Very."

It was her struggle not to cry that touched him. Her eyes were flooding, she was swallowing hard, but her chin came up proudly as she refused to give in to the weakness.

"Go to her, then," Alex whispered.

He waited.

"Go to her!" she cried, flying at him like a shrew. He caught her against his chest as she beat at him with her fists. "Have your fill of her and have done with me!"

He stopped her mouth with his own. Alex struggled and then clung, kissing him with all the fervor built up during her endless wait for his return.

"I haven't touched her," he said when he could talk. "I haven't touched another woman since I met you. I don't want anyone but you. That is my curse, and yours too." He kissed her again.

"Oh, Kevin, I thought you were never coming back," Alex murmured, losing herself in the delicious warmth of his embrace. "The days were so long."

"I want to take you here and now," he said hoarsely, running his hands down her back as if to assure himself of her presence. "I missed you sorely."

There was a slight noise outside the tent,

reminding them both of their precarious position in the middle of the bustling camp, and he released her.

"Can you find your way to the brook alone?" he asked, his breath still coming short.

Alex nodded. She knew the path by now.

"Come at moonrise," he said. "I'll be waiting."

He was gone before she could reply.

The night was cloudy following the rain, and Alex stood at the entrance to the tent, watching the horizon for the pale slip of the quarter moon to show above it. The camp was already still as soldiers rose and bedded early. She had not seen Burke, or the woman with the black hair, since he had left her alone in the tent that morning.

A shaft of light penetrated the trees, and Alex looked up saw the moon. She left the tent and slipped across the camp, smiling at the sentry who looked up at her passage and assumed she was answering nature's call. He nodded and looked away.

She did not see the woman who watched from the shadows, surrounded by a cloud of raven hair.

Under the canopy of leaves the ground was still wet, and it was difficult going in some places where her shoes sank into the soft grass. The moon was high by the time she reached the brook.

The glen beside it was empty. She hesitated, looking around, and then Burke stepped into her path.

Alex jumped. For a man his size, he could be remarkably stealthy when he chose to be.

He opened his arms and she rushed into them.

"Have you been waiting long?" she asked him.

"It seemed long," he replied, cradling her against his shoulder.

"I kept sinking into the mud," she said, drawing back to show him her boots.

"Let's have them off, then," he said, taking her by the hand and leading her further into the clearing. There was a blanket spread on the ground. "It's dry here; the sun shone on it this afternoon."

They sat on the blanket and he tugged off her boots, which were actually Rory's with a rag stuffed into each toe. He rubbed each slender foot as he exposed it.

"Did anyone see you come out here?" he asked.

"Just one of the sentries, but they're used to my going past them at night."

He lay back on his side, his cheek propped on one open palm. He surveyed her fondly as she sat twisting her hands in her lap, avoiding his gaze.

"Alexandra," he said gently.

She looked up at him.

"I'll not ravish you," he said.

Her blush deepened furiously.

"Perhaps you should cut my hair again. That put you in quite a mood," he said.

"You're teasing me," she said miserably.

"I am," he replied, "and I confess I'm a cur for it. Come here to me." He gestured for her to lie beside him, and she did gladly, comforted by the solid strength of his body and relieved that she could escape his penetrating blue gaze.

"Better?" he said.

"Yes." She snuggled closer to his side. "Why did you go off north without telling me?"

"Good-byes are hellish. I spoke to Rory and knew he would look out for you."

"And you were angry with me," she added.

"Was I?"

"For forcing you to face your feelings."

He sat up, and looked down at her. "True," he admitted. "How did a mite like you become so worldly wise?"

"I'm not a mite. Everyone looks small to you. And you are hardly an ancient sage to be acting so superior. How old are you, anyway?"

"Twenty-eight."

"Eleven years. Ten, really, I'll be eighteen soon. It's not such a gulf."

"It's not the years between us that cause the distance, Alexandra," he said.

"I will not think about it," she said. "We have this moment, this time, and while we're here I will not think about it." She put her arms around his neck and drew him down to her.

Burke half lay on her, holding himself up with one hand to protect her from his full weight. He smelled musky and masculine as Alex pressed her face into the hollow of his throat, luxuriating in the sensation of his skin against hers.

His mouth was moving in her hair, one large hand splayed against her waist to hold her to him. She felt the warmth on her ear, her cheek, and then she tilted her head to accept his lips on hers.

His kiss was gentle at first and then gathered intensity until her mouth opened and her head fell back into the crook of his arm. She heard the throaty sound he made when his tongue found hers, and she clasped him to her almost desperately, pulling him toward her until he was pinning her to the ground. One small hand traveled up his back to sink its fingers into the thick wavy hair at the nape of his neck. She shifted her weight beneath him, and he moaned, straddling her.

Alex felt him hard against her thighs as if their double layer of clothing had been burned away by the intensity of their desire. He pressed his face into her shoulder, and burrowed there, and she held him still, thrilled with the feel of him on top of her, anchoring her to the earth.

"Don't move," she whispered.

"I'll hurt you," he said in a muffled voice.

"I never felt a sweeter weight," she said, turning

to trace the shell of his ear with her tongue.

He raised his head to look at her, his eyes brilliant, and then bent again to nuzzle her breast, first mouthing her through the cloth, then pulling on it impatiently. Alex lifted her arms, her eyes still locked with his, and he sat back to draw the tunic over her head.

"Oh, Alex," he whispered when she was revealed. "You are so lovely." Her redhead's skin was milky in the moonlight, lightly freckled like a bird's egg, and her nipples pink brown, puckering with exposure to the night air and her growing excitement.

"I saw you once," he murmured, "taking a bath when you first came here. Do you remember?"

"I didn't know you'd seen me."

"By chance. I think now I lived only to see you again." He tossed the shift aside and knelt next to her, pressing his cheek to the satiny skin of her belly. She tangled her fingers in his hair, the coarse texture of raw silk under her hand, and closed her eyes.

For long seconds he didn't stir, then she felt his tongue trail upward to her navel. She opened her eyes and watched as his brown fingers covered one bare breast and his mouth found the other.

She gasped at the contact and cradled him against her, wrapping her arms around his shoulders and laying her cheek against his golden head. His tongue flicked, then soothed, changing sensations, and then he sucked gently, arousing her to the point where she was tearing at the loose shirt he wore above his leggings.

"Take this off," she moaned, but when he sat up to obey she whimpered at the loss of contact with him. He yanked the shirt over his head, tearing it in the process, and threw it on the pile made by her shift. She reached up to hook her arms around his neck and draw him down again. When his bare flesh met hers she sighed with deep satisfaction, kissing his naked shoulder, running her hands down his muscular arms and up again to the strong column of his throat.

"I feared you so when I first met you," she whispered, her hands fluttering lightly down his broad back, feeling it narrow toward his waist.

"And I thought you were a boy," he said, his mouth against her cheek curving into a smile.

"What think you now?" she whispered, wrapping her bare legs around his hips, feeling her power in his answering groan. She slipped one hand beneath the waistband of his pants and touched the patch of down at the base of his spine.

"Alex," he said hoarsely, raising his head to look at her.

"I know," she said. "I'm ready."

"Are you now?" he said. He eased his weight off her and lay at her side, trailing one hand along the line of her hip to the apex of her thighs. When he slipped his palm between them she sucked in her breath, then moaned at the delicious friction of his touch.

"Oh, please," she gasped.

"What are you wanting?" he asked, his lost brogue resurfacing with his emotion.

"More."

"Of this?" His caress went deeper and her legs fell apart.

"Of everything." She sighed and pressed against his hand.

"Do you know what I'm about to do?"

"Yes."

"It . . . the first time for a woman there is pain, I'm told."

"I can bear it, for the pleasure that comes later."

"So you do know the way of it?" he said, gathering her close, quelling the surging of his loins with an effort that made beads of sweat stand out on his forehead. He wondered whether she really understood the deep waters of the river she was crossing. If she were sorry, after, he would feel the worst brute in the world.

"Teach me," she said, lying back on the blanket, raising her arms above her head in submission.

He could take no more. He stood and pulled off his trousers. Alex looked at his naked body in the moonlight and then averted her gaze. He seemed too big and too strong for her delicate body. When he rejoined her on the ground and pulled her to him, she stiffened.

"Easy," he said soothingly, as if gentling a skittish horse. "Easy now." She could feel him hard against her, and she swallowed nervously. She balled her fists against his back.

His urge to enter her was the strongest he'd ever felt, but he knew if he forced her now she would be lost to him forever.

"No fear," he said, holding her loosely, letting her relax. "No hurry now, we've all night." He kissed her lightly, letting her pull him closer, letting her desire overtake her until they were entwined again in a passionate embrace. But when she locked her legs around him once more, his patience was tried beyond endurance. He lost all control and thrust into her wildly.

She cried out, and he stopped, resisting the overwhelming need to surge and surge again.

"Alex," he gasped.

She ran her hands down his back, slick now with perspiration cooled by the night breeze. She was motionless for a moment and then made a little sound and pulled him tighter.

Burke muttered something in Gaelic and dropped his head to her shoulder.

"I love you," she said into his ear.

When he moved again, she moved with him, in a sensual rhythm as old as time.

Alex was swimming in a pool of dreamy lassitude, her head on Burke's shoulder, safe within the circle of his arm. She opened her eyes and looked up at the dark sky, the gossamer clouds skidding past a crescent moon.

"Asleep?" Burke said.

"Happy," she replied.

"You'll be a mass of bruises in the morning," he said ruefully. "Your happiness will fade before they do."

"No."

"I was too rough. You've a mark on your arm now, there will be more later. I was too eager. It made me clumsy."

"No. My skin is prone to purple, it was ever so."

"Truly?" he said, looking down at her anxiously.

She reached up to touch his face. "Truly. No woman could have a sweeter lover to claim her maidenhead. Till the end of my life I'll remember this spring night and be grateful that you took me with such special care."

He was silent, wondering what the uncertain future would hold for both of them.

Alex traced the outline of his bicep with her finger. "Your body is beautiful," she said. "Like a statue."

"I've seen some statues, my lady," he said. "They don't come ribbed with scars."

"I don't mean the scars."

He grunted.

"I mean the sinews, the way they play beneath the skin."

"All men are made the same, Alex," he said. "You've only just seen me."

Alex didn't answer. He could never see through a woman's eyes, as she did, see that the way a man stood or moved, or turned his head, could single him out from other men and stop the breath in her throat.

"When you were away I thought you never would come back," she said softly.

He caressed her bare shoulder, making no reply.

"Did you reap the reward of your trip?" she asked.

"You might think so," he said. "Scanlon is dead."

"Did you kill him?" she asked, aghast.

"We had a contest," he said shortly. "It was fair."

"A contest?"

"To settle our differences. It was Scanlon who tipped the raid to the castle when I was hurt. And I owed him for you. I should have killed him back then. He was a blight on the whole countryside and surely no loss to the world."

"Did you see Tyrone?"

"I did."

"Kevin?"

"Aye?"

"This trouble between our two countries, why is it your life's work? Why are you so driven by it?"

"Someone should be driven by it."

"But what is it you want for your efforts?"

"Home rule for Ireland, to govern ourselves without the interference of your queen."

"Will you get it?" she asked, sitting up and drawing the blanket around her.

"I believe that it is coming closer."

Alex looked at him.

"Your friend Lord Essex is bungling his mission," Burke said. "He attacked the rebels in Leinster and Munster first, instead of taking on Tyrone as your queen ordered, and is already down by five thousand men. His ranks are being decimated by desertions and disease. Instead of putting down the pockets of rebellion, he's in the midst of a rout."

"Why so?"

"His timing is bad, for a start," Burke said. "Spring is not the season for an Irish campaign. Our roads are cow paths in good weather, and the rains have turned them into ditches, hampering his passage. We are used to the conditions here and can still move while he is stalled. We skirmish from the trees and fens, and the English don't know where to look for hidden enemies. Essex has lost a goodly portion of his force and accomplished nothing. He gets angry letters from your queen with every boat from England."

"How do you know these things?"

"Tyrone's spies are very well informed."

"And of course you were involved in all of it while you were gone," she said lightly.

He looked down at her.

"Well, how did you get this?" she asked, tracing the line of a vicious welt, obviously newly acquired from a knife, which ran the length of his sculpted thigh.

He didn't answer.

"So then why haven't they attacked our camp?" she asked, changing tactics.

He smiled slightly at her use of "they" and "our," and shrugged. "Mayhap they cannot find it."

This seemed possible. She doubted she could find it herself if necessary, and she certainly had not been able to find her way *out* of it when she'd tried. "What will happen?"

"Tyrone wants a truce on our terms, and it seems that Essex may be forced to give it to him. Gloriana's gilded boy is failing at his task. What think you of your uncle's mentor now?"

He had read her mind. If Essex fell, Philip Cummings would not be far behind him.

"I brought you a gift," he said abruptly, changing the subject as he stood and pulled on his pants.

"A gift!" Alex was delighted.

He retrieved a leather pouch from his pile of clothes and handed it to her. She tore it open like a greedy child.

"Paper!" she exclaimed. It was used, of course, the foolscap blank on only one side. There was also a slightly bent quill with a squib of ink.

"Wherever did you get them?"

"There is a monastery on the road to Armagh. I stopped and asked for writing necessaries and made a donation for their trouble."

"You did that for me?"

"For my lessons," he replied, grinning as he rejoined her on the blanket.

She turned over a sheet of the foolscap and examined it.

"What is that writing?" Burke asked.

"Introibo ad altare dei, ad deum qui laetificat juventutem meam," she read aloud.

"Well?"

"It's Latin, the first part of the mass. It must have been written by a monk, an apprentice scribe, maybe, for the practice."

Burke, who'd not been in a church since childhood when his mother had taken him to the castle chapel, would not have recognized it. "That seems fitting, for a monastery," he said. "Can you read Latin well?"

"Church Latin, like this, and some classical."

"You know so much, Alexandra," he said. "Latin, and elephants, and all such stuff as to be found in books. I feel like a child beside you."

Alex stared up at him, moved by the admission. "Everyone has to learn," she said. "I knew no more than you, once."

"When you were playing at nines with your governess?" he asked, smiling.

"Come, let's do some letters."

He pushed his hair back, and his face acquired that look of fierce concentration that she so loved. During his recuperation she had seen it many times as he had fielded his reading lessons. He sat cross-legged next to her now as she dipped the quill and scrawled a line on the paper.

"What is that you write?"

"You must see if you can decipher it." She held the paper under his nose.

He snatched it from her hand and continued to stare down at it. "A pair," he finally announced, looking at her for confirmation.

"Very good. And the rest?"

"Of."

"Yes. A pair of what?"

"St," he said, putting the first two letters of the next word together uncertainly. "Stay?"

She pointed at the sky.

"Star," he said.

She nodded. "You know the next word."

"Cross," he said, proud of himself.

"Crossed. A pair of star-crossed what?"

"Love. A pair of star-crossed love? What is that, a riddle? It makes no sense." He threw the sheet of paper on the ground.

"A pair of star-crossed lovers. That's what we are, and what we may remain," she said sadly.

"What does it mean?" he asked. She saw she had his full attention now.

"Lovers at cross purposes, lovers with an unfavorable conjunction of planets. A pair of lovers whom the fates conspire to separate."

"Is that how you see us?" he asked quietly.

"Am I wrong?"

He couldn't argue. He picked up the paper and

stared down at the words. "Is this your phrase?"

Alex shook her head. "It's a line from a play by Mr. William Shakespeare. I saw it at the Globe Theatre on Bankside last year, in the open air, as the reassembled playhouse was not yet finished."

"What play?"

"*The Tragical History of Romeo and Juliet.* It's an old Italian tale that Mr. Shakespeare took and adapted for his theatrical. The story concerns the children of two enemies who meet and fall in love and suffer for their passion."

"And how does it end?" he asked warily, as if he already knew the answer.

"Badly."

He crumpled the paper and tossed the ball into the trees. Then, as if in response to what she'd said, he pulled the blanket back and drew her, naked, into his arms. When she shivered in the night air, he covered her body with his own.

"Alex, will you stay with me?" he asked, kissing her hair.

"Of course I'll stay with you. What do you mean?"

"Here, in Ireland."

"Yes, yes. Why not?"

"You have no desire to go home, to England?"

"Oh, darling, my home is with you."

When he made love to her again, she matched his ardor with her own.

* * *

The heat of the sun on her face awakened Alex in the morning. She opened her eyes to see Burke sitting on the ground a few feet away, fully dressed and watching her.

"Time to go?" she asked, stretching.

He nodded, handing her the rumpled clothes she had discarded.

She donned them, and they headed back to the camp, holding hands in companionable silence.

Rory was waiting for them at the end of the path. Alex could tell by his expression that something had happened.

"We've heard from the castle," he said to Burke in Gaelic. "They're ready to make the trade for Aidan."

6

Alas, my love, you do me wrong
To cast me off discourteously . . .
          —"Greensleeves," old English air

Burke's expression didn't change, but Alex felt him release her hand slowly, as if he were coming to a reluctant but imperative decision.

"What is it?" she asked, glancing from him to Rory and then back again.

"Go inside the tent, Alex," Burke said quietly, nodding toward the camp.

"What about you?" she said, not liking his tone.

"I'll join you when I can."

Alex hesitated.

"Do as I say," Burke added more sharply. Reluctantly she left him, glancing over her shoulder.

"What are you going to do?" Rory asked Burke

with his usual directness once Alex was out of earshot.

"Why the devil did it take them so long to respond?" Burke countered, thrusting his hands through his hair.

Rory sighed. "There's a faction among the English who wanted Aidan hung as an example to us. They prevented the ransom demands from reaching Cummings. He only found out recently, when one of them confessed. Once he heard that Alex was alive, he sent a message demanding the exchange, but it took some time to reach us. You know they haven't been able to locate the camp and—"

He stopped his explanation when he noticed that Burke was barely listening. The question had been rhetorical. To him, the whys and wherefores of the delay were immaterial now. What mattered was his offer of the trade, and that his integrity demanded he honor it—even now, when it was the last thing on earth he wanted.

"Do the men know?" he asked Rory, looking around at the huddled groups conversing in low tones, certain individuals glancing over at him furtively. At the very edge of the clearing, Deirdre stood watching the scene as her brother saddled their horses.

"Some of them heard Carberry's messenger talking to me," Rory replied. "We were speaking English, of course, but Neary and Flavin can understand enough phrases to make out what was being said. I'm sure the word has spread." He waited a moment and then added, "They want Aidan back."

"As do I," Burke snapped. "Are they worrying I'll keep my English doxy in place of him?"

Rory didn't answer.

Burke stood with his hands on his hips, gazing into the distance. The shadows under his eyes reflected his sleepless night and the dread of this moment, which he had almost convinced himself would never come.

"Send a message back that we'll make the trade at dawn tomorrow at the castle gates," he said finally.

"To give yourself another night with her?" Rory asked, but without bitterness.

"To give me time to explain it to her. And I want it to happen in daylight. Less chance of a trick."

Rory turned to go.

"And Rory? Take the message yourself. And make it clear that if Carberry has any ideas about getting clever I'll kill the girl on the spot."

Rory stared at him.

"Say it just as I have," Burke directed him gruffly.

"But Kevin—"

"Be off with you now." Burke strode past him briskly into the tent.

Alex looked up as he came in, and the expression on his face made her heart jump into her throat. "What's happened?" she whispered. "Tell me."

"Rory heard from your uncle while we were gone. He wants to make the trade for Aidan."

"And?"

"I've set the time for tomorrow morning at dawn."

Alex felt as if he had punched her. "You don't mean you're going through with it?" she finally managed to say.

"I can do no other," he replied, staring at a point in the middle of her forehead, refusing to meet her eyes.

Alex was stunned into silence. And in the silence her anger grew, like a sleeping animal uncoiling and gathering strength to spring.

"What do you mean?" she finally burst out, standing and facing him, her fists clenching and unclenching as if she might strike him. "Tell them you've changed your mind, tell them they've accepted too late, tell them anything!"

Burke was silent as her furious words rained on him.

"You're actually planning to hand me over to them like some plaything which no longer amuses you?"

"Alex, listen to me," he began.

"Are you going to tell me that I've misunderstood, that you have no intention of giving me back?"

He looked away.

"I see," she said quietly. She began to pace. "You knew this all along, didn't you? You returned from your trip to parade that woman under my nose, knowing that this deal had been fixed. You went with me last night anyway, to have your amusement before the chance for it was gone, and all along my replacement was here, waiting for my imminent departure."

It wasn't true, it wasn't fair, but she was past the point where he could reason with her.

"I'll come back later and—" he started to say, but she cut him off in midsentence.

"Don't bother. I have no desire to see you again before I have to. When you come for me in the morning I'll be ready."

He stared at her a long moment and then walked through the tent flap as abruptly as he'd arrived.

Alex sank to the floor, covering her face with her hands. She felt too numb to cry and resolved then and there that she would not. If Burke could hand her over to her uncle with a stone face and nary a loving word, then she could act the same way.

She was awake the night through, but Burke did not come to the tent to attempt another conversation. When dawn began to streak the sky, she washed her face in the pot of cold water Burke kept in the tent, tidied her hair with her hands, and changed into a clean tunic of Rory's. She stepped

through the flap into a chilly, misty morning and
saw that Rory and Burke were dressed and ready,
waiting for her.

Rory was untethering two horses from a tree,
Burke's sorrel and his own dappled gray. Burke
watched her progress toward them and then
mounted his horse. He took the reins from Rory
and extended his hand down to Alex.

Alex had no choice but to grasp his hand. He
hauled her onto the horse in front of him, where
she sat turned into the hollow of his shoulder, her
legs draped over one side of the horse. As they
trotted slowly out of the camp, Rory falling in
behind them, the men emerged from their tents
to see them pass, watching their departure in
silence.

The trip through the woods was agony for Alex.
Burke's physical closeness made the fact that they
would soon be parting even more poignant. She
closed her eyes and savored the pressure of his
arms around her, trying to remember it forever.
The rising sun filtered through the trees, dappling
the leaves and creating shafts of light that pierced
through the foliage to the ground. No one said a
word until they were within sight of the castle and
could make out the trio on horseback waiting
there, the last wisps of the lifting fog swirling
about them.

Alex turned to look up at Burke, but his gaze
was trained ahead, on the men.

"That's Aidan," Rory confirmed behind

them, and Alex looked at the man in the middle, between Lord Carberry and her uncle. He was as big as Burke, but slightly heavier and darker, his wavy hair the color of roasted chestnuts.

"Come up by me," Burke said to Rory.

They came to a halt about fifty feet away from the three men. Aidan was dressed plainly, like his brother, but Carberry was outfitted in dandyish fashion, with a purple doublet and hose and a matching cap trimmed with gold thread perched on his graying hair. Alex's uncle wore his usual sober clothing, but cut from the finest materials. His fingers were heavy with rings, and the Cummings ancestral sword was sheathed at his side.

There was a long silence.

"Well, Burke," Carberry finally said, his voice ringing out in the early morning stillness, "is this how you repay my wife's kindness to your mother?"

"My mother was your wife's chambermaid, for which service she was paid, not well, but very meanly," Burke replied. "And that was the end of it."

Carberry shook his head. "You always were an arrogant pup, and you have grown into a most noisome man. You spent time under my roof, you were my sainted daughter's childhood friend. Well, she is gone to God"—he crossed himself—"and so much the better to avoid what you've become. Have you no memory of those days?

Have you forgotten entirely the regard of my family for yours?"

"My quarrel is not with your lost ladies, but with you," Burke replied.

"Alexandra, are you well?" Philip Cummings called out to her, ignoring this frosty exchange.

"Yes," she replied.

"You've not been harmed?"

She felt Burke stiffen behind her. "No," she said. "I've not been harmed."

"Let her down," Cummings ordered Burke.

"When my brother's by my side."

Carberry and Cummings exchanged glances. This testy meeting could erupt into dangerous hostility at any moment; it behooved them to cooperate. Cummings nodded at Carberry, who unsheathed his knife and leaned over to Aidan, slicing through the rope binding his hands. Aidan nudged his horse and it trotted forward until he brought it around to stand next to Burke.

"A bheil thu math?" Burke asked him. Are you all right?

"Tha," Aidan replied. I am.

"I'll take my niece now," Cummings announced.

Burke jumped off his horse, held his hand up to Alex, and lifted her to the ground. For just an instant, his hands lingered on her waist, and Alex wanted to fling her arms around his neck and beg for him to keep her. But the moment passed and she turned away, glancing briefly at Rory before facing her uncle.

"Come here," he said, and she obeyed, taking up her position next to his horse.

"I trust I'll see no more of you," Carberry said contemptuously to Burke.

"You'll see no more of me when you've left Ireland to the Irish," Burke replied. He looked at Alex a final time, his eyes very blue in the morning sunlight. Then he kicked his horse and galloped for the trees, his brother and Rory following him.

Alex watched them until they had disappeared completely into the forest.

Alex stared down from her tower room at the moat below, the brackish water ruffled by the evening breeze. Sentries patrolled the entrance to the drawbridge, which was down now to receive a contingent of riders. At their head she spotted Lord Essex, his magnificent apparel bedraggled and stained from travel; even from such a distance she could see the dried mud clinging to his clothes and boots. She studied the scene for a moment and then turned away with a sigh. Both she and the queen's favorite had come to grief in Ireland.

Once she'd had time to think about it, she knew she could not blame Burke for what he had done. He had behaved according to his own code of ethics, which was as strict in its way as the lord privy seal's. He had made an offer to his enemy, and when it was accepted he had no choice but to go through with his part of the bargain. He simply could not make his feelings for her more important. An English gentleman would have done the same.

Alex heard the rattle of a key in the lock and braced herself for another interview with her uncle.

He was preceded into the tower room by one of Carberry's servants, who deposited a tray on the serving table near the fire and then scurried out again. Philip Cummings waited until the woman was gone, his hands clasped behind his back in an attitude of forbearance, and then turned to confront Alex when the door closed.

"Well?" he said. "Have you anything more to say?"

Alex looked at him in silence.

"I find it incredible that you could spend such a length of time in the company of that rabble and then have nothing to report about the experience."

"Uncle, would you have me invent some horrifying tale of abuse that you can use for political purposes? As I've already told you, I was well treated, I came to no harm, and now I'm back with you. There's little else to say."

His annoyance with her was apparent. "I hope you understand that all this befell you simply because you defied the rules set out for where you could walk about the grounds."

"I understand that."

"I was humiliated before Carberry and Lord Essex," he said, beginning a familiar diatribe. He went on to describe his humiliation in detail, but she wasn't listening. Rather, she was staring out the window once more at the scene below. The drawbridge was now being raised.

Her view was obstructed when her uncle stepped in front of her and slammed the shutters closed.

"I'll thank you for your attention," he snapped. "You don't seem to realize fully the position your extraordinary behavior has resulted in for me. We've lost a valuable hostage because of you, one that we might have used to better purpose."

"Then why did you redeem me?" she asked.

He pursed his lips, not answering.

"Oh, it's not necessary to reply," she said. "I know how strongly you feel your responsibility concerning me."

"And thankful you should be for my family feeling, else you would still be languishing among those ruffians, little girl."

"They're not ruffians," she said, trying to suppress her anger.

He stared at her, astonished. "That Burke is no better than a highwayman! It's well known that he and his men ambush travelers to the castle and rob them, cutting their purses and stripping their horses."

"He practices robbery on occasion to arm his men, to free their country."

"He practices robbery to line his pockets! His spurious patriotism is an excuse for brigandry of the worst sort."

Alex had seen firsthand how humbly the rebels lived and was tempted to protest, but she realized that perpetuating this argument would only enrage Cummings further and reveal to him where her true feelings lay.

"I can't believe you would defend that gang of hooligans to me," he said.

"I was not defending them," Alex replied, now sorry she had spoken, "merely stating a truth. If they were as bad as you say, I'd be dead or worse, and well you know it."

His eyes narrowed. "Alexandra, you have always baffled me, but never more than at this moment. You were spared in order to trade you for that bandit's brother, and for no other reason. I hope you harbor no romantic ideas about their treasonous rebellion against their lawful queen, and ours."

Alex fell silent again.

"That Burke is well set up, is he not?" he said.

Alex maintained her composure with an effort.

"A handsome man, you might say. Young, and apart from his rebel's rags, quite comely?"

"Elevate your mind, dear uncle," Alex replied, determined to drive him off this dangerous track. "He saw me as a trading chit, nothing more."

Cummings seemed to accept this, probably because he did not want to consider anything else. "You'd best eat that meal," he said. "From the look of your thinly covered bones you've lost a stone since you were gone."

She was surprised he noticed. As he turned to go out she stopped him.

"Uncle Philip? When did you send the message to the rebels holding me that you agreed to the trade?"

He seemed surprised at the question. "Just the day before the trade was made. Why do you ask?"

Alex closed her eyes. So Burke had *not* known he was giving her back when he spent the night with her by the brook. It was something, anyway. She had little enough to hang on to now.

"Alexandra, are you sure you are well?" There was a genuine note of concern in his voice, and Alex felt a sudden stab of sympathy for him. What a curse she must seem, visited upon his late middle age: headstrong, impulsive, and a general bother, she was a blight upon his well-ordered bachelor's life. Yet he clung to his duty, unable to abandon his late brother's child no matter how much he might want to do so.

"I'm sorry for all the trouble I've been to you, Uncle," she said quietly. "It was never my intention to disrupt your life."

"Eat your dinner," he said, and swept from the room. She heard the key turn in the lock after he left.

Alex walked over to the tray and glanced without interest at its contents. The succory pottage was unappetizing, smelling strongly of woad, and the chop looked greasy. She took a sip from the pewter flagon of malmsey and its sticky sweetness almost gagged her. Sighing, she picked up the small loaf of manchet bread and went back to the window and opened the shutters. She nibbled the crust as she peered through the gathering dark at the world of freedom that lay below.

There must be a way out of the tower room.

"I *will* have her back," Burke said.

Rory threw up his hands. "You've lost your mind and no mistake. It's over, Kevin. She is with her own people and better off for all of that. Let it go, man."

"Do you love her?" Aidan asked his brother quietly.

"I ken I must," Burke replied. "What other can this be? I can't sleep, I can't eat, I think of her every minute, and I've gone off other women as if I'd taken holy orders."

"Even Deirdre?" Aidan asked.

"Haven't you seen her pining away all over the camp for lack of encouragement?" Rory asked.

"So you love the English girl," Aidan said. "And you gave her up for me, so I will help you get her back."

Rory stared at Aidan as if he'd announced he was joining forces with Essex. "Don't encourage him in this folly!"

"I'll watch the castle and find out where they're keeping her," Aidan said. "Are you certain they haven't shipped her off to England yet?"

"No boats have left since she went back to Inverary with her uncle," Burke said.

"It shouldn't be too difficult a task to locate her within the castle. After that we'll plan the rest."

"What rest?" Rory called after Adian as he departed. Then he turned to Burke, who sat brooding on a tree stump, chin in hand. "You're not thinking of taking her again?" he asked.

Burke met his eyes, then looked away.

"By force?" Rory demanded. "What makes you think she'd come willingly? She was none too happy with you when she left."

"I'll see her first and explain."

"You'll see her where? In Carberry's reception hall? Will you show up at the gates, peasant cap in hand, and ask His Lordship for an audience? Kevin, leave off this madness now before you get us all killed over this slip of a girl!"

Burke stood and walked away a few steps and then turned to face his cousin. "Rory, I think we've had this talk already, have we not?"

Rory made a dismissive gesture.

Burke held up his hand. "How long have we been fighting the English now?" he asked. "Ten, maybe twelve years? And in all that time, have I ever departed from the path to our goal? What, in all those days and weeks and months, have I asked for myself?"

Rory examined him in silence. They both knew the answer.

"I want this woman," Burke said quietly. "It may be folly, as you say, but I will not let her go back to England without trying to see her and keep her with me. Now, if you won't help me, at least stay silent on the subject."

Rory sighed heavily and passed his hand over his eyes. "I'll help you," he finally said.

"Good. Now come along and we'll work on a plan."

Rory followed Burke back toward the camp.

Two weeks passed, during which Alex pricked her fingers attempting the needlepoint that Carberry's servants supplied, read the reformation religious tracts that made up the castle library, and stared out of the window. The weather was unfavorable for sailing or she probably would have been packed off to England immediately. No boats were going until the spring rains subsided entirely. This meant that mail did not reach them either, so Lord Essex was of uncertain mind as to the full extent of his queen's displeasure. He continued the failing campaign, losing more men by the day, and an aura of gloom pervaded Inverary.

Alex found it difficult to sleep, spending her nights recalling her time with Burke, and on one such night she lay awake with the shutters open to the spring breeze. She could tell the passing of the hours by the calls of the sentries on the leads. It was past three in the morning by her count when she heard a noise at the window.

She sat up in bed, peering into the darkness, illuminated only by the dying fire at the other end of the chamber. Her first thought was that a bird was trapped between the shutter and the wall, as sometimes happened. Then there was a louder thud as a figure jumped from the parapet into the room.

"Don't scream," a low voice said. It was Burke.

Alex scrambled out of the bed and flung herself on him, only to discover that he was soaking wet.

"Run and bar the door," he said, pushing her away and pulling his drenched tunic over his head. Alex did as she was bid, shoving home the heavy wooden crossbar and then rushing back to embrace him, pulling his head down and covering his face with kisses.

"What kept you so long from me? I thought you would never get here, that you had abandoned me."

"Come away from the window," he said, taking her arm and leading her toward the bed. Only then did he embrace her, holding her close to his damp, chilled skin, kissing her cheek, her hair, and finally her mouth. His fingers fumbled with the drawstring neck of the lawn gown she wore, and it was soon puddled at their feet. He sought her breasts with his hands, then with his mouth, as he lifted her and set her back on the bed. Alex tugged at his tight leggings, the wet material fighting her. She yanked on them in frustration until he put her hands away and undressed himself. When he joined her she twined her limbs around him and wrestled him into position, desire giving her a strength that surprised and delighted him. When he entered her she moaned with satisfaction and he covered her mouth with his hand, then his lips.

It was over quickly, both of them too starved for niceties, and they collapsed, panting, in each other's arms. When he could talk once more, Burke whispered, "I'm wondering what became of that trembling virgin I once knew?"

Alex yawned. "Sir, you have corrupted me."

"Madam, how you talk."

She curled her arms around his neck and settled against his shoulder. "However did you get here?"

"I swam the moat and climbed the first parapet, then slipped down into the kitchens and up the inside stairs. From there I waited for the sentry to pass, and crawled out on the leads to your room."

She had forgotten that he knew the castle well, from his childhood. "How could you tell which room it was?"

"Aidan scouted it for me, but the tower always seemed much the best choice to keep you close. I didn't think that in your case Cummings would choose the dungeon."

"Oh, and why so long?" she murmured, turning her head to press her lips to his throat. "I've been going mad here, thinking all sorts of awful things, first among them that you had resolved to let me go and I'd never see you again."

He tightened his arm around her. "I had to wait for the dark of the moon, else the sentry would have seen me cross the water." She felt him stir slightly as he drew the coverlet over them. "And I wasn't sure of my reception."

"Did you think I would turn you away?"

"You weren't speaking to me when you left."

"Well, why didn't you comfort me, say that you would come after me?"

"The less you knew, my lady, the less your uncle could ferret out of you." Alex thought about her outburst during her last conversation with that venerable man and knew Burke was right.

"What happens now?"

"Are you still of the same mind, to stay with

me?" In the uncertain firelight, his eyes flashed like gemstones when he changed the direction of his glance.

Alex stroked the slight cleft in his chin. "How can you even ask me that?"

He shrugged. "Once you were gone, I was . . . unsure."

"Did you think I'd go back happily to the life I had before? Prayer services and tutorials and stitching coverlets?"

"Regular meals and a warm bed and safety from all storms," he countered.

"None of that matters. I craved your presence so much I thought I would die!"

"Truly?"

"Truly. And this I missed most of all," she said, stripping back the coverlet and falling on his naked body.

He laughed. "I've never awakened a virgin before. I must do it again."

"Never!" she said, sitting astride him. "Never again with anyone else. Promise me!"

"Never is a fearful long time."

"Promise!" she said, stroking him.

He closed his eyes.

"Well?"

"I promise." He pulled her onto him.

"And we won't be separated for the rest of our lives."

"Not by me," he replied, rolling her under him.

Alex gave herself up to pleasure, and it was only

later, when she was curled against him again, that he realized she was crying.

"What?" he said, touching her wet face.

"I missed you horribly. I didn't want to live. We will make very sure we aren't parted again."

"Then we must plan." He folded his arms behind his head thoughtfully. "If your uncle has no real regard for you, as you've said, what matter to him if you remain in Ireland?"

"As the consort of the queen's enemy? You jest. Appearances are everything to him. He'd lock me in a cell and toss the key in the Thames before he'd have it known that his ward was so careless of his wants and his name."

"And if it were not known?"

She looked at him and smiled.

"In secret, then," he said.

Alex nodded. "Unless you want to fight it out."

"He won't come after you a second time?"

"Not the first time, either, if Essex hadn't been aware of the situation. I'll just disappear and he will say, 'Silly girl, such a shame,' and add the cost of my keep back into his estate. A mysterious disappearance he could bide, but not my open choice to stay with you. They'll all be leaving Ireland soon anyway, they talk of nothing else at the castle. Essex is expected to be recalled at any moment."

He was staring past her shoulder. "So I'll come again tomorrow, this same time, and leave two horses tethered in the woods."

"Why not tonight?"

"The best time has already passed. The lazy sentry who never walks his whole route falls asleep each night between two and three. We must wait for him again. And it must be tomorrow, because after then the moonlight will return."

"If I meet you at the kitchen entrance, it's an easy path from there," she said, excitement creeping into her voice.

"Is there kitchen staff through the night?"

Alex shook her head. "They come in at six to start the cooking fires. Until then it will be empty."

"Are you afraid of heights?"

"A little."

"No matter. The drop from the kitchen level is small, I can take you on my back. Can you swim?"

"Yes, but I haven't for a long time. Is the moat very deep?"

"Deep enough, but no concern if you stay on the surface."

"I don't suppose there's any way we could go out by the bridge," Alex said wistfully.

He stared at her.

"Disguises?"

He continued to stare.

"I have no confidence about this plan," she admitted.

"Leave it all to me."

There was a knock on the door to the hall.

Burke and Alex exchanged alarmed glances.

"What is it?" Alex called, holding her finger to his lips.

"I've been sent by your uncle to check on you, miss," a woman's voice answered.

Alex pointed to the bed, and Burke dove under the covers, curling into a ball. She bunched the coverlet to disguise him, but he was a big object to hide. For good measure she went to the standing storage wardrobe and grabbed a few of Lady Carberry's gowns, which smelled strongly of the pomanders hung in their midst to preserve them. She tossed them on top of Burke. At the last moment, she snatched his clothes up from the floor, scattering the rushes, and threw them under the bed. Pulling her nightgown back over her head she went to the door and eased back the bolt to admit her visitor.

"Are you all right, miss?" the servant asked.

"Yes, of course. Why not?"

"Your uncle gave me to understand you were sleeping poorly. He thought a glass of honeyed cow's milk might go well." She indicated the tray she carried.

He thought a bit of spying might go well, you mean, Alex thought. "I haven't been sleeping well, it's true," she replied, "and so I've been arranging your late mistress's warm-weather clothes to pass the time, as you can see. I was told to take of them what I wished. But I am fine. I'll take the milk and you can go."

The woman set the tray by the fire and turned to look at Alex with a puzzled expression.

"Well?" Alex wanted to drive the wretch from the room with a spade.

"When I was in the hall outside just now I'd vow on my life I heard voices."

Alex coughed, glancing at the lumpy bed. "I suffer from night terrors. You must have heard me babbling in my sleep."

"While you were airing the clothes?" the woman said.

"I wearied of the task and lay down in the middle of it, so dozed off and had a worrisome dream."

"Why was the door bolted?" the servant inquired.

Am I on the rack? Alex wanted to scream. She kept her expression impassive, aware that the woman would report every inflection to her uncle.

"A portboy stumbled in here on Sunday when I was in a state of undress. To avoid another such accident, I have taken lately to bolting the door."

"I see," the woman said.

"That will be all, thank you."

The servant finally left, glancing over her shoulder, and Alex ran to secure the door after her.

"All right," she whispered, and the gowns cascaded to the floor in a jumble of rich fabrics as Burke's head appeared, the coverlet draped over it like a nun's veil.

"Who was that?"

"An informant, carrying milk and honey. My uncle is uneasy about me, so he sends spies bearing gifts. What he thinks I can get into up here in the middle of the night defies understanding."

Then she realized belatedly what she had said and they both burst out laughing.

"Shh!" Alex said, clapping her hand to her mouth. "Do you want to be taken in my bed?"

"I'd rather take *you* there," he said, snaking out an arm to pull her down to him.

Alex rolled into his embrace and fitted herself to his naked body.

"What's all this?" he said, tugging on the nightgown. "Let's have it off." It joined the muddle on the floor.

"For two whole weeks I dreamed of you every night, when I slept at all," Alex murmured, clinging to him, luxuriating in the feel of his muscular limbs. "Such dreams to make a doxy blush. I longed for you. In my whole life I've never felt anything so wonderful as your hands on my body. When I thought I would never feel them again I wanted to fling myself from this tower room and splinter to little pieces on the bridge below."

"Don't say such things," he said, pulling her closer. "You tempt the fates."

"Lord Essex complains that the Irish are a superstitious bunch."

"We are that, surely."

"Do you think that an excess of happiness draws the envious attention of heaven?" she asked.

"Hush now, you talk nonsense," Burke said, trying to soothe her , but she heard the wary note in his voice. He shared her fears.

"I'll die if I'm parted from you now!" Alex cried, perilously close to tears.

"Who talks of parting?" Burke said. "Not my lovely girl." He put his hands on either side of her waist and lifted her onto him. Alex closed her eyes and clutched his shoulders, penetrated, sinking, surrounding him with herself.

"Do you love me?" she gasped.

He groaned.

"Say it," she commanded, moving on him.

"I love you," he said hoarsely. "How could you doubt it?"

They both fell asleep afterward, and when Alex awoke the sky was ominously lighter.

She shook Burke awake. "You must go," she said urgently, slipping out of the bed and retrieving his clothes.

He stirred drowsily.

"Now," she added, thrusting the clothes at him. They were still damp. She should have spread them out by the fire, but it was too late for that. He would have to wear them as they were.

He stood and pulled them on, grimacing at the

clammy feel against his skin. He strode to the window and squinted at the horizon, then down at the drawbridge.

"Will you get away safely?" Alex asked, shivering in the predawn chill, wrapping a sheet from the bed around her.

"I'll be fine, Alex," he said, embracing her. "If I got up, I'll get down again."

"You'll come again tomorrow night?"

"I will."

She drew back to examine his face. "Think you that we shall see each other again?"

He kissed her lips to silence her. "I'm certain of it."

"Go," she said, pushing him toward the window.

He released her and climbed through it, maneuvering his tall body bit by bit until she heard the thud of his landing on the leads below. She wanted to look after him but was afraid to call attention to his progress, so she went back into the room and sat on the bed disconsolately.

God speed you back to your men, she thought. And then right back to me.

When the time came to meet Burke late the next night, Alex dressed as simply as she could, taking nothing to carry, and crept down the narrow spiral stairs leading to the kitchen. The castle was quiet; she could hear the steps of the sentry in the distant great hall echoing as he strolled to and fro, clanking his lance against the paving stones as he completed each round. She ran through the kitchen and the larder and pushed open the heavy outer door that led to the courtyard.

The moat gleamed below her and the night wind ruffled her hair as she stood waiting, praying that Burke was on his way. She should have known better: he was already there. One large hand clutched her shoulder and the other covered her mouth securely as he stepped up behind her.

"Follow me," he said into her ear.

Alex turned and did so, trailing in his wake. When they reached the edge of the parapet he knelt swiftly and motioned for her to climb onto his back.

She locked her arms around his neck and her legs about his waist. She closed her eyes as they swung over the edge and then swayed free as he went down the wall hand over hand. She didn't know they had reached level ground until he unlocked her death grip on his neck and said softly, "Get you down."

They were facing the rippling water, which looked colder and darker at close range than it had from her window. He took her hand and whispered, "Ease yourself in, now. Don't make a splash."

Alex climbed over the stone barrier and hung

on with her hands, letting her feet touch the water and then lowering herself down the inside surface of the ledge, grabbing for crannies in the rough bricks. She gasped as the cold water closed over her body and then let herself drop, keeping her head above the surface with frantic paddling. Burke joined her seconds later, and then he set off across the water with strong, overarm strokes, slowing his pace to keep Alex with him.

It seemed an eternity before they reached the other side. Alex was freezing cold, her lips blue, as she watched Burke scramble for handholds and climb out and then stretch flat on the ground to reach down for her.

She was almost out of strength. Burke plucked her from the water as if lifting a doll from the nursery floor to place it on a shelf. When she felt the grass under her feet she threw her arms around his neck and sobbed with relief.

"Isn't this a charming sight?" said a voice behind her.

The lovers whirled to find Philip Cummings confronting them with a contingent of armed men, some bearing torches.

Cummings strode up to Alex, his hands on his hips.

"So you were nothing to Burke but a trading chit, eh?" he said, throwing her words back at her. "Did you think you deceived me that easily?" He slapped her face smartly.

"Don't you touch her!" Burke lunged for Cummings and managed to knock him to the ground before Carberry's men dragged him off the older man. They pinned Burke's arms behind his back, and a sword was leveled at his throat. It took three soldiers to hold him.

"Get off of him!" Alex cried, her mind barely able to take in what was happening.

"Such touching devotion," Cummings said. "It seems our Mr. Burke does not lack for female admirers, but he must take care to treat them better." He smiled unpleasantly at Alex and then at Burke, who glared at him in mute fury.

"It was one of them who told us about this little plan to spirit you away, Alexandra," Cummings went on. "Your lover's discarded mistress was only too happy to inform us about an interesting conversation she had overheard in the rebel camp. A buxom lass, frolicsome no doubt, but not too scrupulous. It seems she bears a bitter grudge against your young gallant here for deserting her." He patted her wet shoulder solicitously. "I'm afraid you are not in very exclusive company, my dear."

"Let him go," Alex cried. "I'll stay here with you, just let him go."

"Oh, no, it's much too late for that," Cummings said as if they were discussing a missed appointment. He turned to the castle guard, who were watching him alertly, awaiting direction.

"Take him," he said.

Burke was dragged away, bucking and struggling, as Alex stuffed her fist in her mouth to keep from screaming.

7

I find that I sent wolves and not shepherds to govern Ireland . . .

> —Queen Elizabeth I, upon hearing of massacres conducted there in her name.

Alex was returned to her tower room and confined there for almost a month, eating from trays brought to her three times a day. She saw no one but servants, who were forbidden to speak to her, and had no news of Burke. She watched spring blooming from her window, the comings and goings of the troops, but nothing disturbed the dull routine of her miserable life. Nothing except the knowledge that she had missed her monthly flux for the first time since it had begun when she was twelve years old.

Of Burke's fate, she knew nothing.

One day in late May, after she had watched her uncle departing with Lord Carberry and a contingent of men at dawn, she vomited her breakfast. When the charwoman returned to take the tray and saw the mess she looked at Alex through narrowed eyes.

"I couldn't clean it up myself. I have no washing things here," Alex said.

The woman departed and came back shortly thereafter with a bucket. Alex saw her opportunity and said, "I wish I could walk outside this room for a bit. I would keenly enjoy the fresh air."

The woman continued her task without responding.

"Is my lord of Essex still in residence?" Alex asked, trying to strike up a conversation.

The servant glanced at her but still didn't speak.

"I know you have orders not to converse with me, but if he be here, can you not ask him if I may take some exercise? In my uncle's absence he is in authority and could give me leave to walk in the courtyard."

Alex hoped that the woman would be afraid not to convey her request, and that Essex, always partial to ladies, would be a more lenient jailer than her uncle. She was right on both counts. About an hour after the woman had left, a guard came to her door and said he had orders from Essex to take her out for a walk. Apparently, the ban on talking to her had been lifted also; the young man engaged her in conversation, and Alex found that trading pleasantries with him helped to pass the time and keep her mind off other, weightier matters.

Thereafter the guard came every day, and the longer her uncle was gone the higher Alex's hopes rose. She befriended the boy, an easy enough thing for a pretty girl to do, and on the fifth day she asked him lightly, "Is there an Irish prisoner still in the dungeon, a big man, with hair the color of river rushes?"

"Aye, miss, he's there," the guard responded, not knowing he was speaking of her lover. He had been told that Alex was under guard because she'd been kidnapped once and was therefore a vulnerable target for the rebels.

She withdrew her hand from the folds of her skirt and opened it to reveal the gold bauble lying on her palm. It was one of the few relics she had of her mother, and it was very valuable—a year's wages for this soldier, enough for his greed to overcome his fear.

"I wish to see him," she said.

The boy's eyes grew enormous. He looked from the locket to her face and then back to the gleaming object. She could see his conflict in his rapidly changing expression. Under other circumstances it would have been comical.

"There will be little risk for you if you take the night shift and slip me in after dark. Bribe the regular guard to stand his turn; what you give him will be little enough by comparison with this." She closed her fist and hefted the chain.

"It would be worth my life . . ." he began fearfully.

"No one will see us! We will take great care. My uncle is away, and my lord of Essex is preoccupied with greater troubles than my taking a nocturnal stroll."

He shook his head. "I know not—"

"Come at nine if you decide to be a rich man," she said impatiently, and went into her room, pulling the door closed behind her. She heard him hesitate a long moment before his footsteps receded down the hall.

Alex was nearly in a fever waiting for the hour of nine to arrive. If she had guessed wrong and the guard reported her offer to Essex, Philip Cummings would probably drown her like a puppy when he returned. Did the boy stand to gain more by taking her bribe or by currying favor with his superiors and turning her in to them? Then again, he might do nothing, just ignore her offer and go on as before. She flattened the rushes on the stone floor with her pacing, trying to anticipate what he would do.

Nine o' clock came and went, and nothing happened. Alex was almost weeping with frustration when there was a light tap at her door, about ten minutes after she heard the sentry pass below her on his rounds.

"What is it?" she called, putting her ear to the door.

"'Tis 'Arker, miss."

Alex clasped her hands together in gratitude. The guard had come after all.

She opened the door, and he extended his hand to her, palm up and waiting to be filled.

"Not until I've reached the dungeon," she said.

He shrugged, turned, and set off down the stairs without a word. Alex followed, lifting the skirts of Lady Carberry's old gown clear of the stone steps and descending in a spiral toward the cellars.

Alex had never been this deep into the castle before, and as they went lower the walls became slimy, covered with moss and lichen. The dampness was pervasive. They passed the kitchen level and still kept going down, the stairwell narrowing, until the tidal smell of the moat was overwhelming and the low ceiling pressing in on them fairly dripped moisture. Alex's stomach clenched. Burke had been in this fearful place for how long? One night would be enough to break her spirit. At least the guards could leave it when they went off duty; for Burke, it was home.

Harker stopped short as they came to a level spot and turned a corner, where an open room was divided into a guard post and three barred cells. A torch fitted into a wall sconce showed that two of them were empty. Harker nodded toward the last one, where she could barely see a dim figure prone on a bed of filthy straw.

Harker held out his palm once more, and Alex dropped the necklace into it.

"I'll wait at the foot of the stairs, there," Harker said. "If you hear me speak up, hide around the bend until I come for you."

Alex nodded distractedly, her gaze still on the farthest cell. She walked toward it slowly, wanting to run but alerted by some inner instinct that told her she'd better see him before he knew she was there.

Once outside his cell, she was glad she had been quiet. He was lying full length facing away from her, his wrists manacled and held close together by a length of chain fixed to a peg in the floor. His broad back was striped with whip marks, some of them dried and black, some still oozing. Even in the uncertain torchlight she could see the blue bruises on his arms, the gash on the back of his head that matted and darkened his fair hair.

Alex sank back against the wall, her hand to her throat, trying to catch her breath. She didn't speak. She knew he would never want her to see him like this. They had obviously been tying him up and holding him defenseless while they whipped and abused him. He was a man they could never have defeated in a fair fight.

She felt a surge of cold hatred for her uncle, yet it was mixed with a terrible sense of responsibility on her part for what had happened to Burke. He had come back to the castle for her, and if it hadn't been for her, he would be safe now, with his men, plotting the destruction of his enemies, and blessedly free.

Alex knew what she had to do. She turned and walked back to Harker's station.

"I'm ready to go up to my room now," she said.

Harker looked at her, puzzled. He had heard no conversation, and her payment had been beyond extravagant for a visit so brief. The upper classes had always been a mystery to him, and this lady was no exception. He turned and led the way up the stairs.

When they reached Alex's room, she said to him, "Mr. Harker, I would take it as a favor if you'd leave word for my uncle that I wish to speak to him most urgently when he returns."

Harker looked alarmed.

"Not about you. Our business is done and remains between us. And one thing more. Pray do not tell the prisoner I came to see him."

"I'll say nothing, miss."

"Thank you. Good night."

He waited until the door closed behind her and then hurried down the stairs, fingering the locket in his vest.

Alex waited five more days for her uncle's return, and by then her resolve was firmer than it had been in the dungeon. She looked up from her needlework one afternoon to see him stride into her chamber, fresh from the road, stripping off his riding gloves.

"I've been told you wish to see me," he said.

"Yes."

"Well?"

Alex stood and shook out her skirt, putting the embroidery hoop on her chair. "I wanted to tell you that you've won. I know what's been happening to Burke, I've heard the servants talking. I can't let him be tortured any longer because of me. If you let him go, I'll return to England whenever you like and do whatever you require."

"Tortured?" Cummings said, raising a brow.

"What would you call it?"

"Burke has been interrogated concerning his treasonous activities, which is our practice with any captive rebel. I would encourage you not to dramatize his injuries, or your role in his current situation. Though you will certainly go back to England and obey me in all things, you have no power to bargain for your lover, my dear. You value yourself much too highly. He's been persuaded with the lash because he will not part with information we need. It has little to do with you."

"It doesn't matter what methods you use on him. He will tell you nothing."

"He is human. He will break."

"Why bother to question him at all?" Alex burst out, unable to control herself. "Your cause is lost, Uncle. Lord Essex has forfeited the queen's support, and nothing Burke could tell you will help you at this point."

"What do you know about it?" Cummings

demanded, walking toward her and grasping her shoulders. She squirmed under his painful grip. When he released her suddenly, the room seemed to spin, and she sat down hard on the edge of the bed, almost swooning. When her vision cleared she saw her uncle's boots planted a few inches from her feet. He was staring down at her pensively.

"Feeling poorly?" he asked.

"A bit dizzy."

"I see." He strode away from her and then turned to face her with his arms folded and his legs apart, like a judge at a fencing match.

"The servants tell me that you are often unwell at mornings and have had no flux since you returned from your time among the rebels," Cummings said. "Is this true?"

Watched so closely as she was, it had only been a matter of time before the servants got together and reached the obvious conclusion.

"Your silence is eloquent," her uncle said, when she did not reply.

"What do you wish me to say?"

"You are with child," Cummings stated.

"I know not." She paused. "It may be so."

"By that same august personage who now enjoys the hospitality of Carberry's keep."

Alex said nothing.

"A fine choice for your child's father. Or do you know he's the father? Were you servicing the whole lice-ridden lot of them?"

Alex gave him a look of icy contempt and then stared away from him deliberately. How could she ever have felt sorry for him for being saddled with her? He was as mean as a viper, and she hated him.

"I know better than to ask if he forced you," Cummings observed, disgust plain in his voice. "Christ's sacred blood, Alexandra, I could skin you alive. You are a disgrace, quite beyond hope. You have dishonored me, the memory of your parents, the name of our entire family."

"And you're covering our name with glory, I suppose, slogging through the bogs after Essex, chasing phantoms? You have pistols and gunpowder, men and supplies, the whole might of England behind you, and you still can't put the rebels down. They'll go on fighting even if they're reduced to throwing rocks, don't you see that? Burke would rather die than help you. Punishing him because I love him, or because your gamble in coming here was a bad choice, will not change the outcome of your benighted campaign or make me into the niece you think you deserve."

"I see you have adopted the quaint Irish custom of making boring speeches."

Alex fell silent. She would have to keep reminding herself that talking to him was wasted effort.

"It is clear that I must expedite the plans I had in mind for you," Cummings said.

Alex's heart sank. What did he have in mind?

"I have written recently to my good friend, Lord James Selby of Hampden Manor in Surrey, to offer him your hand in marriage. Do you recall him?"

Alex had a vague impression of an older man, her uncle's contemporary, with grown children and substantial holdings in the county that had been mentioned. More important, though close to the queen, Selby was not an intimate of the Essex contingent and had taken no sides in that group's constant struggle with Cecil's faction. Cummings was clearly carving an alternate route for himself if things continued to deteriorate along their current course.

"What would induce Lord Selby to take me off your loving hands?" she asked.

"A substantial dowry and the promise of my influence at court with Lord Essex."

"Then you'd better step smartly before the Essex influence wanes further," Alex said.

"I wouldn't be so flip if I were you, Alexandra. My letter did not include the news that you would be coming to the marriage bed with a bastard in your belly."

"Perhaps he'll call it off, then."

"We shall see."

"Are you suggesting I should deceive him?"

Cummings gave her a look of mock horror. "You? Practice deception? Perish the thought! In any event, you'd best marry somebody before that brat begins to swell your stomach, and it might as well be Selby. You could do worse."

"I insist that he know about my condition."

"You are not in a position to insist on anything."

"If what he wants is my dowry and your good offices with the queen, he may not care about the child. It is merely that I remember him to be a decent, kindly man and do not wish to see him misled."

"You've acquired a tender conscience? A recent addition, I assume. It did not trouble you while you were consorting with known criminals in defiance of *my* express commands."

"If you don't tell Lord Selby, I will."

"Enough!" Cummings exploded, slamming his fist down on the fireside table so hard that the crockery rattled. Clearly he would not allow Alex's scruples to interfere with his neatly formulated plan to transform her into a respectable country matron and make a valuable political connection at the same time.

"By your leave, sir," a nervous page said from the doorway.

They both looked at the boy, conscious for the first time that Cummings had not closed the bedroom door on his arrival.

"Captain of the guard requests your immediate presence, sir," the page said.

"Bother," Cummings muttered under his breath. In a louder voice he said, "Tell the captain I am now detained and will see him at my first leisure."

The boy hesitated.

"Well?" Cummings said.

The page glanced at Alex, then at her uncle.

Cummings made a sound of exasperation and stalked over to the boy. They conversed in a low tone and then the page hurried off. Cummings turned to look at Alexandra, his expression grim.

"What is it?" she asked.

"Apparently we didn't 'torture' your paramour quite enough. He's escaped."

Alex couldn't control the joyous glow that suffused her countenance.

"You are not heartbroken by this intelligence, I see," Cummings said.

Alex made no reply.

"You realize, of course, that he's deserted you," her uncle added spitefully.

"It gladdens my heart that he is free."

"He's left you with his by-blow and will now return to pursuing the same type of low woman who betrayed him to us. He cares nothing for you, he never did. Despoiling you was part of his revenge on his hated overlords. He played you like a lute, my girl."

Alex sighed and folded her hands, fixing her gaze on the wall behind his head.

"I hope you're not entertaining any notions of his returning here for you. He knows what it would mean for him to do so. He'll forget you and disappear into the fens forever. You should accustom yourself to that notion and arrange your future accordingly."

Cummings whirled about and strode purposefully from the room. Alex ran to the window and looked down at the trees, praying that they would conceal her lover and silently wishing him the choicest of luck.

Burke slid from his stolen horse and hit the ground hard, reaching for a tree trunk to steady himself against it. The world swam for a moment. He pulled the hood from his head and discarded the peasant's cowl on the ground. The man he'd taken it from was lying unconscious with a welt on his brow and would have a thick head in the morning, but Burke was pleased that it had not been necessary to kill him.

He tethered the horse to a low branch by a stream. He wasn't sure how far he'd come from Inverary, but he thought it was safe to take a brief rest. If he tried to push on, he could pass out, and then Carberry's men might come across him. He was unable to tell if he was being pursued, but he thought it likely. They knew he was injured and would therefore expect his progress to be slow.

His back felt as if it were being raked with fingers of fire. His thin tunic was stuck to the oozing wounds, and his flayed skin came away with the cloth when he took off the shift and sank gratefully into the stream.

The cool water eased the burning, and he closed his eyes, thinking about the woman he had left behind at the castle. If only he had been able to take her with him. Getting this far himself had been difficult enough and had taken weeks of planning. Trying to include her would have made the whole scheme impossible. The only way was to go back for her with a force of men when the time was right. In his mind he knew he'd made the only choice, but in his heart he felt that he had abandoned her.

He crawled out onto the bank, trying not to imagine her sitting alone in the tower, wondering what had become of him. She was strong and brave. He smiled to himself when he thought of her intractable behavior when he'd first kidnapped her. She would endure. He would find a way to get a message to her, and they would be together some day. He drifted into a doze, thinking about their life together, their children . . .

Burke shook himself awake. Falling asleep now could be fatal. He dragged himself to his feet and dressed again, pausing to cup his hands and give a drink to the tired horse. He mounted the animal and set off at as brisk a pace as the weary horse could manage, promising himself that it would have a good meal and a warm stall at the end of their journey.

Ten days after Burke's escape, Alex went walking in the courtyard with Harker. Her uncle had permitted her exercise to continue; perhaps he thought that with Burke gone he could relax her security, but she was still unable to leave her room unescorted.

"Fine day, miss," Harker said.

The rain had stopped, leaving the vegetation as green as emeralds and the countryside fresh and renewed. A strengthening sun warmed Alex and her guard as they strolled across the worn flagstones, taking the morning air.

Alex stopped short as a child rushed up to her, clutching a nosegay. The little girl tugged at Alex's skirt and proffered the flowers.

"What's this?" Alex said. She recognized the child, the daughter of a local washerwoman who came in to do day work at the castle. The Irishwoman often brought the girl with her, much as Burke's mother once brought him to the kitchens.

"Posies for you, miss," the child said in English with a pronounced brogue, and curtsied.

"How lovely, thank you," Alex said, smiling. The child's mother stood nearby, watching the scene intently.

"My mam says to look careful among the blooms so you don't get stung," the child added as she handed her the bouquet.

Harker was looking on with a bored expression. As Alex took the flowers she glanced at the little girl's mother, and something in the woman's eyes made her realize that this was indeed a special bouquet.

Alex nodded. "Please tell your mother that I

understand," she said loudly, and turned away before her own face betrayed her.

Harker moved on and Alex kept up the pretense of the walk for another few minutes before she said, "I think we should go back. I'm a little tired today."

Harker took her back to her room, and the second she was left alone Alex tore the bouquet apart. There was a note concealed at the base of it, where the twisted stems were held together by a piece of twine.

"Exspectaru me," she read. *"Ego per te reddereo."* Wait for me. I'll be back for you.

Alex read it again, her hands shaking, and then sank slowly onto her chair.

How on earth had Burke gotten the message translated into Latin? Another trip to the Armagh monastery? It was a sensible precaution; if the note had fallen into the wrong hands, only a few people could decipher it.

She closed her eyes for a long moment, then opened them again and tore the note to bits, tossing the fragments on the fire in the grate and watching as they burned to ashes.

I'll be back for you.

But what would be his fate if he came back? The fighting could go on for years, as it already had, and as long as Burke was a wanted man, it was not safe for him to return to Inverary.

* * *

On her next walk with Harker, Alex waited until he had returned her to her door and then said, "Tell me something, please. The prisoner I visited, the man who escaped–if he were to be taken again, what would happen to him?"

Harker's eyes met hers and then slid away.

"Tell me," she repeated.

"I think they would kill him, miss. He's already shown he won't give up any information, so the next best thing would be for them to deprive the rebels of his leadership."

Alex sighed and nodded. She had thought as much. "Will you do me another service?" she asked him.

"If I can."

"You know the mother of the child who gave me the flowers. She's a laundress, I believe?"

He nodded.

"Will you send her to me the next time you see her? I wish to speak to her about the way my linens are being done."

"Yes, miss, I'll see to it."

It was several days before the woman finally appeared, late one day, with Harker in tow. She was obviously wary, her posture stiff and her expression withdrawn.

"It's all right, Harker, I'll see this lady and you can go," Alex said to him.

He looked from one to the other.

"Unless you want to hear a discussion on the uses of lime wash and tallow soap," Alex added.

"I'll be just down the hall," he said as he left.

When he was gone, Alex took the woman's arm and led her to the other end of the room. "Don't be afraid, I mean you no harm," she whispered.

The woman stared at her, wide-eyed.

"Do you speak English as well as your daughter?"

"Well enough."

"Who gave you the bouquet of flowers for me?"

The woman shook her head. "I was told to say nothing, miss, to make sure you got it but to say nary a word else about it."

"By whom were you told?"

She shook her head again and looked at the floor.

Alex tried to hide her impatience. Pressing the woman would only make her say less. She had learned from Burke that when uncertain, they all shut up like a guildsman's vise.

"What's your name?" Alex asked gently.

The woman looked up at her. "Maura."

"Maura, listen to me. There was a note concealed in the flowers, and the person who wrote it is dearer to me than anyone else in the world. He's one of your own people, the father of the child I'm now carrying. My love for him is the reason I'm kept under lock and key here. Do you understand?"

Maura hesitated, then nodded.

"Do you know where he is? Is he safe?"

"He's safe."

Alex grasped the woman's hand and held it to

her lips. "Thank you," she said, her eyes filling. "Oh, thank you for telling me."

If Maura had any doubts, Alex's reaction to the news of Burke's safety convinced her of the Englishwoman's sincerity. She withdrew her hand slowly, taking pity on this lonely lady who was clearly unhappy and desperate for word of her Irish lover.

"He's well," Maura said. "They did their worst to him belowstairs, as you might know, but it takes a powerful lot to fell that one."

"Will you tell him something for me?"

"When I see him. I don't know when that will be. They're always moving about."

"When you see him, then."

Maura waited.

"Tell him that I've gone back to England, to do my uncle's bidding. Tell him"—and here her voice faltered, but she forced herself to go on—"tell him to forget me."

"Are you certain you want me to say that, miss?"

"Yes, just that," Alex said, wiping her eyes. "It's the only way. If he comes back to the castle after me, they'll kill him. Tell him there's nothing here for him, that I've gone home. Do that for me, Maura? Will you promise?"

"I promise," Maura said quietly.

Alex pressed her hand again. "I have nothing to give you." The last of her mother's jewelry had gone to Harker and she had no money.

"I want nothing."

"Are you ladies finished?" Harker said from the doorway.

"Yes," Alex replied, turning away to hide her tears. "And I'll expect my instructions to be followed to the letter, Maura. No more mistakes, is that clear?"

"Yes, miss."

"You may go."

Alex watched her leave, hoping that Maura could be trusted but aware that she had no choice in the matter.

The next boat brought a letter saying that Lord Selby would take Alex to wife under Cummings' conditions, and she was told that same day to ready herself to depart within the week. The weather continued to be clear, and a crossing might be made at any time.

There was almost nothing to pack, as she'd come dressed as a boy and was going back home in a dead woman's clothes. But she was taking from Ireland a host of memories that would have to last her for the rest of her life.

"Good-bye, Harker," Alex said to her guard as he lifted her single bag and placed it outside the door. "If ever I need a compassionate jailer to keep a prisoner close confined, I shall send for you."

Harker looked embarrassed, shifting his feet.

"What is it?" Alex asked.

He withdrew the locket she had given him from his blouse and handed it to her. "I think you should have this back, miss. I don't feel good about taking it from such a forsaken lady as yourself, kept locked up here all this time and so grievously troubled."

Alex pressed it back into his hand. "It's yours, Harker, for your many good offices toward me."

"I've done nothing, miss," he mumbled.

"Oh, but you have. You've been a friend to me when I needed one sorely. God keep you."

She walked into her room and Harker went off with her sack, wishing that such a goodly young lady had a happier life.

When Alex boarded ship on a warm morning in June, the one thought sustaining her was that Burke's child was safe in her body and she would have it to remember him. The trip across the channel was horrendous; the nausea of early pregnancy combined with seasickness kept her prone and miserable for the greater part of the journey. Philip Cummings allowed her to return to his house long enough to take some of her belongings, but then she was packed off to Surrey almost immediately, as if the bridegroom might decamp if kept waiting too long.

Alex and Lord Selby were very formal and correct with each other. She was past two months pregnant at their first meeting at his house in the country, near Richmond Palace, and she informed him of that fact immediately.

"Don't distract yourself about that, my dear, there's room enough in my household for another child," he said.

So her uncle had gotten to him first, or else Selby had not been blind to the indecent haste of the proceedings.

"The father . . ." she began.

He waved his hand dismissively. "No matter. You and your offspring will have my name and my protection, and there's an end to it. Now shall we discuss the details of the wedding?"

8

Blarney!

> —Queen Elizabeth I, in response
> to excuses offered for her military's
> inability to subdue the Irish.

Alex was married in the chapel of Selby's manor house the day after her arrival. As she listened to the minister droning the words of the service, she heard herself saying to Burke, "I will marry where my heart lies, and nowhere else."

My love, forgive me, she thought. I do this for your sake, and for the child's.

The ceremony was mercifully brief, and afterward Selby took her into his study. The room, like the rest of the house, was richly appointed, with silk hangings and a Turkish carpet, and Alex found herself wondering again how a man who seemed to be so wealthy had been induced to marry her for a dowry. Maybe Selby was in debt; she knew her uncle sometimes kept up appearances while juggling creditors and chattel mortgages. Or perhaps Selby really did want the Cummings influence at court. Things had happened so fast that it was all beyond her. She felt like a cork bobbing at sea, carried on by the current and fighting every minute just to stay afloat.

"How are you feeling, my dear?" Selby said. He smoothed back his graying hair and adjusted his doublet. He was in his late fifties and when young, must have been a handsome enough man.

"Fine."

"Good, good. Sit you down there and rest comfortably whilst I sort through some things here."

Alex sank gratefully onto a plush chair with a velvet seat cushion and an elaborately carved back. She watched him rustling through a stack of papers on a Spanish oak desk. A globe of costly Venetian glass at his elbow held a handful of quills, and the inkwell cut into the desk was full.

"Now, then," he said as he found what he wanted. "As I am sure your uncle has told you, I am attached to the staff of the ambassador to the Netherlands, a grace and favor appointment which keeps me away in the Low Countries most of the time on the queen's business."

Alex nodded.

"I shall be leaving for Amsterdam on the morrow, and I wanted to take this time to instruct you on the supervision of the house and the handling of the servants."

Alex listened as he described the daily routine of Hampden, which was overseen by a Mrs. Curry, a housekeeper Alex would be meeting shortly. Mrs. Curry had been in charge of running the estate when Selby's late wife had been alive. It didn't sound as though Alex would have much to do; there was a clerk to keep the books and pay the bills, Mrs. Curry to supervise the staff, a groom and stable boy to care for the horses, and a driver to take her out in a carriage if she wished to go anywhere. In other words, she was to be installed at Hampden to await the birth of her baby while Selby was off on business and the servants handled everything else. It was a tidy solution to her problems, she had to grant her uncle that. She would avoid certain disgrace, and the child would be born legitimate. That Alex would also be alone and miserable during her approaching confinement did not seem to concern anyone.

"Does that sound satisfactory, my dear?" Selby said, interrupting her reverie.

"Yes indeed."

"My children from my first wife, Margaret and John, are both married and long gone from this house. Margaret is living in Italy with her husband, and John is called to the bar at Lincoln's Inn and seldom comes out this way, but if either of them require the hospitality of this house in my absence, I expect that you will offer it to them."

"Of course."

"I have agreed with your uncle to make provision for you in my will, and a copy of that document is in his hands right now."

Alex nodded. She had not expected Cummings to waste any time.

"My children's share has already been distributed to them, inter vivos, and the bulk of the estate is entailed for my son, so it is all settled, and you will have no cares on that score."

"I'm sure everything is in order," she murmured. She didn't care what arrangements had been made, but she was sure that Philip Cummings had driven a good bargain.

Selby stood up. "It occurs to me that you might be troubled on another matter."

Alex waited.

"I do not expect you to fulfill your obligations on the physical side of marriage."

Alex looked at him blankly.

"Neither one of us has entered into this arrangement for that reason," he continued. "As you are already with child, I think it will ease your mind to know my mind on the subject. I have had a room prepared for you next to mine, where you will have privacy and comfort and can live unmolested. There is a connecting door between the two rooms for form's sake, but I shall not be using it."

Alex tried not to show the relief she was feeling. Thank you, merciful God, she thought. She had been prepared to go through with all of it, but the thought of sleeping with this man after her passionate lovemaking with Burke had given her some awful moments.

She found her voice. "I'm very grateful," she said. "You've rescued me from a questionable fate and seem to be asking for nothing in return."

Selby held up his hand. "I do ask that you serve as lady-in-waiting to Her Majesty when she is in residence at Nonsuch, Oatlands, and perhaps Richmond."

"Oh?" Alex had not known she would be shouldering this duty, and it was typical of her uncle to have omitted the information.

"The queen is not often at Oatlands, except in hunting season. She prefers Nonsuch, or Richmond, which is warm in winter, closer to London, and big enough to cater to her entire court. But it has always been the custom of the women of this house to attend her whenever she is close at hand. I doubt it will be in summer, as she progresses through the south from Greenwich then, but if she wishes you to follow her to Richmond, or indeed anywhere else, you must do so, and leave Mrs. Curry in charge here. As you may know, the queen is abrupt and changeable, and if she takes a fancy to you will expect you to wait upon her at her behest. Beyond that, it is true that little will be demanded of you, and that your uncle has made this marriage very much worth my while."

"How?" Alex couldn't resist asking.

"He has been assigned partial revenues from the

import of sweet wines, in perpetuity, and has agreed to a limited partnership in the enterprise with me."

"That franchise belonged to Lord Essex," Alex said in surprise.

"He has transferred a fifth portion of it to your uncle."

Alex smiled thinly. "And your taking on the charge of me was part of the deal," she said.

"Your kinsman hopes that marriage and the responsibility for a child will settle you."

"I could hardly do worse than previously, in his opinion," Alex said, sighing. "I fear my uncle is severely disappointed in me."

"High-spirited young girls are often settled by a stable marriage. You will be well treated here and can recover from an experience that I'm sure was something of an ordeal."

Alex looked at him with alarm. What on earth had Cummings told the man about her time in Ireland?

"I loved the father of my baby, Lord Selby," Alex said. "I still do. If it were at all possible, I would be with him now."

"Oh, I'm sure, I'm sure that is very true," Selby said. "Now, in view of our contract lately made, don't you think you should call me James?"

Throughout the summer, the rebels continued to fight the English to a standstill. The armistice

was declared in September. Essex met with Hugh
O'Neill, earl of Tyrone, at the River Langan—
Essex on the shore and Tyrone astride a horse in
the water. The two men agreed to an immediate
cessation of hostilities and a future devise of home
rule for Ireland. Then Essex returned to England
and an irate queen, who put him under house
arrest for ignoring her orders. The world waited to
see what his eventual fate would be. He had
calmed her and won her to his side often before,
and bets were heavy that his charm would claim
the day again and he would once more dominate
the court.

Burke left Tyrone in the north and rode for
Inverary the same day peace was declared. Aidan
and Rory insisted on going with him. The truce
should protect them, but it was new and fragile,
and no one could predict what Carberry's reaction
to their arrival would be.

When the trio rode up to the gates of the castle,
the guards presented arms.

"Kevin Burke seeking admission for an audience
with Master Carberry," Burke called out in English.

Carberry's men stared at him, lately a prisoner in
their dungeon, now demanding to see the lord of
the castle.

"Did you not know that the peace has been
made, and that you must honor it?" he asked them,
smiling slightly.

They glanced at each other nervously, and
finally the captain of the guard broke from his

position and called for the drawbridge to be lowered. It creaked down and shuddered slowly into place, and then the captain strode across it and disappeared into the cavernous entrance of the castle.

They all waited in silence for his return, the Englishmen lined up with their lances at the ready, the mounted Irish gazing straight ahead and controlling their restive horses.

The captain returned minutes later, stopped at the nether end of the drawbridge, and called loudly through his cupped hands, "Admit the visitors!"

The English parted ranks, and the Irish rode between them across the bridge, their horses' hooves clomping loudly. When they dismounted in the courtyard, pages came forward to take the horses and Kevin strode purposefully through the entrance, his brother and his cousin slightly behind him.

Carberry and Cummings were waiting in the great central hall, and Burke noticed with a distinct feeling of unease the expression on Cummings' face. He didn't look like a man whose cause had recently been defeated.

"Where is she?" Burke demanded.

Cummings smiled unpleasantly.

"Have you still got her locked up in that tower room?"

"I assume you are referring to my niece," Cummings said.

"I am, and well you know it. Where is she?"

"She is not here."

"What have you done with her?"

"She's gone."

Burke stared at him, his fists balled at his sides. "What do you mean, gone? Gone where?"

Aidan and Rory exchanged glances.

"Gone back home to England, where she'll be safe from you and all of your kind. She was very glad to go and to put all of this, and her captivity with you, well behind her," Cummings said.

"I don't believe a word," Burke said as he took a step forward.

Two guards closed in, and Rory grabbed Burke's arm.

"Mind yourself, man, you could forfeit the peace over this," Rory said to him in Gaelic.

"And so could they!" Burke fired back.

"He may be telling you the truth," Aidan said to his brother.

Burke eyed Cummings. "I want to see the room where she was kept," he said. He made for the stairs in long strides before anyone could stop him.

The guards started after him, but Carberry waved his hand dismissively. "Let him go. He'll find nothing."

Burke stormed up the stairs two at a time and burst into the tower chamber where Alex had been confined. The room had obviously been abandoned for months; it smelled musty, the cupboard was empty, and the window was barred with dusty shutters.

Burke ran back down the stairs and confronted Cummings. "What have you done with her?" he cried again, this time in anguish, the cords standing out in his neck.

"Did you think to find her here, knitting a kirtle and waiting for you like patient Griselda while you fought your nasty little war?" Cummings said.

"If you've harmed her, I'll kill you," Burke said flatly.

"Harmed her? I think not. She has made a splendid marriage and is most content and settled in her homeland, quite undisturbed by thoughts of you, I feel certain."

"Marriage?" Burke said incredulously.

"Kevin, leave this and let's away," Rory said quietly in Gaelic. "You heard the man, she's married."

"You expect me to take this blackguard's word for that?" Burke demanded in English.

"It's quite true, Burke, I assure you," Carberry interjected, speaking for the first time. "She left here in June and married upon her return to England. She's been a wife for months."

"To whom?" Burke whispered, his expression terrible. "To whom is she a wife?"

"I'll tell you nothing more," Cummings said, his lip curled and his tone supercilious. "Now be gone from this place before I lose patience and treat you as you deserve."

Burke, stunned by the information he had just received, allowed his kinsmen to lead him out of the hall and to the castle entrance. Then he suddenly thrust off Aidan's restraining hands and rushed back to Cummings. He was stopped by a trio of guards, who took hold of him as he wrestled to get free.

"Tell me where she is!" he shouted at Cummings.

"I know where she is," one of the guards said in Burke's ear as Rory once more joined the fray, trying to restrain his cousin.

Burke stared at the guard.

"Stop bucking like a horse, go quietly outside, and I'll tell you," the man added.

Burke paused, astonished, and then recovered enough to look away. He straightened as the men holding him back gradually let go of him. He faced Carberry and Cummings, similarly dressed and standing side by side, like a child's wooden soldiers.

"You've lost your dominion here, and you think to take your petty revenge on me by keeping me from Alexandra," Burke said. "I would advise you to think again."

"Your words are as worthless as your loathsome country," Cummings said. "I make haste to put the memory of it, and you, long behind me." He turned and left the room, Carberry following closely after him.

"Come along, Kevin, there's nothing more for you here," said Aidan.

The men filed out, and when they went for the horses the guard who had spoken to Burke earlier held out his reins.

"I know you," Burke said in a low voice, searching the other man's face for confirmation.

"I sometimes had the charge of the dungeon whilst you were imprisoned there. You may have seen me with the turnkey at searching time."

"What have you to say to me?"

"She is married to Selby, Lord James Selby of Hampden Manor in Surrey," the guard said quickly. "I took the letters down to the boat and saw the address."

Burke repeated the information to himself and then said, "Why do you tell me this?"

"My name is Harker," the guard said, looking over his shoulder as another guard approached them. "Commend me to your lady with all good wishes."

"I will, surely," Burke murmured as the other man thrust the reins into his hand and moved quickly away.

The Irishmen mounted and rode across the drawbridge, which began to ascend the moment they left it. Burke called a halt as soon as they entered the trees and were out of sight of the castle.

"I know her husband's name," he said to Aidan and Rory. "The guard told me as I left."

Rory snorted. "Why would one of them tell us anything? He made up a tale to throw you wide of the mark."

"I think not. I ken he was well intentioned and meant to help."

"Help us?" Aidan said. "You're dreaming, man! You want to believe, so you do. Give it up." His voice changed, took on a kinder timbre. "She thought you had abandoned her and so she went home and married her uncle's choice for her. It follows. Girls like that are raised to do as they're told, to obey their elders."

"Not Alex," Burke said softly.

"It's no slight to you, her feeling for you was true, I saw that," Rory added in his cousin's support. "Her kinsman must have left her little choice."

All three looked up at a noise in the underbrush. A woman, red-faced and disheveled, burst into the clearing.

"Maura!" Burke said, handing his reins to Rory and dismounting. "I have been searching everywhere for you."

The washerwoman indicated she was too out of breath to talk as he took both of her hands in his.

"Easy now," Burke said soothingly. "Take a moment to get your wind, I'll wait."

"I saw you," Maura finally said in a rush, "entering the castle as I was going home. I waited until you left and then ran after you. I never would have caught up if you hadn't stopped here."

"Well, you're with me now."

"Is it true that Tyrone got a peace pact from the English?" she asked him breathlessly.

"It's true."

Maura pressed his hands and smiled. "No small thanks to you, I'll warrant."

"Did you deliver the message in the flowers as I asked?" he said impatiently.

Maura nodded. "That same day, back in June."

"And?"

"She was most happy to hear that you were safe away and out of English hands."

"And?" he prodded further.

Maura hesitated. "She gave me a reply. She made me repeat it to get it by heart."

Burke waited, his eyes fixed on her.

"She said, 'Tell him that I've gone back to England, to do my uncle's bidding. Tell him to forget me.'"

Burke closed his eyes.

"She was sore afraid for you," Maura added. "She thought you would be killed if you came back after her."

"So she thought if she left I would be safe?" Burke demanded, throwing up his hands. "Damned headstrong, impossible woman! All she had to do was wait! Why the devil couldn't she wait?"

Maura looked away from him.

"What?" Burke said to her. "What is it?"

"She was with child. She told me so herself."

Burke didn't move, but he looked much as if he might collapse. "My child," he whispered.

"Your child," said Maura.

Burke looked back in the direction of the castle

and said between his teeth, "I should gut that bloody bastard like a flounder. He knew and never told me."

"There's nothing to be done for it now, Kevin," Aidan said. "Leave it alone. We've won the peace on our terms and the girl is gone. Let it go."

"There's something to be done, right enough," Burke said. "I'm going after her."

"To England?" Aidan said in astonishment.

"To England. That's where she is, I'm told."

Aidan looked at Rory, who shook his head. It was no use talking to Kevin on this subject; Rory had already tried many times.

"You can't leave now. We've just stopped fighting, and there's much to be done," Aidan protested.

"Nothing you can't handle on your own," Burke replied. "The difficult part is over, and you don't need me for the rest."

"How do you plan to get there?" Rory asked.

"I'll get a curragh from the fishermen."

"A fishing boat is not meant to cross the Channel," Aidan pointed out.

"I'll tar it well and outfit it fully for the voyage."

"It's foolhardy," Rory said, stating his opinion for the first time. "But of course you must know that."

Burke ignored him and raised Maura's hand to his lips. "I owe you a debt I can never repay."

"I've done nothing," Maura said, embarrassed. "I pray that you might swiftly find your much-put-upon lady." She withdrew her hand from Burke's grasp and headed off through the thicket of trees, leaving the men alone.

In the morning Aidan and Rory stood on the shore as Burke, his boat loaded with provisions, a compass and a borrowed sextant and several flasks of water, pushed the curragh into the sea.

"We'll never see him again," Aidan said.

"Would you have chained him to a stake in the ground?" Rory countered. "That would be the only way to keep him here."

"I only hope she's worth it."

"He thinks she is, and that's all that matters."

"Even if he gets there, he'll never find her. England is a vast place, many more people than here, spread about the countryside in hamlets big and small, as well as teeming towns with folk packed in like rabbits in a warren."

"He'll find her," Rory said.

"And then what? She'll welcome him when she's married to another? A rich man, no doubt, whom she'll reject in favor of my brother? He's an idiot who thinks so."

"She's carrying your brother's child," Rory reminded him.

"All the more reason for her to stay with the man who could best provide for it," Aidan said.

There was a pause while they watched the waves and the vanishing figure in the curragh.

"Well, good cess to him," Rory said, clapping

Aidan on the back. "He's doing what he wants, and so should we all. Let's go back to the camp and have a drop on it."

The prospect of a drink cheered Aidan, and the two men headed inland as the departing boat grew smaller in the distance, heading toward the horizon.

9

The word must is not to be used to princes . . .
—Queen Elizabeth I

"Lady Selby!"

Alexandra whirled at the sound of her name to see Mary Howard running toward her, skirts flouncing.

"The queen!" Mary said, gesturing in the direction of the privy council chamber at Richmond Palace. As Alex looked past her, the elaborately carved doors burst open and the helmeted guards stationed on either side of them banged their axes on the floor.

"No more war, my lords!" the queen announced, concluding the council session an hour early. She strode purposefully out of the room and into the hall. Mary and Alex floated to the floor in curtsies as she swept past them, calling, "Attend me!" over her shoulder.

The two women stood up and hurried after her, exchanging glances as the old lady muttered her usual postcouncil imprecations about "bankrupting my treasury with their military exploits" and "impotent old fools playing at toy soldiers." The councilors streamed out of the room behind her, murmuring to each other as they packed up their papers. Among them was the principal secretary, hunchbacked Robert Cecil, son of gouty old Lord Burghley. The younger Cecil, nicknamed "Pygmy" by the queen for his stunted stature, had inherited leadership of the anti-Essex faction from his dead father. The men stopped to confer in small clusters, casting apprehensive glances at the queen as she marched away, still in a pother.

Guardsmen snapped to attention as she passed, and her path cleared before her as if by magic. Elizabeth walked briskly along the paved stone corridor, the courtiers she passed bowing from the waist and the ladies sinking gracefully to mark her progress.

"I will hear no more of Ireland!" she said to no one in particular as Alex and Mary hastened to keep up with her. "Three years ago I sent thirty-five hundred men to that benighted place, and within a year twenty-five hundred of them were dead, fled, or converted to the Irish. My soldiers disappear into those bogs as if melted by the fairy mist."

She turned in at her privy chamber, and the door flew open before her. A startled Lady Warwick put aside one of the silk wigs she had been combing and curtsied abruptly. Two tirewomen making up the royal bed in the next room fell to their knees in fright.

"And Essex!" the old lady went on, taking no notice of the response of her servants. "I followed up his flagship last spring with sixteen thousand foot soldiers and thirteen hundred horsemen. And what have I to show for it? Not defeat for the rebels, as I was promised, but a *truce*, thank you very much. A truce, by Jesu's wounds, with that wily, scheming, thieving rascal Tyrone!"

Alex was careful to shift her glance away from that of her mistress. The debacle in Ireland had been worse than she ever could have imagined.

"And now these varlets ask for *more* money for *another* campaign under Mountjoy! They will drive me to distraction with their demands. I will replace every one of them and have some blessed peace in my kingdom for my beleaguered and overtaxed people. Far better for my councilors to serve my interests by laboring on the charter for the East India Company and leave off Ireland altogether."

The queen seemed to notice suddenly that everyone in the room had frozen. "Get up, get up," she said, waving aside their obeisances. "Go about your business again. I merely wish to change my costume before receiving the French ambassador, but these two ladies can do for me well enough."

Lady Warwick fled as Alex and Mary moved in on the queen, and Alex began to unlace her bodice when she gave the sign.

"Think you that Mr. Hurault de Maisse will like the silver cloth with the crimson kirtle and the slashed sleeves?" the queen asked.

"It's a lovely dress, ma'am," Mary said.

"The red taffeta lining becomes me not," the queen said, fishing for a compliment.

"Your Majesty looks very well in red," Mary said.

"But not so well as in some other colors," Elizabeth said.

This was a trap, and both women knew it.

"Your Majesty can wear any color to excellent effect," Alex said smoothly, "but perhaps the ambassador would prefer the red since it is new from France. It has always pleasured him to see you in his country's latest fashions."

"Well said," Elizabeth remarked approvingly. She had spent her life fencing with diplomats, and she could recognize one anywhere. She stood still as the women dressed her in the new outfit and then said, "Bring the curled wig. This one is too heavy, and it tires me."

Mary lifted the auburn wig from the old woman's head and repinned the sparse gray hair it had covered. When the new wig was brought, Mary set it on the royal head gently. She had been cuffed more than once when she was deemed too rough.

"Ah, better," the great lady said, examining her image in her looking glass.

She gestured for her jewel box and added the touch of a circlet of rubies and pearls to match the pearl drops in her ears. Elizabeth lifted her long fingered hands, of which she was very proud, and studied the rings she wore, exchanging a heavy carnelian set with diamonds for a star sapphire embedded in gold.

"There," she said when the sapphire was settled on her finger. "Now bring me the attar of roses scent the ambassador sent ahead of him. If I wear it, he may recognize it."

Alex brought the crystalline bottle, and the old lady uncapped it and held the stopper to her nose.

"Bah!" she said, slamming the bottle down on her dressing table, where the contents slopped over onto the lace cover and stained it dark.

"This potion reeks. The man would have me stinking like a whore in the Southwark stews. Take it away."

Alex, who knew the queen's sensitive nose, removed both the bottle and the lace doily and put them in the other room.

"I will have the marjoram," the queen said, indicating a pot of her favorite, lighter scent.

Mary fetched it for her, and Elizabeth sprinkled herself liberally with the perfume.

"Now I am ready," the queen announced, handing the jar back to Mary. Her wrinkled face, heavily painted with alum and borax to enhance its natural whiteness, crinkled as she smiled at them, exposing the gap on the left side of her mouth where most of the teeth were missing. It was said that her physician kept fenugreek at hand to draw her teeth, since so many of them were yellowed and rotten— a consequence, Dr. Butts believed, of the queen's fondness for sweets. Still, bejeweled and attired in rich clothes, she made an impressive figure for an ancient crone of sixty-six. And her intellect, as all who served her knew, was as sharp as the day she had ascended the throne forty-one years earlier.

"You are dismissed," the queen said to Mary and Alex. "Remain here and await my return."

She swept out to her audience with the ambassador, and the two younger women collapsed onto chairs as soon as she was gone.

"Aye me," Mary said, adjusting her headdress. "What a tizzy she's in! I would not change places with my lord of Essex for a chest full of silver guilders."

Alex had seen him shortly after she had begun to serve the queen, the night he'd arrived back from Ireland, fresh off his horse, his face and clothes still splashed with mud from the wild ride. He had taken the queen by surprise at Nonsuch, bursting into her apartments when she was still in her nightclothes, surrounded by her women, her gray hair about her shoulders. The old lady had been speech-

less at his apparition; she had thought him still in
Ireland and suddenly found him on his knees
before her, covering her hands with kisses and begging her indulgence to let him explain his abrupt
and unsanctioned return.

That had been the beginning of the end for him.

"How are the mighty fallen," Alex said.

"Favorites change. When you've been at court
longer, you'll learn." Mary brightened suddenly.
"How is the babe?"

Alex winced. "Kicking."

"When is it due to be born?"

"January, Dr. Butts says."

"It will arrive with the new year and the new
century," Mary said. "It's a good omen."

Alex smiled and nodded. Mary, a distant cousin
of hers with the dark eyes and hair of her mother's
people, was near her age. She had a homely philos-
ophy of life and was given to such remarks.

"The father will be so proud," Mary said.

The father will never see it, Alex thought, turning her face away so Mary would not notice her
expression.

Mary laughed. "And who would have thought
this of old Selby? There's no cure for the ills of age
like making merry with a young girl. As my childhood nurse was wont to say, you shouldn't put an
old horse out to pasture before his true time, there
still might be some seed left in him."

Alex said nothing. She had been careful to let
everyone think that Selby had sired her child,

but it still bothered her whenever people talked about it.

The baby's real father lived in her mind as vividly as if she had left him yesterday, and it was difficult for her to pretend otherwise. She felt like a traitor going along with the fiction, a traitor to herself and to her memory of Burke, but for the future of the child she carried she had no choice.

"Her Majesty may want to play the virginals when she returns," said Mary. "She asked for some new Italian sheet music, madrigals, I think, this morning. Perhaps we should alert the singers, as she'll want them to take their parts."

Alex sighed. She did not share her monarch's passion for the harpsichord, and after several hours of listening to the queen pound the instrument, especially when accompanied by her chorale, Alex usually wound up with an aching head.

"I'm so happy we got her dressed without incident." Mary stood and checked the next room, empty now, and then opened the door to the hall and looked into the corridor. She returned and whispered to Alex, "She gets worse every day. On Tuesday she kicked me when I told her that my lord chamberlain had said there was no more of that small beer she likes for her dinner."

Poor Mary seemed to come in for the worst of it. Once, when she wore a fancy dress that the queen thought too grand for her station as lady-in-waiting,

Elizabeth took it away and kept it, even though it did not fit her.

"We've ordered vats of that light ale," Mary went on, "but she goes through it like it's water."

"It almost is. She insists on diluting it so much I don't know how she can tell the difference," Alex replied.

Capricious, the queen certainly was, and exasperating, but those who served her endured her tantrums not only because they had to, but because her essential nature inspired devotion. She was in love with the romance of her own reputation as a great lady, and she always eventually lived up to it, even if others did not agree with her estimation of what that required. She never forgot an act of kindness or fealty, and she repaid loyalty with loyalty, like with like.

"I'd best get rid of this perfume before Her Majesty returns," Alex said, rising and clearing away the debris. She rinsed her hands at a wall laver, but the heavy smell still clung to them, making her head light and her stomach unsteady.

"You'd think that Frenchman would learn that giving her strong scent is a poor idea," said Mary.

"It's a premier product of his country."

"But not highly regarded in these hallowed precincts." They both giggled.

Lady Warwick returned, carrying a folded stack of the queen's silk chemises. "Help me sort through these before the queen returns," she said. "She's been complaining that the seams are too thick on some of them and are thus chafing her skin."

The women exchanged glances, but then set to the work in silence, ruled once more by a magisterial whim.

Burke had been at sea two days when a fierce storm swamped his small boat and tossed him into the churning waves. He saw a ship in the distance and swam for it, going under several times before he reached its side and was pulled aboard, half-drowned and coughing water. He passed out on deck.

When he woke up he found himself confronted by a sunburned blond man in a surprisingly neat uniform.

"What's your name?" the captain of the vessel demanded in English as Burke blinked salt rime from his eyes.

Burke was silent.

"What were you doing at sea?"

"Trying to get to England," Burke grudgingly replied.

"From Ireland, I assume."

Burke said nothing.

"Oh, you'll get to England all right," the captain said. He turned to one of the men at his elbow and said, "Let him sleep 'til morning and then feed him a good breakfast. He looks fit enough, he should be ready to work by then. Set him to repairing the mainsail." The captain surveyed him. "Congratulations, paddy, you are now a sailor in the British Imperial Navy. You'll take your orders on this ship and obey them smartly. If you disobey, you will be shot. If you desert, you will be shot. You are entitled to wages of two pounds a month at Her Majesty's grace, though I wouldn't count on it if I were you. We haven't been paid in a year."

He turned away abruptly, and both Englishmen disappeared.

Burke fell back on the deck, not as unhappy as he might have been. Impressment of seamen was common, and he could certainly do his share of the work long enough to get to England. He was alive and intact, and he knew that sooner or later the vessel would have to put in to port.

When it did, he would jump ship and find Alexandra.

The cold winds of autumn gave way to the freezing sleet of winter. In late November, Alex and Mary were gathered with a small group of courtiers surrounding the queen as she sat next to the fire, playing chess with Sir Walter Raleigh.

Elizabeth was dressed in one of the fantastic outfits of her old age, a black velvet dress with pink slashes, her wig drawn up into a gold net spangled with sequins and pearls. In these later years she favored black and white, both colors admirably suited to a pale-skinned woman with red hair. Raleigh was himself arrayed in the fine apparel he typically cultivated—he'd once paid six hundred Spanish maravedis, part of his seafaring booty, for a pair of Italian shoes. Today his long, lean frame was graced by a burgundy velvet doublet embroidered with silver and gold thread, and his elegant legs were encased in costly silken hose. He studied the chess board intently, stroking his full beard, the firelight gleaming on his thick black hair, as Elizabeth fingered one piece dreamily and then seized another.

"An error, Water," she said gleefully, using her nickname for him. "If you had used such tactics in Cadiz, methinks you would have emerged from that fray no hero."

"You outwit me at every turn, madam," Raleigh said in his broad Devonshire accent, inclining his head.

Alex looked on, admiring the adept way he handled the queen. In his youth he had been as hotheaded and impetuous as the banished Essex, but now he was a favorite, an older man who had learned to temper his behavior. Poet, businessman, warrior and courtier, as versatile as he was mercurial, Raleigh had years earlier fallen out of favor for violating a lady-in-waiting and getting her with child. He had lost his position as captain of the guard, and everyone at court had written him off as a fallen power, never to rise again.

But Raleigh knew how to play a waiting game. As time passed he had worked his way back into the queen's good graces, unlike the boyish Essex, who had been known to turn his back on the queen in contempt and had even drawn his sword when she'd refused his advice on the touchy subject of Ireland.

"Your Majesty is a strategist. You should have field command of the army," an onlooker said from the sidelines.

"Think you that I could do better than some who have lately been in Ireland?" Elizabeth asked.

"You have not lost there, Your Majesty, only stayed the fight for another, better day," said Sir John Harington, her godson and Essex's friend, knighted by him in Ireland.

"That may well be true, ma'am," Raleigh said. As Essex's constant rival in glorious naval exploits as well as in the queen's affections, he could afford to be gracious now that Essex was in prison and in disgrace.

"That fight should have been concluded ere this," said another onlooker, Francis Bacon, a former friend of the defrocked favorite.

"We shall see, we shall see," said Elizabeth. She looked up to notice Alex and Mary Howard standing in the background.

"Lady Selby," she called, "some wine to quench our thirst. And a plate of those almond sweetmeats my Walter favors."

It was the queen who favored the candy, but no one contradicted her. Alex walked over to a sideboard and poured Alicante wine and water into a goblet, mixing the liquids three-quarters water and one-quarter wine as the queen liked. She filled another goblet with the undiluted wine for Raleigh and added a pile of sugared almonds to a gold plate, placed all of it on a heavy inlaid tray, and carried it to the chess table.

The queen gestured impatiently for her to put it down. "There will do, Alex."

"Alex, what manner of name is that for an English child?" Raleigh asked. "What can your father have been thinking of, Lady Selby?"

"Lady Selby was named for Alexander of old, so she tells me, for the respect her father bore that ancient ruler," the queen said. "And so he should have done, and so should we all, for the many lessons his noble story has to teach us," she added with finality, settling the matter.

"Lady Selby or Alex, you're looking well," said Raleigh, surveying her figure with the practiced eye of an expert. "Impending motherhood becomes you."

Alex glanced at the queen nervously. The monarch was known to be jealous of male attention and notoriously disapproving of compliments paid to other women in her presence.

"When is your confinement?" the queen asked abruptly.

"January, ma'am."

"And will your husband return?"

"No, Your Majesty. He is now in Antwerp, securing loans for the Crown, and that business should keep him well into the spring of the new year."

"Oh, yes," Elizabeth said, remembering. "So, should you like to go home to Hampden Manor for the birth?"

"Yes, very much," Alex said, relieved that she did not have to bring it up herself. She had been waiting for an opportune moment to broach the subject.

"Very well, then, you are dismissed. And take your kinswoman with you," she added, gesturing to Mary Howard. "Her husband is also away, and you can keep each other company for Christmastide and to await the coming of the child."

Both Alex and Mary sank to the floor in deep curtsies, hardly able to believe their good fortune. They rose gracefully and walked unhurriedly to the door, waiting until they were outside in the hall to fall into each other's arms.

"Praise be Jesus, He owed me a favor," Mary said. "I thought my ears were playing tricks. What do you suppose possessed Her Majesty?"

"I'm not going to stop to find out," Alex said. "Let's pack and go before she changes her mind."

They were on the road to Hampden Manor in Surrey early the next morning, Alex in a litter because of her advanced stage of pregnancy and Mary following on a horse, their belongings strapped to pack animals in the rear. The way was bumpy and slick with ice, and the babe in Alex's belly protested every time they hit a rut. By the time they reached Hampden it seemed every muscle in her body was aching, and when Mrs. Curry met the two women in the entry hall with flagons of mulled wine, Alex felt she was never so glad to see anyone in her life.

"Oh, my lady," the housekeeper clucked, "just look at yourself, almost asleep on your feet. And Lady Mary, you look half-frozen. What was the queen thinking of to send you off in the middle of winter this way? When I got word that you were coming from the rider Her Majesty sent ahead, I thought that all of you must have taken leave of your senses."

"I'm fine, Mrs. Curry, we're both fine," Alex said. "I'd much prefer to be here, and there was really no risk. We proceeded slowly and took two gentlemen pensioners with us for our protection. By the by, would you see that they are fed in the kitchens? And the horses need attention, too, they're as tired as we are."

Mrs. Curry gave the orders to two underlings as she took the ladies' outer garments and led them to the fire roaring in the great room. The women sank onto cushioned chairs and ate from the trays the housekeeper gave them as they caught up on the local news.

"Has there been any word from Lord Selby?" Alex asked.

"A letter came for you yesterday. I was going to

send it on to Richmond with tomorrow's post. Would you like to see it?"

Alex nodded.

Mrs. Curry left to get it, and Alex looked around the room at the fine furnishings and appointments. Although she was legally married to Selby, she did not think of any of it as hers but felt rather like an honored guest in a hostelry who was given the best treatment and the full attention of the staff.

"This mutton is tasty," Mary said with her mouth full.

"Shoe leather would taste good to me tonight," Alex answered. "I'm starving."

"The babe makes you eat. The appetite will go once it is born."

"It is to be hoped so." She felt like Jonah's whale; she could never pass for a boy now, as she had not so very long ago. At least her hair had grown in; it was now long enough to brush to her shoulders and pin up in back.

Mrs. Curry returned with the letter and a file. Alex burst the sealing wax with the opener.

"There's also another letter from your uncle in Ireland," Mrs. Curry said cautiously. Alex had refused all previous correspondence from him.

"Is he still there?" Alex asked. "I thought they had all returned home by now."

"It came by boat from Dublin."

Alex held her hand out for it reluctantly as she read through the letter from her husband. "Lord

Selby says he should be back in March," she announced.

"His son should be two months old by then," Mary said.

"How do you know it's a boy?" Alex asked.

"You carry it so low below the waist."

"She's right, you know," Mrs. Curry said. "It's a boy, certainly, I'm never wrong."

Alex tucked the letter from her uncle inside her sleeve and sighed. Maybe she would force herself to read it later.

"I've ordered the fires lit in your bedroom and the south guest suite, my lady," Mrs. Curry said. "That way you can have Lady Howard close by you if you have need of her."

"Thank you, Mrs. Curry. That will be all," Alex said.

Mrs. Curry left the room in a whisper of skirts and Mary said, "She's a jewel, isn't she?"

"Yes, we're very lucky to have her. She's been here a long time and is devoted to Lord Selby."

"Why do you always call him that? You never refer to your husband as your husband, but always 'Lord Selby.'"

Alex was suddenly very tired of the whole charade and longed to confide in Mary, who had an understanding nature and was the closest friend she had in her new life.

She finally spoke. "Perhaps because he's not my husband, not in the sense that most people think of the word, anyway."

Mary stared at her. "You're married, aren't you?"

"In name only. We went through the ceremony last June. We don't share a bed and have hardly shared board since that time."

"Then who is the baby's father?" Mary inquired breathlessly, her eyes round.

Alex sighed again, overwhelmed by the enormity of the story she was about to tell. "Do you remember that I once told you I spent some time in Ireland with my uncle before I came to court?"

"Yes. I thought it odd when you said it. Whatever were you doing in Ireland? It's such a barbaric place, full of rebels and witches dreaming up charms and such, isn't it?"

"I met the baby's father there. He's Irish. One of the rebels you mentioned, actually."

Mary's mouth fell open.

"Are you sure you want to hear this?" Alex asked.

Mary nodded vigorously.

Alex told her all of it, sparing but a few of the details. Mary sat spellbound.

When Alex finished, Mary got up to add a log to the lowering fire, not wishing to call one of the servants, and then said, "Does the queen know?"

"About the baby?"

"Yes."

"She thinks it's Selby's."

"Best keep it that way. She's very stiff-backed in such matters, especially where her ladies are concerned. You must remember what happened to Raleigh. And poor Bess must still keep close to their house at Sherborne. She's not permitted at court."

"Selby will say nothing."

"How can you be sure?"

"He's profited handsomely from the marriage, and beyond that, he's really a kind man who took pity on my plight. He thinks of me in a fatherly fashion; his daughter is older than I am. He's much more interested in his business and diplomatic advancement than he is in me."

"And the baby's father, this man Burke?"

"I've given up hope of ever seeing him again." She thought she had learned to live with that fact, but saying it aloud made her eyes fill, and before she knew it she was crying.

"There, there." Mary came and knelt next to her chair, patting her arm. "All will be well. You'll have the baby soon, and that will make you happy."

"What can I do, Mary? I keep telling myself that I must learn to live without him, but I feel I simply cannot."

Mary shook her head slowly. "I never would have guessed all this. You seemed so quiet, so contained, ready always to do Her Majesty's bidding and ask naught else, very different from the bold little girl I recalled from our childhood."

"You see what a mummery I've been making, putting on a show as the dutiful wife. I've tried to accept my lot, but at night in my dreams Burke comes to me, real as life, and I wake up longing for him so badly that I think I must go mad."

They both looked up as Mrs. Curry entered the room, carrying a tumbler of hot milk. "To rest your stomach for the night," she said, handing it to Alex. "Your beds are all turned down and ready, the warming pans in place." She took a closer look at Alex's face. "Are you all right, Lady Selby?"

"Yes, fine," Alex replied, wiping at the tears on her cheeks. "I get a little weepy now and then, too often, really, I expect it's just that I'm breeding."

Mrs. Curry tsked loudly. "Very true, and on top of that you must be exhausted. Come along now, let's go on up to your room and get you settled in bed."

Alex rose, sipping the milk, and the three women went upstairs.

Burke's vessel docked in Southampton a week before Christmas. Half the sailors were given immediate shore leave, and when he walked off the ship he simply kept on walking and never looked back.

He had no idea where he was; he had never been in England in his life. Since he had made a habit of keeping strictly to himself on board the ship, refusing to answer questions or be drawn into conversation, no one had confided their destination. He was not popular, but he was left alone, too big and agile to be the target of harassment, and that suited him fine. The less the sailors knew of him the better; it would make him more difficult to track once he was gone.

The port city was filled with diverse accents, both foreign and domestic, some country brogues so thick it hardly seemed that the people were speaking English. He kept his mouth shut and listened, strolling a good distance along the quays and then spotting a seaside tavern with rooms to let on the upper floor. The pub announced its name to the largely illiterate population with a hanging picture of a ram's head, which swung, clanking, in the ocean breeze. He crossed the thoroughfare and shouldered his way through the crowded doorway.

It was dim and close inside, filled with drunken sailors and the overpowering smell of unwashed bodies. Burke ordered a mug of beer and a pasty by gesturing for them to the landlord. When the barmaid brought his order she set it down smartly in front of him and said, "There you go, old son. A strapping fellow like you must need his food, so call for seconds if you've a want of them."

He was sure he heard a lilt of the west country in her voice and decided to take a chance.

"What town is this?"

"What town, you're asking? God's teeth, you *are* lost, aren't you, lad?"

"I'm Irish, just like you, picked up at sea and forced into the English navy."

She looked around furtively and said in a low voice, "Keep that to yourself, boyo."

"But where am I?"

"You're in Southampton, on the southern coast of England hard by Portsmouth," she said, wiping the scarred table before him with a filthy rag.

Burke shook his head. "That doesn't help me. Where is Surrey from here?"

She blinked. "Surrey? Why, that's just south of London, the county bordering it. You're in Hampshire County now."

"Is it far from here?"

"No, not so very far. Just travel north and east, it's perhaps two days' ride."

Burke's spirits lifted perceptibly.

"But the county is big, what part of it are you wanting?"

"Hampden Manor."

The woman shrugged. "Never heard of it."

"Lord Selby?"

She grinned, displaying yellowed incisors. "We don't get too many lords in here, if you take my meaning."

He smiled back at her.

"Best advice would be to head for Surrey and ask the locals when you get closer."

Burke nodded. "I've no money for this," he said apologetically, indicating the food.

"I'll see to it."

The barkeep screamed, "Maeve!" and made a rude gesture.

"Must go," the woman said. "Good cess to you." She lumbered away, and Burke took a long pull on his beer.

The first thing, of course, was to steal a horse.

Burke waited for nightfall and then scouted out the local stables. There was a livery half a mile in from the dockside that offered a selection of sorry nags for daily hire. After having peered into the stalls, Burke wished he could liberate all the horses and treat each of them to a good meal of ale-soaked oats and sugar-cane mash. But he noticed that one bay looked a little less ragged than the others and singled it out as his choice.

When a stableboy approached him and asked, "Which will you have?" Burke cuffed him behind the ear and caught him when he fell, settling his limp body on a tack chest. He checked to make sure the boy was still breathing and then led the bay out into the street, hoping it was strong enough to carry him where he had to go.

North and east, the barmaid had said. He figured north from the memory of the setting sun and set off in that direction.

* * *

There was a snowfall three days before Christmas, and the countryside around Hampden Manor was muffled and white, as soft and quiet as if covered with a down quilt. The stillness of the house was most unlike what would be taking place at court, as Mary had described it to her. There would be masques and balls in honor of the season, and all the courtiers would be trying to outdo each other with a New Year's gift for the queen. The halls of the palace would be hung with holly and ivy, and music and spiced wine and general gaiety would prevail in every corner of the court.

Alex looked out the leaded window at the frost-covered fields, glad to be away from the Yuletide clamor. She felt contemplative, in need of peace and quiet.

"How are you this afternoon?" Mary asked, entering Alex's bedroom.

"A little tired, but otherwise well."

"The fatigue will pass."

Alex laughed. "You seem to know a lot about it for a woman who has not yet birthed a child."

"My elder sister has six children."

"Daphne, who went to live in Sussex?"

"The same. I stayed with her while she was expecting the last two. You'll have energy enough once the babe is born."

"I'm sure I'll need it."

"Have you been reading?" Mary asked, nodding toward the book open on Alex's chair.

"Yes. Aristotle. Would you like to hear what he says about Burke's forebears?" Alex picked up the book and found the page she wanted. "'We have no word for the man who is excessively fearless; perhaps one may call such a man mad or bereft of feeling, who fears nothing . . . as they say of the Celts.'"

"Was Burke like that?"

"He was bold, assuredly, but not to the wild extreme of foolishness. And he certainly could not be called 'bereft of feeling.'"

"Is the book interesting?"

"Yes, it is. The queen gave it to me, she says it's a good translation. I have to take her word for it since I can't read the original. She's deluged me with Greek works in honor of my name, which she considers a pleasant novelty."

"Better pleasant than not. She's sent people out of her service for having the wrong name, the wrong face, the wrong clothes, too many jewels, or too few teeth."

Alex smiled. "You'll get your dress back, Mary. She'll have second thoughts and return it to you."

"She doesn't always. She kept Lady Derby's locket."

Mrs. Curry entered with Alex's lunch tray. "Will you take your luncheon in here with my mistress, Lady Mary?"

"No, I think I will leave Alex to rest. You can serve me in my room." She shook her finger at

Alex. "Not too much reading now, it will sour your milk."

Mary was good-hearted but sometimes her homilies defied comprehension.

"I'll bring your meal up shortly," Mrs. Curry said to Mary in the hall. "There's been a delay in the kitchen, a beggar off the roads arrived late this morning and was fed the capon I had ordered for your luncheon before I knew of it."

"No matter. A little soup will do."

"The cook feels sorry for such fellows," Mrs. Curry said huffily. "I abhor the advantage they take, coming at Yuletide because they think they won't be turned away."

"But some of them are truly starving, surely. Since the dissolution of the monasteries in late King Henry's time many of the former clergy have no livelihood and no place to go, so they roam the roads."

"This is no aged priest, he's a young man, a great big fellow fit enough to work."

"Maybe he was turned off his land for taxes."

"Who can say? He has a cunning approach, I'll give him that. He asked if Lord Selby were in residence, and when I told him my lord was away this ruffian said that he *knew* Lady Selby and demanded to see her. Can you imagine? As if I would bother my lady in her late pregnancy with such street rabble. I told the cook to give him some food for the road and turn him out."

"But why would he say he knew Alex?" Mary

asked, knitting her brow, her eyes fixed on the housekeeper's face. "The lie could be so easily disproved."

"Some of them will say anything for a meal. Lying comes as naturally as sleeping in the dark." She paused for a moment. "He had most peculiar speech, though, for a vagabond, talked like a gentleman."

"Was he Irish?"

"Irish! Saint George, I've never met one of them and hope to die in ignorance of the experience."

"What did he look like?" Mary asked, already hurrying toward the stairs.

"Big, as I said. Dirty and scrawny, with long tangled hair and a fearsome beard." Mrs. Curry stared at her in amazement. "Where are you going?"

"Is he still in the kitchens?" Mary called over her shoulder.

"I imagine so," the housekeeper replied, bewildered.

"Stay there," Mary said as she rounded the corner. "And say nothing to Lady Alex until you hear from me."

Mrs. Curry looked after Alex's departing houseguest in undisguised shock.

Mary flew past the servants, who looked around in consternation as she passed. She charged into the kitchen, startling the cook, who dropped her wooden spoon into the broth she was stirring.

"Where is the man who was here?" Mary demanded.

"What man?" the cook said defensively.

"The man who came to the door off the road." Mary guessed the reason for the cook's attitude and said, "I'm not going to chide you for feeding him, just tell me where he is."

The woman sighed. "He said he wouldn't take charity, insisted on working off his meal. He wanted to feed his horse, too, so I set him to chopping wood in the stables." She lowered her voice. "Don't tell Mrs. Curry about it, or I'll come in for another lecture."

"Clear your mind on that account. If Mrs. Curry finds out about it, I'll tell her you acted on my orders."

"Thank you, ma'am." Now that she was off the hook, the cook grew chatty. "Any Christian soul would have done the same. You could see he was proud, how it pained him to ask for anything. Half-dead from hunger and cold, too, and the horse not much better, from what I could see through the window." She picked up the spoon again and scattered parsley into the crock with a practiced hand. "Most peculiar the way he asked for Lady Alex. Mrs. Curry would have none of it, of course, but I had the idea he wanted to work to prolong his time here, find a way in to see the mistress." She grinned wickedly, wiping her hands on her apron. "For a moment I thought he would grab my knife and hold it to Mrs. Curry's throat, force her to take him to my lady, but then he seemed to think better of it."

Mary reached for the cook's cloak, hanging on a peg by the wall. "I need to borrow this," she said, pulling it around her shoulders and dropping the hood over her head. "I'll return it shortly."

"Yes, ma'am."

"I'm in a hurry," Mary explained, seeing the woman's surprised expression. She opened the door to the cobbled courtyard, letting in a fine mist of blowing snow. The cold hit her like a blow, and she hurried across the yard to the stables, almost slipping once on the icy paving stones. The snow had been cleared by the staff but it was mounded at the edges of the walk and the wind sifted it into her face as she walked. By the time she reached the stables her cheeks were wet and stinging. She yanked the door open, and then slammed it closed against the wind, pushing the hood back off her hair.

The stableboy, Tim, looked up at her in surprise. He was polishing a bridle next to a small fire in a corner grate. From the back of the barn, Mary could hear the rhythmic sound of an ax falling at intervals.

"Lady Mary," the boy said.

"Carry on with what you're doing. I want a word with the man who's chopping wood."

"Yes, ma'am," Tim said, going back to his work.

Mary walked past the horse stalls, ignoring the whinnying and stomping her presence aroused. She slowed as she caught sight of the vagabond Mrs. Curry had described.

He was very tall, indeed, and had once been heavier, judging from the way his clothes hung on him. It was obvious that he had recently washed, from the bucket and stained rag sitting on the bench, but he was still much the worse for wear—his apparel bedraggled as well as too large, his hair smoothed with water but not fully combed. He was working his way through a pile of logs, splitting them and piling them neatly at his side. A few feet away a skinny nag, recently groomed, was munching a bucket of oats contentedly, with two woolen blankets strapped to its meager flanks.

The man stopped in the act of swinging the ax when he caught sight of her. He planted its blade in the earth and leaned on the handle as he watched her, waiting for her to speak.

"Who are you?" Mary asked.

He said nothing, his blue eyes like twin candle flames in his bearded face.

"Where did you come from?"

Still no response.

"What are you doing here?" Mary demanded more testily, annoyed at his silence.

"Working, as you see," he replied shortly, moving to loosen the ax from the dirt.

"I mean, why have you come to this house?"

"If that shrew of a housekeeper has sent you to turn me out, you can take your ease. I'll not leave until I've seen Alexandra," he said.

Just the way he said her friend's name nearly

convinced her. "You're not English," she said.

He snorted. "I am not."

"Have you traveled a great distance?"

"Look at me and answer that for yourself."

"Are you Burke?" she whispered.

The man dropped the ax and came forward to seize her hands. He towered over her, and his grip was so strong that Mary flinched.

"How do you know that name?" he said hoarsely.

"Alexandra told me about you. Are you truly the man she left behind in Ireland?"

"I am."

Mary hesitated.

"Am I not as she described?" he demanded. "I've looked better in my life, it's true, but surely you can judge from her own words if I deserve to see her."

"I don't know, I don't know," Mary said. "I don't want to upset her, she is far gone with child and a shock could cause her serious harm."

"I'll not do that. Jesus, woman, I've crossed the ocean to find her. Do you think I would be capable of harming her?"

"She thinks she has lost you forever."

"Then let her see me and know she's wrong."

Mary's dark eyes were locked with his bright ones.

"Take me to her," he said softly. "Don't make me gain entrance by force."

Mary closed her eyes, then opened them again and removed her hands from his grasp.

"Follow me."

She led the way across the courtyard and back into the house. When the pair entered the kitchen the cook whirled to face them, her eyes going from Mary to Burke and then back again.

Mary held her finger to her lips. "I'll explain later," she said. "Where is Mrs. Curry?"

"Going over the household bills with the fishmonger's man in Lord Selby's study."

Mary returned the cloak she had worn to its peg and said, "Good. She won't see us if we go up the back stairs." She proceeded through the kitchen and Burke hurried in her wake, almost treading on her heels in his anxiety.

"You must let me go in first," Mary said quietly to him as they went up the steps.

He nodded.

"You know she is married?"

He nodded again, his eyes distant. "But the babe is mine."

Mary stopped outside Alex's door, which was ajar. She tapped and then pushed it open to find Alex dozing on her chair, her book closed on her lap.

"Alex?" Mary called softly.

Alex's eyes opened and focused on Mary. She smiled.

"There is someone here to see you."

Alex sat up, arranging her skirts. "Yes?"

Mary stepped aside, and Burke entered the room. When Alex caught sight of him she held both hands to her mouth, gasping, as her book slid to the floor.

He went to her side and fell to his knees, putting his arms around her middle and his head in her lap.

Alex bent to embrace him, her cheek against his hair.

Mary watched for a few seconds, her eyes wet, and then went out quietly and closed the door behind her.

10

Sleep after toil, port after stormy seas,
Ease after war . . . does greatly please . . .
—Edmund Spenser,
The Faerie Queen

"How?" Alex said when she had regained
the power of speech. "How did you get here?"

"No matter," Burke replied. "I found you." He
put his hands on her mounded belly and looked up
into her face.

"Did you know?" she asked.

"Maura told me."

"Would you have come after me anyway?"

He took her hand and held it to his mouth.
"How can you ask?" he said, and closed his eyes as
her fingers curled against his cheek.

"You have a beard now," she said, smiling.

"More than that, probably, crawling in my clothes. I've been on the road for several days and before that on a ship."

"I thought never to see you again," she whispered.

"I'm a hard man to be rid of," he said, and grinned, his teeth white against his brown beard.

"You're so thin," Alex said.

"I've not eaten much since I left the navy."

"The navy!"

"I'll tell you about it later. Now we must go." He stood up and offered her his hand.

"Go where?"

"Why, out of this house. You're coming with me."

"I can't just run off with you, Kevin!"

"Why not? You did once before."

"For one thing, I'm having your baby in a matter of weeks. Do you want me to drop it by the side of the road?"

"Well, all right. We'll wait until you have the baby."

Alex stood also, still trying to absorb his presence. "For another thing," she said slowly, "I'm married."

"You don't love him, whoever he is. You love me."

She moved closer to him and took his hands. "Kevin, try to understand. I took vows, I made promises. I am married according to the rite of the Church of England."

"You have suddenly become religious?"

"That's a poor jest. You take my meaning very well. I can't just walk out the door with you, without a care, pretending that it never happened."

Burke snatched his hands from hers. "What you mean is you prefer this"—he gestured at the room—"and this"—he grabbed a handful of her velvet dress—"and this"—he took a silver goblet from a tray and threw it on the floor—"to what you could have with me!"

Alex merely stared at him until he lowered his eyes.

"Kevin, I was alone," she said finally. "You had gone back to your men and I thought you would be killed if you ever returned to Inverary. I was with child and had to give the babe a name."

"So you married Selby."

"My uncle had the match in mind for some time. When I knew I was pregnant I saw no other way for me."

"Selby is rich, of course."

"He is a kind man and has been very good to me."

"He is old?"

"Yes."

"How old?"

Alex sighed. "Fifty-eight."

"Has he bedded you?" Burke said tightly.

"No."

"Has he tried?"

Mrs. Curry tapped on the door and then pushed

it open and entered the room. When she saw Burke she stopped dead in her tracks.

"What are you doing in here?" she said with a gasp.

"Visiting," Burke said, enjoying her shock.

"Oh, my lady, I'm so sorry. To think that you should be disturbed in this way by such road rabble. I'll call Mr. Evans and have this man ejected immediately."

Mr. Evans served as footman, houseman, and horsemaster, the only person on the estate large enough to have even a chance of removing Burke by force.

"Mrs. Curry, this is Mr. Kevin Burke, an old friend of mine," Alex said. "Why should you think I would want him removed?"

Mrs. Curry stared at her, silenced for perhaps the first time in her life.

"I asked you a question," Alex said.

"He came to the door this morning and I thought he was a beggar asking for food," Mrs. Curry said.

"I asked to see Alexandra."

Mrs. Curry reddened. "I'm sorry, Your Ladyship, if I erred in handling the situation."

"You did," Burke said.

Alex gave him an exasperated look.

"From his appearance I took Mr. Burke to be a roamer on the roads," Mrs. Curry said.

"I told you otherwise," Burke said.

"I made the judgment not to disturb you. These people come all the time, especially at Christmas, and—"

"That's all right, Mrs. Curry," Alex said. "No harm has been done. I would like you to order a hot bath prepared for Mr. Burke, with soap and a razor, some shears as well, and look for some fresh clothes for him."

"He's too big," Mrs. Curry said stiffly. "We've nothing here to fit him."

"Then set Mrs. Fagin from the village to sewing some things for him. In the meanwhile take out some of Master John's clothes, the ones stored in the cellars. He is almost as tall as Mr. Burke, and they will do for now."

Mrs. Curry didn't move.

"Mrs. Curry, did you hear me?"

"Yes, ma'am."

"Surely the task cannot be difficult?"

"Yes, ma'am." Mrs. Curry inclined her head and hurried from the room.

"About as fond of me as your beloved uncle, that one," Burke said.

"You look like trouble to her."

"She's right about that."

"I think she's frightened of your beard. And with that hair you appear as fierce as the Medusa."

"The what?"

"The Me . . . Never mind. Go and have your bath."

"Don't order me about as you do that woman."

Alex eyed him uncertainly, not sure why he was offended.

"I see you've taken right easily to giving orders. You always were a great lady with command of servants, I suppose, and I just didn't notice it while I was lying in the long grass with you."

"Kevin, what is this?"

"Am I too dirty for you, then?"

"No, I only want you to be comfortable!"

"And I want you back the way you were in Ireland!" he burst out.

Alex took a step, then another, and then ran into his arms. "I am that girl," she said against his shoulder. "I would be that girl again, but my case is altered now."

"You have not been with him?" he said fiercely into her ear.

"Never."

"But he's your husband!"

"He's not, the marriage is a paper transaction. My uncle paid him off to marry me, but Selby has been kind and I won't disgrace him. He doesn't deserve it." She paused. "I think I've already done enough disgracing for a lifetime. I'll be a mother soon. I must be responsible and think of what my behavior will mean for the future of the baby."

"Then what can we do?" he said, holding her off to look at her. "You surely can't expect me to leave you in this house with my child and another man."

"He's never here."

"What difference does that make? I want you with me!"

There was a cough from the hall, and they sprang apart. Mary waited a respectful moment and then stepped inside.

"Is all well?" she asked Alex.

"Yes, Mary, you did the right thing in bringing him here. Thank you so much."

Mary relaxed visibly and smiled.

"This is Mr. Kevin Burke, of whom you have heard so much. Kevin, Lady Howard."

"We've met," Mary said, her smile widening.

Kevin went to Mary's side and took her hand, kissing it lingeringly and bowing. Alex looked on in amazement; she had never seen him behave so, and his rough look was at such variance with his actions. He seemed a fantasy figure, a creature of the firelight and her nightly, longing dreams.

"Let me add my thanks to Alex's," he said. "I'll never forget your kindness."

Mary looked up at him, entranced.

"What is it?" Alex asked, breaking the spell. "Why have you come?"

"Oh," Mary said, stepping back from Burke. "Mrs. Curry has found some suitable clothes, and the cook is heating a vat of water in the kitchen."

"And Mrs. Curry sent you up here to tell us that?"

Mary nodded. "I think she is embarrassed," she added in a low tone to Alex.

"I'll go," Burke said. "Perhaps I should take Lady Howard along to protect me."

"I'll show you the way back to the kitchens," Mary said, preceding him to the door.

Burke looked back over his shoulder at Alex, standing in the center of the Afghan rug.

"I won't be long," he said.

Alex nodded.

Mary shot her a glance that spoke volumes and then ushered Burke from the room.

When Mary returned she found Alex standing in front of the fire, staring into the flames.

"What are you going to do?" she asked.

Alex turned, pressing her hands to her hot cheeks, and shook her head.

"You can't just keep him here."

"I know that."

"And I doubt he's going to leave of his own accord."

"I know that, too."

"It won't be long before Mrs. Curry solves the puzzle and guesses the truth."

Alex grabbed her friend's arm. "She knows Lord Selby is not the baby's father?"

"I think she's too flustered to conclude anything at the moment. But the way Burke looks at you, it . . . it doesn't betoken friendship. And once he's cleaned up she'll see what he looks like."

"What do you mean?"

"I mean she'll see that he's a much more likely candidate for your lover than Lord Selby."

"Jesu help me," Alex whispered. "What am I to do?"

"Are you sorry that he came here?"

"Oh, God in heaven, no. When I saw him all I wanted to do was take his hand and run out the door, get as far away from the cares of this place as my feet could take me, and be with him forever."

"But you can't do that."

"You know I can't. Even if I disregarded Lord Selby, which would be most unfeeling and ungrateful of me, I would give my child an adulteress for a mother. I care nothing for my own reputation, but it's not fair to brand a child for its mother's misdeeds."

"So you are caught in a net."

"Of my own making, I'm afraid."

"They are usually the tightest traps, are they not?"

"It will be very difficult to persuade Burke to go."

"Do you really want him to?"

"No."

"That's why it will be difficult. He knows you, he can tell what you feel."

"I must talk to him tonight at dinner," Alex said, thinking aloud. "The very least I can do is offer him a good hearty meal. He looks half-starved."

"I fear he must have gone through quite a lot to get to you," Mary observed quietly.

"I don't even want to think about it." Alex

caught her friend's eye. "He said something about the navy."

"The navy?"

Alex swallowed. "I think he deserted."

"Deserted!" Mary gasped. "They hang deserters, doesn't he know that?"

"They hang them if they catch them. I don't think he's planning on getting caught."

"He's a fugitive, then."

"Probably."

"He doesn't seem at all bothered by the fact."

"He's accustomed to it. He was a fugitive in Ireland for many years."

"This gets worse every minute," Mary said with despair in her voice.

"One thing at a time." Alex folded her hands, trying to stay calm. "Would you please ask Mrs. Curry to supervise an excellent dinner, perhaps the venison stored in the smokehouse from the last deer Evans got in November."

"I'm not sure how much of it is left."

"Ask. And I'll want the Rhenish wine, and some of those glazed figs Lord Selby had sent from Italy, and the honey cakes the cook gets from the bee-keeper's wife in the village."

"I'll attend to it," Mary said.

"And tell her I do not wish to eat in the dining room."

"Why?"

"I will have no appetite, surrounded by all the portraits of Lord Selby's ancestors on the walls," Alex said.

"I can't tell Mrs. Curry that."

"Tell her it's too chilly in that great room, the heat of the fire never penetrates its corners, and I desire to be served in here."

Mary nodded.

"And wish me luck."

"I do so, with all my heart."

Alex watched her friend's departing back until the door had closed behind her.

That evening the food was everything Alex could have wished, and Burke ate as if he were consuming a condemned man's last meal. Alex watched him raptly, devouring the sight of him as he devoured the dinner. Shorn of the beard and the excess hair, he looked much like his old self, even though his wrists protruded from John Selby's sleeves and the prominent bones of his face made him resemble a sprouting teenager. He finally sat back with a goblet of wine in his hand and surveyed Alex across the makeshift dining table.

"What's all this in aid of?" he said. "Are you fattening me up for the kill?"

"Don't joke about it," Alex said. "I have a good idea you're on the run from the navy, and I know what the penalty for that is."

"They won't find me," he said, taking a sip from his silver cup.

"Oh, how do you know? Why do you take such chances?"

"I had little choice." He told her about his adventures on the high seas and concluded, "So it was either spend the rest of my life on one of Her Majesty's ships or come here and find you."

"Does that happen all the time, vessels just kidnapping people at sea and forcing them into the navy?"

He looked at her as if she were incredibly naive. "Yes, Alexandra, it does. That's only one of the many reasons my people were so unhappy with your queen's government."

"But they may be looking for you," Alex said.

"I doubt it."

"Why not?"

"I wasn't a very skilled seaman, I did nothing another could not do as well in my place. They'll replace my body with somebody else's in short order and forget me."

"I hope that you are right."

"So is there anything else we can talk about?" he asked. "The sun, the moon, the latest predictions of the future from Dr. Dee, the deserts of Arabia? You've done a fine job of avoiding the topic most heavily on both our minds."

"I don't know what to say about it."

"Yes, you do. You have a speech all prepared, I'll warrant. You're waiting for the right moment to tell me that we must make the ultimate sacrifice. You must stay with your old goat of a husband and I must go . . . to hell, I suppose."

"Please," Alex said, looking away from him.

"Oh, have I put it badly? Perhaps you would like to rephrase it for me."

"You phrased it well enough."

He stood abruptly, almost upsetting his chair. "You have turned into such a prig, Alexandra! There was a time, short months ago, when you would have done anything to be with me. Now you sit there with your little whey face, swathed in maternal stateliness like a nun in her habit, and tell me to go scratch. If I had known motherhood would do this to you I never would have touched you."

"That's a terrible thing to say."

"I feel terrible. You're more concerned with getting your husband's fortune for the babe than you are with me."

"My husband's estate is entailed for his existing son," Alex said.

"Entailed, what is that?"

"All the property goes to him, with support provisions for his sister, Selby's daughter, and a small legacy for me."

"Then why not come with me?"

Alex put her palms flat on the table and was silent a long moment. Then she answered him with a question.

"Do you know what it's like for a woman to bear an illegitimate child in this kingdom?" she asked. "I'm not talking about a peasant woman or a slattern, but a woman of good family, whose conduct at court, and in all of England, is watched and noticed, a woman like myself?"

He was silent, watching her.

"Ostracism is the best that can happen to her, becoming a charge upon a charity is a strong possibility, beggary is the worst. When I thought I could stay in Ireland with you, the propriety of my conduct did not matter, but when I knew I must come back here, well . . ." She trailed off. "Eight years ago," she went on, "when one of Her Majesty's waiting maids became pregnant by Walter Raleigh, and it seemed for a time that Raleigh would not marry her, the maid tried to kill herself. Twice. Even after they were married and the child was born, the queen sent them both to the Tower to contemplate their misdeed."

Burke made as if to speak, but she held up her hand.

"Allow me to finish. When it was discovered that Lady Mary Grey had made a secret marriage without the queen's permission, Her Majesty had the husband thrown into prison for three years. His wife never saw him again, and when he died, even her request to wear mourning was refused."

"Are you telling me that your queen is a tyrant? Lady, this much I know!"

"I am describing to you the state you left me in, the state from which James Selby rescued me. I won't forget that, no matter how skillfully you might play upon my feelings to get me to do so. If I went off with you now, he would be a laughing-stock, not to mention the effect upon the child I carry, who would never be able to live in this country without accompanying whispers of scandal. This may not be the fate I would have chosen, but it is the one which was chosen for me by my untimely pregnancy."

"I never meant to leave you in such a miserable case, Alex," he said softly.

"I know, and I don't blame you. I was more eager to bed you than you were to take me."

"I would not say that," he replied, smiling slightly.

"Then let's say that neither of us considered the possible consequences. Is that fairly stated?"

He said nothing.

"I had to do something to help myself. This is what I did, and I intend to fulfill my part of the bargain," she said.

He studied her face, then looked away. "As stubborn as ever," he said. "But this is the first time it has been turned against me."

"I'm not against you, Kevin," she said, willing herself not to cry. "I wish with every fiber of my being that I could do what you want. But I can't."

She would never forget the look on his face as he finally understood that she really, truly meant it. He stared hard at her, took a deep breath, and then bent his gaze upon the floor. In all the time she'd known him, he had not once looked defeated, but he did so in that moment.

"Do you want me to go now?"

"No!" she gasped, and stood, reaching out for him before she could stop herself.

He was at her side in two strides, pulling her into his arms and kissing her as she had wanted him to from her first sight of him that day. She responded helplessly, but as he grew wilder, trying to make up for their separation in these stolen moments, she pulled away, stumbling blindly a few steps until he caught her again.

"Don't," she moaned. "I haven't the strength, don't press me."

He released her, easing her back onto her chair. "I'm sorry," he said. "I don't want to upset you. I'll go."

She caught his hand as he moved away. "You can stay in John's room, Mrs. Curry made it up for you."

"Can I see you in the morning?"

She shook her head, her eyes brimming. "It's best this way."

"All right. I'll leave at first light."

"Good-bye," Alex whispered.

"I love you," he said. "I always will."

"Please go," she murmured, raising her palm to her lips to seal them. She didn't move until she heard the door close behind him, and then she buried her face in her hands.

Alex awoke in the middle of the night with the worst backache she'd ever had in her life. She shifted position to get more comfortable and then realized the bed beneath her was soaking wet.

The fire was dying in the grate and the room was cold. She felt for the candle on her nightstand and lurched out of bed, wincing as pain spread outward through her abdomen. She lit the candle from the embers and made her way slowly to the hall, pausing every time a wave of pain engulfed her.

"Mary!" she hissed as she entered her friend's room, sagging against the wall.

Mary stirred but didn't wake.

Alex staggered a few more steps and sat heavily on the edge of the bed. "Mary!" she said more loudly, shaking the other woman's shoulder firmly.

"What is it?" Mary said thickly, rolling over and surveying Alex with her hair draped over one eye.

"I think the baby's coming," Alex said.

Mary sat bolt upright, instantly awake. "Are you sure?"

"Well, I have these pains, and I lost all this water . . ."

Mary threw off the covers, standing up in her shift and looking around for her robe. "Isn't it too soon?"

"By a few weeks, but Mrs. Curry said the first one often comes early."

"I was afraid his showing up here would bring this on," Mary said, fastening her robe and taking the candle from Alex's hand.

"Don't blame Burke for this," Alex said, seizing Mary's arm. "Oh, my God, this can't be happening with him here! Mary, you have to take charge of him, make sure he doesn't do anything—" She gasped and bent double, her face going white.

"You leave him to me," Mary said. "You must stay alone for a moment, I need to wake Mrs. Curry. Evans has to go for the midwife. Will you be all right?"

Alex nodded, unable to speak. Sweat was beading on her forehead and she could feel it running down her sides under her nightgown, despite the chill of the room.

Mary ran out, and Alex waited in a haze of pain for her return. When she came back Mrs. Curry was with her and both women hurried to settle Alex down on the bed.

"Don't you worry about a thing, my lady," Mrs. Curry said. "I've had five children of my own, and Mother Gansey, the midwife, has seen more children into the world than you have seen sunrises. You'll be just fine, and before very long that bonny babe of yours will be sleeping in your arms."

Alex bit her lip to keep from screaming. The pains were coming faster and stronger. She grabbed Mary's hand and gasped, "Mary, remember what I said."

"I will."

"What did she say?" Mrs. Curry asked.

"It's nothing, she was babbling," Mary said.

"Can you stay with her? I want to see that Evans has gone."

Mrs. Curry patted Alex's hand. "We'll be quite well, won't we, my lady?"

Mary slipped from the room and scurried down the hall to Burke's chamber. When she tapped he opened the door immediately, wearing John Selby's too short riding breeches and nothing else.

"What's going on?" he said. "I heard voices."

"Burke, you must listen to me," Mary said.

"What is it? Is Alex all right?"

"She's started."

"Started what?"

"The baby is coming."

Comprehension dawned, and he thrust her aside to push past her, but Mary seized his arm and hung on for dear life. When he moved to shake her off she twined her leg with his to trip him.

"Leave off me!" he said, trying not to hurt her but still determined to proceed.

"If you burst in there now, Mrs. Curry will know that you're the father. Is that what you want, after Alex has worked so hard to keep it a secret and ensure the child's future?"

"But I have to see that she's well!"

"I will keep you informed. You must stay here, and I promise I will report to you on her progress."

They both looked up as a faint cry pierced the stillness of the winter night.

"She's dying," he said, agonized.

"She's not dying, on my oath she is not dying. Birthing babies is a painful process. You must have seen your village women so engaged back home."

"They weren't Alex," he said as if that explained everything. Then his expression darkened further. "Childbed fever is a great hazard, women expire of it all the time."

"We will take strict loving care of her," Mary said. "Most women have come through this experience as hale and hearty as combatants in a tilt-yard."

"They weren't having my child!"

"You must not say so!" Mary hissed. "To anyone!"

"And the infants often die, too. It is a common experience, is it not?" he said with a moan.

Mary took his hand and led him back into the room, and he followed as meekly as a child. He sank onto the edge of his bed and thrust his hands into his already disordered hair.

"You must cease this foolishness," she said, kindly but sternly. "My care must be all for Alex. I can't be worried about what you might do while I am attending her. I promised her that I would control you, but if I stay with you and indulge these fancies of yours, I cannot be with her. You must bear your concern in silence, and I must go to assist with the birth. Do you understand me?"

He nodded miserably, chastened.

"I'll be back as soon as I am able. Give me your word that you will stay here and say nothing to anyone."

"You have my word on it," he said quietly.

When Mary left the room, Burke was overcome with loneliness. Fear for Alex produced such a longing to be with her that only Mary's warning kept him where he was.

There was little mystery about childbirth for him; as Mary had said, village women had been having children practically under his nose for most of his life. But he had never been so emotionally involved before, and the thought that his love for Alex might be the indirect cause of her death drove him to distraction. The subdued cries and anxious voices floating down the hall did nothing to help his state of mind. There was a commotion when the midwife arrived, and Burke finally got up and shut the door completely to block out whatever he could of the sounds accompanying the drama.

The night seemed endless. He could not judge the time, but it seemed like weeks before dawn streaked the sky and he heard, or thought he heard, the thin, piercing cry of a newborn babe.

Mary finally appeared, and he seized her as she came through the door.

"What?" he demanded.

"You have a son," Mary said, beaming.

"Alex?"

"She'll be fine," Mary said. "She's a bit tired now, of course, but everything went splendidly well, and both she and the baby look to be very healthy."

Tears of relief came to Burke's eyes, and Mary patted his hand awkwardly. He seemed stunned, but that was only to be expected; women always took first parenthood more in stride.

"I want to see her," he finally said.

Mary shook her head. "Mrs. Curry is still with her, and the wet nurse Mother Gansey brought."

"Wet nurse? Why does she need a wet nurse?"

"Her milk has not come in yet. With the first one it sometimes takes a few days. There's no cause for alarm."

"But I must be able to see her."

"She's probably sleeping now, and in any case we'll have to wait until Mrs. Curry goes to bed and everyone else has left. I suggest you try to get some rest, too. I'll come back for you as soon as it's safe for you to go in to see her."

Burke wasn't happy, but he saw the wisdom in what she was saying. "Lady Howard," he began.

"Mary."

"Mary. I can't thank you enough for all that you have done for Alex and me."

"Alex is a good friend, and when she told me the story of her time with you I could not help but have compassion for her situation."

"Not mine?" he said.

"Yours as well."

"You know that she wants me to leave her."

Mary sighed.

"How can I do it?"

"Because you must."

He shook his head. "What a tangle. My thoughts are like the knot garden at that house, the childhood home of your queen."

"Hatfield?"

"The same." He noticed Mary's tired face and said, "Forgive me for keeping you. You must be depleted of strength. Please go and rest yourself."

"I'll come back for you when I can."

He nodded and sagged back on the bed when she left. He stared at the ceiling as the sun rose, casting shafts of light across the wooden planks of the floor. Hampden Manor was a country house, not a castle, and wood and glass were much more in evidence than they were back home in Ireland. He did not miss the damp chill of stone floors and mossy walls, but he did miss Aidan and Rory, the comfort of their camaraderie in this pivotal moment of his life.

He had a son. His blood would endure, mixed with the fragile ichor of the child's English mother, down through the generations to a time, perhaps, when their descendants would not be enemies and could live together in peace.

He did not think he could sleep, but he must have, for when Mary touched his shoulder the sun was higher, and its buttery light spread across the bed.

"She's awake," Mary said. "You can come and see her now."

Burke leaped off the bed, stopping only to pull a shirt over his head, and then followed her down the hall to Alex's room.

His first thought upon entering was that she looked very small and white in the large bed, the baby even tinier nestled into the curve of her arm. As he approached, her gaze lifted from the child to him and she smiled dreamily.

"What do you think of him?" she asked as Burke bent to kiss her forehead.

Burke gazed at the red, wrinkled face and said, "He looks like a monkey."

"You've never seen a monkey!"

"A little old man, then. A little old man with apoplexy."

"I think he's beautiful. See his hair? The same lovely color as yours."

"Poor little scrapper, he would have done much better to look like you."

"I'm going to call him Michael. That was your father's name, wasn't it?"

Burke nodded mutely.

"It's a good English name, too. No one will ever know," she said softly.

"No one will ever know," he repeated in a despairing tone, clutching her hand.

Alex's eyes closed and Mary laid her hand on his shoulder. "Best to come away now," she said.

Burke raised Alex's hand to his mouth and

kissed it, then put it gently back on the bedcover. He touched the baby's eyes with his second and third fingers, said something in Gaelic and then abruptly left the room.

When Alex awoke again it was late afternoon, and Mary was sitting beside her bed.

"The baby?" she said.

"With the nurse."

"And Burke?"

Mary's expression changed.

"He's gone."

11

Come live with me, and be my love;
And we will all the pleasures prove . . .
>   —Christopher Marlowe,
>   "The Passionate Shepherd to His Love"

"*Gone?*" Alex echoed.

"As you requested," Mary reminded her.

"But . . ."

"You didn't think he would leave so soon?"

Alex looked away.

"You didn't think he would leave at all?"

"Mary, stop."

"You can hardly fault him for doing what you asked after you were so insistent upon it."

"But he only saw the baby once!"

"Would it be easier for him to go if he remained to see the baby on a daily basis?"

Alex closed her eyes. "I can hardly absorb it," she whispered. "Here and gone, so fast. As if he were a fantasy."

"He was no fantasy. I saw him, too."

"Did he say anything to you before he left?"

Mary shook her head. "No."

Alex was silent for almost a minute and then said, "Would you mind leaving me alone for a time, Mary?"

Mary rose and slipped quietly from the room, closing the door behind her.

Alex turned her face into the pillow and wept.

Burke was not gone, or rather, he had not gone far. He was, in fact, in the stables at Hampden Manor, making himself useful. On the day of his son's birth, instead of setting out on the road, he had convinced Evans to take him on to do whatever work was required in exchange for room and board. The Welshman, who did the hiring for the jobs on the estate outside the main house, saw Burke's size and apparent agility and looked no farther. Since Tim, the stableboy, lived in the village and went home at night, there was room for another full-time hand.

In the winter no one rode for sport, and Burke correctly guessed that a new mother like Alex would not be taking exercise for a couple of months, until the weather improved. In the meantime, he contented himself with feeding on scraps of information about his lover and son from the casual remarks Evans made: "The mistress has recovered right smartly from the birth" or "The young master is as fair a child as was ever born in this kingdom, I'll warrant." Burke listened and said nothing. He filed away all the information and did his assigned chores with efficiency and without complaint. At the end of a couple of months, Evans was pleased at his good fortune in acquiring such reliable help. It enabled him to put his feet up and act in a supervisory capacity while Burke did most of the work. He didn't know why Burke had turned up after a snowstorm and didn't ask, afraid that too much curiosity would cause Burke's ready hands and strong back to disappear as quickly as they had arrived.

Alex, for her part, was lonely. Mary had returned to her own house shortly after Michael was born, and even though the baby kept her busy, the short cold days and long cold nights, with only the servants for company, made her realize fully how much she had lost. She felt housebound and stifled. On the first warm day in early April she announced to Mrs. Curry her intention of taking a ride, and she set out for the stables.

The last of the snow was melting, softening the ground underfoot, and the clumps of forsythia bushes along the path from the house were just bringing forth their yellow buds. Alex's spirits lifted in the thin sunshine as she listened to the birds and tried not think of where she was and what she'd been doing at the same time the previous year. As she swept through the door into the stable, Evans, who had been seated on a crate, whittling, leapt to his feet.

"My lady," he said in surprise. "We haven't seen you down here in a good while. How can I be of service?"

"Good morning, Evans. I thought as the morning was fine I might take a short jaunt, get myself back in riding trim. Which horse might be suitable, do you think?"

Evans cast a brief glance at the stalls and then seemed to have an idea.

"We've a new bay, ma'am, with a frisky temperament and a fine step. Would you like to try him out?"

"Very well. Where is he?"

"Being curried in the back. He'll be all fresh for Your Ladyship. I'll send the new man out with him."

"What new man?" Alex asked.

"Oh, a lad I took on over the winter, a good hand with horseflesh. I'll go and find him."

Alex tapped her riding gloves against her thigh as she waited for the horse to arrive. She was examining a new bridle hanging on the wall, wondering where Tim was, when she heard a step behind her. She turned to see Burke facing her, holding the reins of the bay.

She was so astonished that words failed her. He looked wonderful, so healthy and handsome, which didn't help her self-control. She licked her lips and then said in a carefully controlled voice, "Are you the 'new man' Evans described?"

"I am."

"How new?"

"Almost three months."

"You've been here the whole time. You never left the estate at all?"

He inclined his head.

"Oh, you are a devious man," Alex said.

"I'd never deny it."

"Did Mary know?"

"No one knows, except you and me. Evans thinks I came in off the roads and decided to stay until the spring, when traveling would become easier."

"You did this just to be near me?" she whispered.

"You made it clear you wouldn't have me in the house."

The bay whinnied, and Burke stroked its nose. The horse, considerably fatter and happier than it had been in Southampton, stamped its feet, wanting the promised exercise.

"Are you going to turn me out again?" Burke asked.

"I don't know what to do where you're concerned. I never have," she answered softly.

"What do you think of the bay?" Evans said behind them.

"He's a handsome horse, Evans," Alex replied, trying to keep her voice level.

"He arrived with Kevin here, looking something the worse for the trip, as did his master," Evans said, chuckling. "But we've built him up, and now he exceeds most of the others in strength and speed, and he's as keen as a whetstone, too. Takes orders like a military brute, doesn't he, Kevin?"

"He does," Burke said.

"What's his name?" Alex asked, making conversation for Evans' benefit.

"Dealanach," Burke said. "Gaelic for 'lightning.'"

"That's a mouthful. I think I'll call him Dee."

"He responds to that," Evans said.

"Since this is my first ride since my confinement, I am loath to go out alone," Alex said. "I'd like to take Kevin along with me, if you don't need him."

Burke was silent, watching her face.

"Certainly, my lady," Evans said, beaming, glad of the opportunity to display his new assistant as well as the fine new horse.

"I think I'll ride Dee. Do you have a suitable mount for . . . for Kevin?"

"How about Jasper?"

Burke nodded. "I'll get him ready." He selected a bridle from a peg on the tack wall and went down the row of stalls.

"How are you feeling, my lady?" Evans asked. "You gave us all quite a fright when the baby came early. I had a wild ride to get the midwife, that much I can tell you."

"Yes, and I don't think I ever thanked you properly for it, Evans, so let me do so now."

"And the young master?"

"Beautiful. Thriving."

"Ah, that is happy news. I always ask Mrs. Curry when I see her and she has nothing but good to say of his habits. Sleeps through the night, does he?"

"Yes."

"You are lucky in that. I remember that my first son was almost a year old before he slept through. Drove my wife, God rest her soul, almost to distraction. Now my daughter, she was quite different. . . ."

Burke returned, leading the second horse and sparing Alex a recital on the nocturnal behavior of all six of Evans' children.

"You'll be riding astride?" Evans asked Alex, noting her boyish attire.

"Yes, I don't like sidesaddle unless I am forced into it by my clothing."

They walked the horses outside, and Evans gave her a leg up while Burke mounted smoothly and turned his horse to watch her. Alex patted the horse's neck and then kicked him sharply. He surged ahead, sprinting for the road, and Burke had no choice but to follow.

Alex ran him flat out for a couple of miles, throwing up mud and tussocks of grass, not slowing until she reached the edge of the trees bordering Hampden Park. Then she allowed the horse to canter into the shade.

Burke pulled up alongside her. "What were you trying to prove?" he asked. "That you could lose me?"

"That would have been foolish," Alex said, dismounting and tethering Dee to a tree. "I know no one can outride you."

"I thought Dee had been turned into a pookah," Burke said, tying his mount beside hers.

"What's that?"

"A spirit horse, with breath of fire and crystalline eyes," he replied, running his hand along Jasper's flank.

"Evans would be very surprised to find one of those in his stable," Alex said. She sat on the damp ground and drew up her knees. "You should be ashamed of yourself for taking advantage of a trusting, genial soul like him."

"I'm not taking advantage of him. He's getting a powerful load of work out of me. He's very happy with his bargain. Ask him."

"That's not at all what I meant, and you know it," Alex replied.

Burke knelt in front of her and took her chin in his hand, forcing her to look at him. "Aren't you happy to see me at all?" he asked quietly.

"Of course I am."

"Doesn't seem like it."

"It's just that . . ."

"You thought your problem was solved, and here I am turning up again."

"That's not how I would put it."

"Well?"

"How I am supposed to resist you now?" she burst out. "I'm not pregnant anymore, I can't use that as an excuse, and you're no longer half-starved and exhausted. You look like you did in Ireland when I could hardly keep my hands off you!"

He reached for her, but she twisted out of his grasp. "It isn't fair," she moaned.

"Don't resist me," he said. "Give in."

"I'm a married woman!"

"Oh, don't start harping on that string again. You're about as married as I am, and that's not much." He seized her and pulled her down onto the wet grass, crushing her mouth with his.

Alex had known this would happen, she had brought him with her for this reason. She missed him and longed for him so—his touch, his smell, the feel of his mouth on hers. She had conjured them so often in her dreams that the reality was irresistible. She clung to him, yielding, fitting her body to his. He felt her submission and pressed her closer, bearing her down to the ground. Alex sighed, and he pressed his advantage.

Yet when it came right down to it, she couldn't go through with the betrayal.

"No!" she said, pulling away from him.

"Are you going to give me another speech about your wedding vows?" he demanded, his face inches from hers.

"Let me go or I'll slap you," she said between her teeth.

He released her so suddenly that she slid into the muck, splashing her clothes.

"Excuse me, Your Ladyship," he said bitterly. "I must have gotten the wrong impression, I thought you'd asked for my company. I wager I'm hearing things."

"I asked for your company, but not this."

"What did you think was going to happen, with the two of us out here alone? I *want* you, Alexandra. Why do you ken I've been sleeping in that freezing barn for three months, because I like listening to Evans snore?"

"The barn is not freezing, we keep it very warm." She wiped her clothes ineffectually.

"So, am I being dismissed again?" He stood, hands on hips, surveying her. "Since I am such a temptation, I'm guessing you won't want me so close by."

"Don't ridicule me," she said, her lower lip trembling.

"Do you think you could restrain yourself until the thaw is over? A couple of weeks, maybe?"

"Oh, shut your mouth."

"Two weeks?" he persisted.

"Yes, all right, two weeks!" she almost screamed.

"That is kind of you, I'm sure. I will try to keep out of your way until then. I wouldn't want you to throw yourself on my neck and start the servants talking."

"You can be such a bastard, Burke," she said,

almost in tears. How dare he act as if she were in the wrong. She was the one trying to honor her vows.

"I'll see my son before I go," he said, undoing the knot in his horse's reins.

"Wait a minute," Alex said, sitting up.

"I said I'll see my son, and I'll pick the time for the visit. Until then don't disturb yourself. You won't be bothered by me. If you come to the stables for a ride I'll stay out of your way, and Evans or Tim can assist you."

He mounted before she could protest and was off in a flurry of hooves, galloping away.

Alex sat sniveling on the ground, staring down miserably at her soiled clothes and wondering how on earth she was going to explain them to Mrs. Curry.

Burke was as good as his word. Alex did not see him again, and it was maddening to know that he was nearby at the stables, within easy reach. She had to restrain herself from going down there several times a day. The certainty that he knew exactly what he was putting her through made her want to kill him and drag him into bed at the same time. A week passed, the weather turned warmer, and by the end of a fortnight Alex jumped every time a door opened or closed. She had no idea when he would appear or how she would explain his presence when he did, but she wanted to see him.

On a crisp day in late April Mrs. Curry came into her room when she was feeding the baby. "Messenger from the queen, my lady," she said.

Alex handed her the baby and refastened her bodice. "Make sure you rock him before you put him down," she said. This was supposed to ward off colic.

The housekeeper nodded, cooing to the child.

"You can send him in," Alex said.

The yeoman of the guard entered as Mrs. Curry left. "Lady Selby," he said, bowing.

"Good morning."

"I am requested by Her Majesty to inform you that she requires your presence to attend upon her at Whitehall."

"I am always happy to do Her Majesty's bidding," Alex replied.

The guardsman inclined his head.

"Do you know if a similar message has been sent to Lady Howard?"

The guard looked surprised. "Why, yes, madam."

Alex nodded. Apparently their holiday was at an end.

"I am also instructed to offer you this humble gift as a token of Her Majesty's regard in celebration of your son's birth," the man said.

Alex extended her hand for the package.

The gift was a silver-and-gilt porringer. It was engraved "For Michael Selby, on the occasion of his arrival into this our realm, from his loving princess, Elizabeth R." It was further inscribed with the baby's birth date.

There was a note enclosed, handwritten in Elizabeth's beautiful, flowing script.

"Little Greek: It is our pleasure to welcome you back to our service. We look forward to your presence at court and are certain that your son will enjoy the pleasures of the Surrey countryside in your absence. Make haste to join us as we are in dire want of your most excellent company."

In other words, come yourself but leave the baby behind. It was the typical Elizabethan treatment: a kiss and a blow at the same time.

"You may tell Her Majesty that I will leave for London tomorrow morning," Alex said. "Stop off at the kitchen if you are so inclined, I will send word to feed you. Do you need to exchange horses?"

"I would be obliged if I could, madam."

"Very well, then. Take your pick of the stables, and I will bring your horse back with me when I come to court. Will there be anything else?"

The man made a sweeping bow.

"Good-bye," Alex said. "Godspeed on your return trip."

Mrs. Curry came back in as the guardsman left. "Well?" she said.

"Back to court," Alex sighed. "Without Michael."

"Oh, I am sorry. Are you certain you can't bring the baby?"

"Her Majesty wrote to me herself to make it clear."

"I thought she liked children."

"At a distance, apparently. Or for short visits. Not resident in her house and crying in her ear."

"Perhaps she won't keep you away long."

"It will depend on her whim, I suppose. As it always does."

"I expect I should start packing for you."

Alex nodded. When the housekeeper had left, she braced herself and walked down to the stables to talk to Burke.

He was grooming Jasper, absorbed in the work, and barely looked up at her arrival.

"Does Your Ladyship wish to ride?"

"Are you happy here, Kevin?" she asked, ignoring his question.

"Oh, I am happy to be so near to Your Ladyship. It gladdens my heart," he said, flicking the curry comb to free it of hair.

"Your sarcasm does not become you."

"Your masquerade does not become you, Lady Selby," he countered, emphasizing the title.

Alex decided to overlook his behavior, determined to accomplish her mission. "I've had a message from the queen," she said.

"Indeed. I saw the messenger. He went off with Evans to try out Dealanach. It might be he means to take him back to London."

Alex looked at him, suddenly realizing the situation.

"Didn't you offer him his pick of the horses?"

"I never thought . . ." she began.

"You never do."

"I'll tell him the horse is mine, he can take any of the others."

"Your Ladyship is most gracious."

"If you call me that once more I'll—"

"Slap me? You've threatened me before, I recall."

"Don't provoke me, Kevin, I'm trying to talk to you!"

He put down the comb and leaned against the stall, folding his arms. "Talk," he said.

"I have to go to London, the queen has recalled me to her service. She is at Whitehall."

"Moves around a bit, doesn't she?" he said dryly.

"Yes."

"Why does she want you back?"

"I don't know, she is whimsical. I was at court during the fall, before I had the baby."

"Perhaps she likes you. And why not? You're pretty, intelligent, surely light-footed to do her bidding. I imagine you grace her court very well."

Alex said nothing.

"Did your husband request that you attend the queen?"

"It was part of the bargain that I made with him."

"But of course you hate going to court, those

fine people and fancy trappings, all of that bores you, I'm sure."

"I am nothing but a servant there. I would prefer to be here, with my son."

"My son," he said.

"Our son."

"And with me?" Burke asked.

"I am not with you," Alex replied. "But at least I get to see you, sometimes."

Burke reached out for her as Evans and the guardsman came through the stable door. He snatched his hand back and picked up the curry comb.

"I have made an error," Alex said to the guardsman. "The horse you were trying is mine, as I should have said."

"No harm done," the man said. "I'll take another, he's a bit too tetchy for my taste anyway."

"When will you be leaving for London, my lady?" Evans asked.

"Tomorrow."

"Will you want me to accompany you, or is the queen sending an escort?"

"I will be escorting Her Ladyship to London," Burke said.

All three turned to stare at him.

"Was that not your desire?" Burke asked innocently, glancing at Alex. She wanted to kick him.

"I . . . I thought he could be spared more easily than you, Evans, and he is familiar with the roads in these parts," Alex said.

"Is that so?" Evans said.

"I was traveling for a good while before I came here," Burke replied, which was not a lie.

"Come outside with me," Alex said, putting an end to the charade. "I want to instruct you about outfitting the horses for the journey."

Burke followed her, and when they were safely away he said, "What was that about the horses, my lady?"

Alex whirled and faced him. "You enjoy making me miserable, don't you?"

"And why not? It makes two of us. There's nobody in this whole country more miserable than I am."

"Then why do you stay?"

He stared down at her, a muscle twitching in his jaw. "You know why I stay," he said in a low, furious tone. "I might catch a glimpse of you, or hear something from Evans about my boy, or if I'm dead lucky and say my prayers, you might even speak to me."

"Oh, Kevin, I would have things very different if I could make them so."

"Do you remember all that about star-crossed lovers, that rubbish you told me back in Ireland?"

"It wasn't rubbish," she said, looking away from him.

"I suppose not, considering that I am now beginning to believe it."

"Kevin, you can't come to London with me," she said.

"Why? If you could take Evans, you could take me, and I'm better able to protect you. I'm bigger and stronger and younger than he is."

"That's the point."

"What is?"

"We'll have to stay overnight in an inn."

"Ah. Her Ladyship doesn't trust herself."

"No," she whispered, looking up at him and then down at her hands. "I don't."

"Alexandra," he said in a strong voice, taking a step closer to her.

"Kevin, stay back. We're in full view of the house."

"Oh, damn them all to hell, what do I care what they think," he said, clenching his fists.

"You can come with me if you promise—"

"I'll make no promises! I've a good mind to leave you at that bloody palace . . . what is it, York Place?"

"Whitehall. It is now called Whitehall."

"Whatever in blazes it's called, leave you there and go right on to the quays, and catch the next boat sailing for Ireland."

Alex said nothing.

"Well? Would you have me do that?"

"If you want."

"If I want!" He uttered an oath in Gaelic and then said, "How much more of this torment do you think I can take, knowing how close you are, wanting you every minute, all the while pretending that we hardly know each other? I don't recognize myself, I've turned into a whimpering oaf, waiting every day for a scrap, a word, a crumb of your regard. It turns my gut to water to think of what I've become, all for love of you!"

Mrs. Curry came out of the kitchen door and called, "My lady, the baby won't settle. Could you come in? He always quietens so nicely for you."

They both looked up at the housekeeper, who cast a disapproving glance at Burke and then went back inside.

"She doesn't favor your working here," Alex said to him.

"Devil take her."

"You should tell Evans to have everything ready at dawn tomorrow," Alex advised him hastily, determined to get away from him.

"I want to see Michael before we go."

"You will," Alex replied, and walked on up the path.

Inside the house she tended to Michael, but her mind was elsewhere. She knew the enormous risk she was taking, going on the trip with Burke, but if he did leave for home from London, it would be the last time she'd ever see him.

Alex was awake all night, her things packed for travel, her mind in turmoil. The baby was fretful, perhaps sensing her distraction, and the thought of leaving him had her close to tears. Why did she have all these rules to obey? Why couldn't she just do as she pleased?

In the morning, she insisted that Mrs. Curry carry the baby outside to see her off. When Burke approached leading their mounts she took the child and brought him over, ostensibly to see the horses.

"He's a brawny boy," Burke said, swallowing hard as he looked down at the squirming bundle. The baby was boxing the air with his fists and keeping time with his feet.

"He's already big for his age," Alex said

"More power to him."

Mrs. Curry was looking on with interest, so Alex hurried back and handed him to the housekeeper before she or Burke did anything foolish.

"Take very good care of him," she said, looking away from the tiny face.

"I will, my lady."

Alex was shaky when Burke grasped her hand and helped her onto her horse. He mounted Dealanach and strapped her bags onto the messenger's horse, and the little procession set out for London.

They rode steadily for two hours before Burke slowed and indicated a clearing where they could take a rest. When Alex got down she spread her skirts cautiously on the ground and then shook her head when he offered her a flask of water.

"What is it?" he asked, crouching next to her.

"It's not fair to make me leave him when he is so little," she whispered.

He made a mock salute. "Your queen must be obeyed."

"There's many others to serve her who aren't leaving nurslings behind. We had to get the wet nurse to return, and who knows if he'll take to her milk again? What if he sickens? By the time word gets to me in London, he could be dead."

"When was the last time you had the nurse?" Burke asked.

"Two weeks ago when I had the green fever."

"Two weeks?"

"Yes."

"I ken the child will be fine," he said, smiling.

"Oh, what do you know? You're not his mother."

"You love him very much, don't you?"

Alex toyed with her ruff. It was a question that did not require an answer.

"As much as you once loved me?"

Alex blinked rapidly. Why was she always dissolving into tears at every opportunity? "I love you as much as ever, and you know it, you scoundrel," she said bitterly. "Do you say provocative things like that just to torture me?"

Burke didn't answer for a long while, and then he observed, "We've come to a pretty pass, haven't we?"

Alex stared past him at the pale green, budding trees. They certainly had.

"Do you wish you'd never met me?" he asked, twisting a blade of grass between his fingers.

Alex looked at him, his blue eyes, the long lashes,

the wild hair she loved to caress, even now curling over his brow in front and into the neck of his tunic in back.

"How could I wish that?" she said softly. "I have memories I'll treasure for the rest of my life."

"And Michael."

"Yes, and Michael."

"But not me."

Alex wiped her eyes with the back of her hand. "Let's not do this, Kevin, we'll both be bleeding all over this grass."

It was several seconds before she looked at him, and she was startled to see that he was smiling.

"What?" she said.

"You're talking like an Irishman."

She finally smiled, too. "I always knew you were a bad influence, Burke."

When he stood and offered her his hand she took it, and they remained holding hands for an instant. Then he lifted her onto her horse and the moment passed.

They stopped once more, to eat the meal Mrs. Curry had packed, and then at dusk they rode up to the inn Alex had mentioned earlier. It was really a tavern with rooms to let, like the Boar's Head in Southampton. It was obvious that a roistering crowd was already well into a roaring good time inside the bar.

"Are you certain about this place?" Burke asked, surveying the establishment with a practiced eye.

"Well, we could ride on to Coldstream House, the Ashley estate, and spend the night with Lady Ashley, but it's another hour on the road. I'm tired, the horse is tired, and it's not safe to be on the highway after dark."

"This trip could have been better planned."

"Actually, there are several houses along the way where we could have stayed, but they all belong to Lord Selby's friends," Alex confessed. "I don't feel comfortable with them. They always ask . . . embarrassing questions."

"I see." Burke slipped off his horse, lifting Alex to the ground and then taking their mounts around back to the lean-to that served as a stable. When he returned he said, "Let me get you settled inside and then I'll see to the horses."

They went through the door together and paused as the din from the tavern swirled around them. Burke waylaid the barkeep and said loudly, "We need two rooms to pass the night, as far away from this rabble as possible."

"One room left," the landlord said gruffly. "A shilling for the room, tuppence on top for a meal along with it."

"We need two rooms. This is Lady Selby of Hampden Manor—"

"I don't care if she's Queen Bess herself," the man said. "One room at the top back, take it or leave it."

"Look, you," Burke began, but Alex laid her hand on his arm.

"It's all right, take the room," she said. "I'm too weary to argue, we'll make do."

"And we will need something to eat," Burke said.

"I'll send the barmaid up with bread and ale."

"Is that all you have?" Burke asked as he handed the man the coins for payment.

"Might be some sausage and cheese, unless the cheese has gone off," the barman replied, already pushing his way back through the crowd.

"So this is civilized England," Burke said as they waited at the foot of a crooked staircase.

"I've seen it more civilized than this," Alex replied.

Presently the barmaid appeared, carrying a battered tray and bearing a candle. She looked at Alex's fine clothes and Burke's stableyard attire and raised her brows.

She led the way to the second floor, which featured a beamed ceiling so low that Burke banged his head as they reached the top of the stairs.

"Mind yer 'ead, laddie," the woman said, too late.

The room was about the size of a pin box, but it had a reasonably clean bed with a feather ticking mattress, and there was a welcome fire going in the grate. Though the day had been warm, the spring evening had turned chilly.

"'Ere ye go," the woman said, setting the tray on the battered dresser. "Come down if ye need aught else." The door slammed behind her.

Alex and Burke were left staring at each other.

"Go and take care of the horses. I'll be fine here," Alex said, sitting on the bed.

Burke hesitated as the noise from the drinkers below came up through the floor. "Don't go out of this room," he cautioned, as he left.

He returned ten minutes later. "All fed and set for the night," he said, looking around him again. On second look, the floor was dusty and the single window grimed with chimney soot. A chamber pot covered with a graying napkin stood in a corner.

"Not exactly Hampden Manor, is it," he said, sitting on the one wooden chair since he could not possibly stand. With his legs stretched before him, his feet touched the bedstead.

"Oh, we can bear it for a night. We've borne worse back in Ireland, if you recall." Alex settled on the bed.

"Some would say that was better," he said softly. "I would."

Burke reached for the tray and poured two tankards of the ale. He leaned over to hand one to Alex and then took a gulp of his. "Not bad," he said, smacking his lips.

Alex took a sip and made a face.

"Ah, I was forgetting. Only the finest Madeira for you these days."

"What is there to eat?" Alex asked, ignoring his comment.

"A lump of cheese, hard at the edges, a loaf of

wheat bread, and the promised sausage. Dry as dirt, it is. Oh, and an apple. He didn't mention that."

"We shouldn't have eaten everything Mrs. Curry gave us."

"But then we never do what we should, do we, Alex?" Burke removed a knife from his belt, sliced all the portions in half, and handed Alex her share.

"Apple's fresh," she said, biting into it.

"Our landlord probably stole it from the orchard we saw down the road," Burke said, deftly carving the core out of the fruit.

"Do you remember that knife you had at the camp near Inverary?" Alex asked, watching him.

"Indeed I do. I wish I had it now."

"You were always brandishing it at me. You had me quite terrified," she said.

"That was the idea, my lady. You were a saucy piece of baggage to handle."

"What happened to the knife?"

"Lost it at sea when my boat was swamped in a storm. I was lucky to get out of that with my skin intact, so I counted myself a winner even so."

"You almost died then, didn't you?"

He shrugged. "I can swim—everybody who grows up on an island can swim right enough. But if a ship hadn't been passing, I would have gone under, as I was halfway through the passage and no land in sight."

"You've gone through quite a lot for me, haven't you?" she said, echoing Mary Howard's words.

"Don't fret yourself about that. I did what I pleased, most times do."

"Not always. You're not doing what you want with me now."

"Well, there I need your help, and you're not giving any."

"I can't," she said, and put down her fruit, suddenly losing her appetite.

"You'll feel better after some sleep," Burke said, watching her face. "The floor will do for me. And rest easy, you'll have no company that you're not wanting."

"I know that," Alex said. She got up and pulled the coverlet off the bed, setting it on the floor for him. He stood and unfastened his jerkin, doffing it and untying the neck of the cotton shirt beneath it until it lay open on his chest and then yanking the garment over his head. Alex looked away.

"You can take off your gown if you want, for comfort," he said. "I've seen you in less."

Alex stood up and turned for him to unhook her bodice and help her out of her gown with its heavy underskirt. She removed the ruff and waist bolster and stepped out of the farthingale.

"How can you court women bear to wear all this underneath your clothes?" he asked, shaking his head.

"I've often wondered," Alex said. In recent years the rage for Spanish fashions had caused the skirts to become wider and fuller, until movement was severely restricted. There were many times she longed to be wearing breeches again. She draped her things across the foot of the bed and slipped under the sheet in her chemise.

"I wanted to dress boyishly and ride astride for this trip but many of the people in this area know Lord Selby and I feared it would not look seemly."

Burke lay down on the floor and propped his chin in his hand. "You have changed, Alex," he said, looking up at her. "You now have more rules for yourself than a cloistered nun."

"I feel my responsibility to Lord Selby very keenly."

"So you've said."

"It must dictate my behavior."

"That much," he said in a tired voice, "I have understood."

A long silence fell, and Alex thought he was asleep until he murmured, "Micheali."

"What?" Alex said.

"That's how you say his name in Gaelic."

"Whose name?"

"Our son's."

"Oh."

After that he said no more, and Alex, worn out from the ride and the stress of watching her every move with Burke, quickly fell asleep. But her mind

could not dismiss him, and she drifted into a restless dream that put her back at Inverary Castle,
hurrying down the staircase to the dungeon that
imprisoned her lover. She smelled the dampness,
felt the lichen on the walls, and finally saw Burke,
abused and bleeding, chained in his cell. She had
to get him out of there, had to help him, but she
was powerless against her uncle. . . .

Burke was awakened by the noises Alex was
making, helpless whimpering that drew him to her
side. She was twitching and moaning, her hands
crumpling the sheet that covered her. When he
touched her shoulder, she gasped and pulled away
from him.

"Alex, wake up, it's me, it's Burke. Alex, you're
dreaming."

She opened her eyes and saw him, and in the
moment of relief that he was all right, not a prisoner but with her and uninjured, she threw her arms
around his neck.

"Easy now," he murmured. "Easy, it was just a
dream, no more."

"I thought you were back in the dungeon at
Inverary," she whispered, clutching him.

"Not at all, not at all. I'm free as the air, as you
can tell for yourself."

"I saw the whip marks, and the bruises, how
they had mistreated you," she mumbled against his
shoulder, still in the grip of the nightmare.

He held her off to look at her. "When? When
did you see that?"

She was trapped but there was really no good reason to lie about it now.

"I saw you once, when you were being held in the dungeon. I bribed a guard to bring me down to you, but when I saw how badly you'd been beaten, I knew you would not want me there, so I left before you were aware of my presence."

"Harker," Burke muttered, pulling her back into his arms.

"Yes, that was the guard's name."

"He told me where you were in England, asked me to give you his regards."

"He helped me when I most needed a friend."

"I never knew you saw me in such a bad way. I'm that sorry, Alex, I would have spared you the sight."

"That's why I left Ireland when I did. I couldn't risk your being taken and tortured like that again."

"Oh, darling," he said, drawing her closer, his lips moving in her hair. *"Tha gaol agam ort."*

"What does that mean?"

"I love you."

"It sounds better in Gaelic."

He turned his head, and almost against her will, Alex moved so that her mouth met his.

He kissed her tenderly at first, but it wasn't long before the embrace escalated and Alex was lying in his arms, nothing between them but the thin material of her chemise. He trailed his lips down her neck and inside the gown, seeking her breasts. Alex's head fell back, and he loosened the drawstrings of her gown with his free hand, pulling it off her shoulders. She gasped as the loose material fell to her waist and his mouth closed over her nipple, sucking gently as he tasted the milk that fed his son. She dug her fingers into the muscles of his shoulders and sighed.

"Please," he said hoarsely, finding the valley between her breasts with his tongue.

"Yes," she whispered.

Burke sat up and lifted her back on the bed, pulling the undergarment off her body and lying next to her. Alex watched him in a daze, submitting blissfully as he began to caress her again. His hands on her body were like a feast after the famine of the last year. She hooked an arm around his neck and drew him on top of her, wrapping her legs around his hips as his weight pressed her back into the bed.

"I'll put another boy in you, so I will," he said in her ear, and as he did Alex caught sight of the wedding band on her finger, the glint of gold almost lost in the golden mass of his hair.

She went limp and bit her lip.

Burke felt the change and looked down into her face. "What's amiss?" he said.

Alex didn't answer, but closed her eyes and turned her head away from him.

He sat up, dropping his legs over the side of the bed, his head bowed and his forearms propped on his thighs. She saw that his hands were shaking.

"I'll not force you, Alex, no matter how much you might want me to," he said

"I'm sorry," she whispered.

He picked his cambric shirt and leather jerkin off the floor, shrugged into them, and then stood up, adjusting his pants. "I'll be down in the tavern," he said. "I'll see you in the morning and take you the rest of the way into London."

He paused only to add a log to the dying fire before he closed the door behind him.

Alex pulled the sheet over her naked body and stared, dry-eyed, at the ceiling.

Burke did not get drunk; he was sober and wordless and waiting for Alex when she arrived in the tavern the next morning. She had slept fitfully for the rest of the night after he had left her, but if he noticed her drawn, tight face he said nothing about it.

They conducted the rest of the trip in silence, entering south London in late morning. Alex took the lead since she knew the city. Burke observed the confusion and noise with awe; Southampton had been nothing in comparison with this, and before that he had known only Ireland.

They proceeded slowly up King Street, passing the stalls of fishmongers and herb sellers and bakers and sweetmeat vendors, all hawking their wares. Riders had to take care not to trample the children and dogs and beggars who threatened to run under their horses at any moment. The tidal smell of the river, the food offered for sale, and the press of unclean people was so overwhelming that Burke was tempted to cover his nose.

Alex turned north through Holbein Gate, passing the connecting route between Charing Cross and Westminster, and thereafter the passage grew wider and less congested until they reached Whitehall Gate, the entrance to the palace. She dismounted and signaled for Burke to do the same. She handed what looked like a letter to the guard, and after examining it he indicated that they should pass and walked over to take their mounts.

Burke hesitated. "I'm not handing over my horse to that dressed-up dummy," he said to Alex in a low voice. It was the first sentence he had spoken to her that day.

"Dee will be perfectly all right. He'll go to the palace stables, where he'll be well tended. You can have him back when you leave."

"I'm leaving now," he said, holding her gaze.

"Oh, please, Kevin, not here, at least let me say a proper good-bye!"

"I said I would get you here, and I have," he told her. "I'm done with this business, and with you."

"Are you punishing me for last night?"

He was spared a reply by a commotion coming from the direction of the elaborate gardens that led down toward the river. They looked up to a see a woman in the distance, striding briskly toward them, followed by a group of four men who were hurrying to keep up with her.

"Oh, my God," Alex whispered.

"What is it?" Burke asked.

"The queen." The guard, who had joined them, answered his question, taking the horses and leading them back to his post.

"Listen to me," Alex said quickly. "Bow low when she approaches and then just remain still. Say nothing unless she speaks directly to you, and then answer briefly and respectfully. Kevin, do you hear me?"

"I hear," he replied dully, resisting an overpowering urge to flee. These people, all so recently his enemies—especially this old woman bearing down on him—made him feel as though he were voluntarily entering a prison camp. Everything in him rose up screaming, telling him not to take another step closer to the fire.

He drew a deep breath and stood his ground.

"My little Greek!" Elizabeth said, extending her hand for Alex to kiss. Alex sank to the ground in a curtsy and pressed her lips to the old lady's long, slender fingers, glittering with rings. Burke stared, fascinated, and then remembered to bow.

The old lady was wearing a pale yellow gown with a deeper buttercup underskirt and a surcoat of amber velvet. A pair of cloth-of-gold slippers peeped from under her voluminous skirts and there were huge white pearls in her intricately designed wig.

"Your Majesty," Alex murmured.

Elizabeth indicated they should rise and stood beaming at Alex while her councilors huddled in the background.

"Welcome back to court," the queen said graciously. "And how is your son?"

"Thriving, ma'am."

"I'm sure, I'm sure. What think you of his gift?"

"Overwhelmingly generous, Your Majesty. I cannot compose a proper expression of gratitude."

Elizabeth waved her hand dismissively. "Master Cecil had a letter from your husband. His business goes well and he expects to return and give his report in a month's time."

"So I understand."

"And who is this?" Elizabeth said, turning her sharp gaze on Burke, who stood uneasily a few paces behind Alex.

"My manservant," Alex said, her heart racing. "He accompanied me from Surrey and will be returning there."

"Nonsense," Elizabeth said, moving closer to Burke and looking him up and down. "He shall stay overnight at the palace and rest himself. Time enough to return tomorrow."

"Most gracious, ma'am," Alex said, despairing inwardly. She shot a meaningful glance at Burke, and he bowed again.

"A long lad," the queen said, observing his

height. "I like a long lad. Why have you been keeping this beauty hidden away in Surrey, Alexandra? He should be assisting you at court."

"My husband's manager is needful of his skill with horses on the estate, Your Majesty," Alex said.

"Ah, well, I would not disturb your domestic harmony, Lady Selby," the queen said. "But you will stay the night with us, even so," she added, addressing Burke, "and attend upon us tomorrow morning before you leave."

"I will, and thank you, ma'am," Burke said in his best Inverary Castle accent.

"Done," the queen said briskly. "Cantwell, see to his accommodations," she said to one of her councilors. "Lady Alex, you will come with us."

Alex followed the queen, casting one final glance over her shoulder at Burke, who looked after her longingly.

Burke stared into the leaping flames of the fireplace in his assigned room at Whitehall, wondering at the fate that had led him to his present ridiculous circumstances. Here he was, sitting in the palace of the woman whose forces he had recently been fighting, waiting for an audience with that same lady, who had no idea who he really was.

What would his fellow Irishmen think of this? Rory would be yelling his head off, no doubt, and

Aidan would be laughing, holding his sides and crying with mirth at the sight of the great Kevin Burke, cavalier of Ireland, waiting for an audience with Elizabeth I of England like a lazy boy called before his tutor.

Burke got up and looked for a window to open. There was none. The fire was too high, and the room felt like an oven. He had noticed the servants lighting all the fires at dusk, even without being requested to do so. Well, old people felt the cold, and the queen doubtless suffered from the river damp.

But he was young, and sweating.

He looked at the door to the hall, trying to remember the route he had taken from the courtyard. He felt certain he could get away, simply slip out of the palace under cover of night, but then Alex would be left to explain his absence in the morning. He wasn't sure the queen would notice it, but judging from the lively interest in her eyes when she had looked at him, he had a sinking feeling she might, which could leave Alex in a tight spot.

Alex. She said she still loved him, but more than that, he *knew* she did. He could see it in her face, her eyes, and had felt it in her touch the previous night at the inn. But she was as immovable as the Rock of Cashel when it came to her marriage, her duty to an old man he had never met. It maddened him, but at the same time he had to respect her tenacity. Adherence to a promise was a quality much admired by the Irish.

Burke stripped to the waist and moved his chair back from the fire, settling in to wait.

He had an idea this would be his second night in a row without sleep.

In the morning Alex stood nervously next to Mary Howard in the presence chamber, waiting for the queen to appear. She had told Mary about recent events, and when Burke came in with a yeoman of the guard Alex felt Mary grow tense beside her.

When the queen came in there was rustle of garments as the people made their obeisances. The old lady was in deep green taffeta with a celadon silk underskirt, her ears and wrists and fingers hung with emeralds, her billowing sleeves and starched ruff white as alabaster. As the courtiers looked on she conducted interviews and dispensed with petty business matters, pausing to tally the company with her eyes, making sure that all who had been requested to appear were present. Finally she concluded with a flourish and said, "Now we will see Captain Markham of my navy, who has much to report to us."

A naval commander in full regalia swept into the room. His eyes passed over the onlookers as he walked up to the throne, and then he stopped in his tracks when he saw Burke.

There was an awful, pregnant silence as the two

men surveyed each other, and Alex felt her heart drop into her shoes.

"Seize him!" Markham cried, pointing to Burke.

Everyone stared at the two men, aghast.

"Captain Markham, what is the meaning of this?" the queen demanded.

"Your Majesty, I do beg your pardon for this insult to your presence, but he must be taken at once. He's absent without leave from my ship, a foul traitor. This man is a deserter!"

12

If all the world and love were young,
And truth in every shepherd's tongue,
These pretty pleasures might me move
To live with thee, and be thy love.

—Walter Raleigh,
"The Nymph's Reply"

"*Lady Selby, I demand* an explanation," the queen said. "Is this man your servant, or is he not?" She pointed to Burke with one forefinger.

"I . . . ah . . . he is, Your Majesty," Alex replied.

"Then what is this story of Captain Markham's?" Elizabeth asked. "I do not enjoy being trifled with, and Markham has leveled a serious charge. It wants answering."

"I can explain, ma'am," Burke said, stepping forward.

Markham moved toward Burke, his hand on his sword hilt.

"I heartily wish someone would," Elizabeth replied, tapping her foot.

"I went absent from the captain's ship some days before I joined Lady Selby's staff. I was hired by her horsemaster to work in the stables. No one at Hampden Manor knew anything at all of my previous life."

Alex willed herself not to react visibly. She could see how this was going, Burke was planning to take responsibility on himself and keep her out of it.

"So you admit the desertion?" the queen asked.

"I left the ship as the captain says, but I did not regard my leaving as a desertion," Burke said.

The queen waved her hand and guards from either side of the room moved in on Burke and took hold of him. He made no resistance, merely stood his ground, not looking at Alex.

"An insolent reply," Elizabeth said to him. "I would like an account of it."

"I was taken at sea and forced into service aboard the captain's ship. Since my participation had not been rightly obtained, I felt it no crime to end it."

The queen looked at Markham, who was shifting his feet uncomfortably. Everyone else was immobilized, spellbound by the unexpected drama taking place.

"Is this true, Markham?" the queen demanded.

"It is a common practice, ma'am," Markham said.

"Have you not enough legitimate sailors to populate my navy?"

"This ingrate would have drowned had we not saved him!" Markham cried, losing his temper. "Demanding that he serve on board was little enough payment for his life, I'll warrant."

Elizabeth sighed. "Where is your home?" she asked Burke, her expression grim.

Alex closed her eyes.

"Ireland, ma'am."

Elizabeth's faint reddish eyebrows shot up toward her artificial hairline. "You speak English very well for an Irishman."

Alex waited for Burke to make some acid reply, but he let it pass, for which she was grateful. Before the interchange could reach the subject of Burke's involvement with the rebels, she stepped forward.

"Your Majesty, I feel responsible for bringing this man into your presence and causing this disturbance. Please allow me to apologize and make amends," Alex said.

Elizabeth regarded her thoughtfully. "This man is your servant, Lady Selby. What would you have me do with him?"

Alex took a deep breath. "If he was taken unlawfully, as he says and Captain Markham does not deny, perhaps you should let him go."

"And give that example to every beggar who's

planning to jump ship in the next port?" Markham yelled. "Your Majesty, I beg you, refrain from doing so severe an injury to your navy and to me."

"Perhaps if you treated my sailors better they would not be induced to flee at their earliest opportunity to do so, Captain Markham," Elizabeth snapped.

Markham subsided prudently as they all waited for the queen's decision.

"Take him away," she finally said. "Detain him at Ludgate whilst I bethink myself on the subject."

Alex watched helplessly as Burke was marched out of the room between two uniformed guards.

"Now, Captain Markham, if we can avoid any further theatricals, I am ready to receive your report," Elizabeth said, drumming her fingers on the carved arm of her throne.

Alex cast one stricken glance at Mary Howard and then looked away, afraid that the other courtiers would notice her distress.

The doors of the presence chamber opened and closed as Burke was taken away.

"Can you believe the miserable mischance that brought Burke together with that naval captain on the very same day?" Alex said to Mary Howard later, when they were alone. "I find it hard to keep my courage up when luck moves against us at every turn!"

"The bad luck was in Burke showing up here,"

Mary replied. "Captain Markham has been at court for over a month. It could have been any day during that time."

"Oh, why did I let Burke come with me?" Alex moaned. "I knew in my bones that it was an ill-bethought scheme, but I could not endure to leave him again."

The two women were supposed to be airing the queen's summer clothes, but the rich garments lay piled about them on the canopied bed and other furniture in the privy chamber as they discussed Burke's plight.

"Best to leave off these recriminations and think how to get him out of jail," Mary said.

"I'm going to ask the queen's permission to visit him."

"Do you think that's wise? You should be wary of showing too much interest in him. He's supposed to be a servant, after all."

"I have to talk to him, find out what he wants me to do. If I act without his knowledge, he may thwart my efforts, thinking to protect me or to pursue some other plan of his own."

"Pray tell him not to attempt flight, it will only worsen his case. Even if he got away, he would be a fugitive forever more."

"Try explaining that to him," Alex said. "I'm certain he's planning his escape right now, and that's one reason why I must get to him quickly."

Mary sighed. "You should catch the queen early in the day, when she is in a good humor. Once the council sessions start . . ." She rolled her eyes and shook her head.

"Maybe tomorrow morning, after breakfast."

"Not tomorrow," Mary said. "Lady Essex is coming to plead her husband's case. It will not be a good day."

"He's not still at Grafton?" Essex had formerly been placed under house arrest at the Oxfordshire house of his uncle, Sir William Knollys.

"No, but the queen will not hear his name spoken. She flies into a rage or falls mutinously silent if any so much as mention him."

"Is there any chance for him?"

Mary shrugged. "When Lady Rich wrote the queen a letter pleading for her brother, the queen placed her under house arrest, too."

"Oh, no," Alex said. What chance did an Irish deserter stand if the queen's one-time favorite could tumble into such a pit?

"What are you thinking?"

"Maybe I could tell Her Majesty the truth, throw myself upon her mercy."

Mary stared at her in horror.

"She likes me," Alex said. "You've said as much yourself."

"Alex, you've taken leave of your senses. Don't even consider it."

"I may have no choice."

"Have you forgotten that less than a year ago Burke was fighting Her Majesty's forces in Ireland? Right now she thinks he's a mistreated, albeit miscreant, sailor, and he's already in Ludgate. Can you imagine what might happen if she finds out he was one of those men who forced Essex to a truce, a truce she abhors and which resulted in Devereaux's disgrace?"

"She might admire Burke's courage."

Mary closed her eyes.

"All right," Alex said, "don't disturb yourself on that account, I'm getting ahead of myself in any event. I must make suit to see him first."

"Wait a goodly time after Lady Essex visits. I'm told she's bringing the child, Frances, in hope that seeing the babe will soften Her Majesty's heart toward its father."

"That may not have the exact result Lady Essex anticipates."

Mary nodded. A crying, fretful child would not help the Essex cause at all.

"Three days. I'll wait three days," Alex said.

Mary picked up a silken ruff and shook it out firmly, examining it for wear.

Alex followed suit, and her hands became busy while her mind wandered elsewhere.

"Your Majesty, I crave a boon of you," Alex said as she removed Elizabeth's breakfast tray. The old lady was still in her dressing gown, but fresh and seemingly well favored at the beginning of the day.

"What is it?" the queen said.

Alex exchanged a glance with Mary, who was

laying out the queen's clothes for the morning. Alex put down the tray and moved a step closer to the queen.

"I would have your permission to visit my servant, the man who was taken into custody on Captain Markham's testimony of desertion."

"Why do you wish to see him?"

"I would make certain that he is well treated," Alex said, and then regretted it.

The queen looked at her with one eyebrow raised. "Think you that my prisons are charnel houses?"

"Certainly not, Your Majesty," Alex said hastily. "I merely wish to inquire if I can be of any service in his case. My estate manager set great store by the man's services and would be extremely sorry to lose him."

"And you, Lady Selby?" the queen asked. "Would you be sorry to lose him?"

Alex looked back at her, unable to reply. Was it possible that the old lady, intuitive as she was, suspected Alex's true relationship with Burke?

"He's very decorative, is he not?" the queen asked.

Alex looked at Mary, who looked alarmed. "I . . . why, I suppose so, Your Majesty," Alex said.

"I myself once had a most decorative horsemaster. Have you ever heard tell of him?"

Both Alex and Mary froze.

Alex decided that honesty would be the best tactic. "Yes, Your Majesty. You are referring to Robert Dudley, the earl of Leicester."

The old lady nodded slowly. "Dead these twelve years. It is a fearful thing to outlive all those you love, Lady Selby. Life becomes a lonely place."

Alex said nothing.

"For I did love him," the queen went on, "so much that I raised him high and thus gave others reason to attach scandal to my name. When Robin's first wife died, Mary of Scots was heard to say, 'The queen of England is about to marry her horsemaster, who has murdered his wife to make room for her.'"

Alex listened silently, touched to see the old lady's eyes fill with tears.

"Pretty Amy fell down a flight of stairs and broke her neck," the queen continued. "She'd been ill, and the inquest deemed it an accident, but since Robin was my chosen cavalier many thought I had wished him free and so contrived at Amy's death."

"No, Your Majesty," Alex said.

"Oh, yes. I had to send him right away, and I missed him sorely. I was at his wedding, of course you would not know that. As a young princess I danced to enhance his marital joy but was later accused of ending it."

Alex didn't know what to say.

"I did love him," the queen repeated softly. She blinked rapidly and raised her head. "Go and see your horsemaster, Lady Selby. I will send word for the guard to admit you this afternoon."

Alex curtsied deeply and left the room speedily, taking the tray with her.

* * *

The prison at Ludgate was used for petty criminals, debtors and such, and for detainees in transition whose cases had not yet been settled. Burke fell into the latter category. So far he had been charged with nothing, but he was being held while the queen decided whether his behavior merited prosecution.

"Why didn't you ask the queen if she was planning to let Burke go?" Mary Howard inquired breathlessly, panting from the climb up the hill as the two women entered the stone building, passing armed guards at the door.

"It's too soon to press his case. I have to proceed slowly with her, let her think that leniency is her own idea."

"She's not that easily led, don't underestimate her," Mary said. "And don't forget how rapidly she changes suits. She's of one mind on Sunday and another on Monday."

"Yes, I know."

They halted at the warder's desk, where Alex showed a pass from the queen's lord chamberlain. Mary was detained in the corridor while an attendant took Alex into an anteroom containing a table and several chairs. She waited a short time and then Burke, his wrists manacled together, was led inside. The guard shoved him forward and then took up a position in the corner.

"Her Majesty did promise me privacy for this

interview," Alex said to him, stretching the truth.

The guard shrugged. "I'll be right outside the door, miss," he said, and went out, closing the door behind him.

"How are you?" Alex said to Burke, who was surveying her expressionlessly.

"Grand, considering I'm back behind bars again."

"You must admit that this place is an improvement over Carberry's dungeon."

"Are you saying I should be happy here?"

"I'll get you out."

He snorted. "And how do you propose doing that?"

"I'm working on it."

"How?"

"With the queen."

He shook his head. "Alex, abandon this cause. Abandon me. Isn't it clear by now that you were right? We aren't meant to be together. I was planning to leave you at Whitehall and go back home. Just pretend I've done that and leave off this visiting." He looked away. "It won't help me to forget you."

"I don't want you to forget me."

"Do you want me pining, is that it?"

"I want you free."

"Some hopes."

"Are you giving up?"

"I'm giving in, Alex—to fate, to the will of your vengeful English God, whatever it is that has the scales so weighted against us, and against me."

"I've never heard you talk like this."

"Are you surprised that I've finally had enough?"

"But you don't know what the queen will do!"

He threw up his hands. "I deserted from her navy, Alex, the pride of England, the reason for the victory against the Armada. She's not going to forgive that."

"She didn't like the story of how you were taken on board. She might yet be influenced."

"You heard Markham. They must make an example of deserters, else they'll be knee deep in them."

"Just bide your time here and let me try."

"I don't want you to risk your position with the queen, your future and that of my son, in annoying her by pleading for me."

"She was not annoyed when I asked to see you. She expected me to take a hand in your case. She interests herself in the problems of her loyal servants. Why should I be different?"

"Her sympathy would vanish if she knew our true situation."

"I'm not so sure of that," Alex said softly.

He lifted his chin. "Why do you say so?"

"She was once in love with someone she couldn't have."

"But what of all those tales you told me about her harsh treatment of those guilty of indiscretions?"

"Those tales are true."

"Then you are dreaming. As I said before, think

of yourself and the child, and relinquish all efforts
on my behalf."

Alex rose. "I see that you are in no mood to listen to my counsel. I will be back as soon as I am
given leave to visit you."

"It would be easier for me if you did not
return," he said.

"Will you refuse to see me?" Alex demanded,
putting up a brave front. Inside, she was quaking.
She had never seen Burke so hopeless.

He smiled slightly. "I don't think I could ever do
that."

"Then look for me."

"Always," he replied, and Alex felt a little surge
of encouragement as she left the room.

"Everything all right, miss?" the guard asked
her politely as she passed.

"Everything is fine."

Alex went down the hall to join Mary, who was
waiting for her.

"How is he?" Mary asked.

"Resigned."

"I can't say that I blame him."

"Nor can I."

The women nodded to the guards as they left
the prison and stepped out into the pleasant spring
afternoon.

Alex bided her time for several days, waiting
for an opportune moment to plead Burke's case.

But the queen remained in a foul temper over reports of malcontents such as Southampton and his friends gathering at Essex House, so Alex kept quiet. She was trying to gather her nerve one morning on which the queen seemed somewhat brighter, when Mary Howard took her aside.

"I have some bad news," Mary said in a low tone.

"Is there any other kind?"

"Brace yourself, it's very bad."

"Oh, Mary, just tell me."

"Markham has gotten word of Burke's past. He knows what Burke was about in Ireland and is preparing a brief for the queen on the subject."

"Oh, my precious Lord! How could he have come by such information?"

"Does it matter? Markham was furious that Burke told the queen about the impressment of seamen. You know she doesn't like to hear such stories. She wants her navy at full complement, but she doesn't care to know how it's done, especially if the means used are suspect. Markham has been determined to see Burke hang, and now he has the evidence to get a warrant."

"Who told you all this?"

"John Harington. He was in the room when Markham was preparing the case against Burke."

"Why did he tell you?"

"It's common knowledge that we are friends as

well as kin, and he knows that Burke came here with you."

"I must prevent Markham from getting to the queen!" Alex said wildly, starting to run.

Mary blocked her path. "Alex, listen to me, you can't. If Markham doesn't tell her, someone else will. The story is all over the court. You must stay silent and see what happens. There is no other course open to you. At least by keeping out of the fray you may be able to help Burke in the future."

"When the queen hears this she will have no mercy," Alex said miserably. "The rebels have been a thorn in her side for years, and she will see Burke drawn and quartered. Hanging will surely be deemed too good for him." She closed her eyes. "Oh, why did I let him accompany me here? I was selfish and wanted to spend some last moments with him, and look where that has led. This cursed happenstance is all my fault!"

Mary took her by the shoulders and shook her hard. "Stop this caterwauling!" she said sharply. "Bewailing your fate and his will not help him now. You must keep your wits about you and act wisely or all will be lost!"

Alex took a deep breath, swallowed hard, and nodded.

"Now, we must go about our business as if nothing is amiss. We are scheduled to display the gifts for the Venetian envoys. Come with me and let us do so."

Alex trailed in Mary's wake, forcing herself to remain calm.

What Mary said was true. She was Burke's only hope.

It was late afternoon when a page came into the room where Mary and Alex and a circle of court ladies were sewing. Alex was staring down at her unfinished work, blinded by silent tears.

"Her Majesty requests Lady Selby's presence in her privy chamber," the boy said.

Alex rose from her chair, looked once at Mary, and then followed the boy into the hall.

The queen was standing on a pedestal with two seamstresses at her feet fitting her for a new gown. Alex curtsied.

"Well, Lady Selby," the queen greeted her, "it seems your horsemaster has a colorful past."

Alex said nothing.

"You've heard the charges Captain Markham has brought against your man Burke?"

"Yes, ma'am."

"I have sent Sir John Harington to speak to the prisoner, and Harington reports that Burke swears you knew nothing of his previous doings when he was hired. Is that true?"

Alex looked at the two fitters, who were poised, fascinated, listening to every word.

The queen saw the direction of her gaze and said, "You are dismissed," to the seamstresses.

The women, visibly disappointed, took up their things and left. The queen waited until the door had closed behind them and then said, "Well, Alexandra? Were you ignorant of this man Burke's past when he came to you?"

The time for dissembling was long gone. She decided to follow her initial instinct to reveal all and hope for a compassionate reception. Burke could hardly be in a worse case if the truth failed to help him now.

"No, Your Majesty," she said quietly. "I knew who he was."

"Hmm," Elizabeth said, watching Alex closely. "And how came you by that knowledge?"

"I knew him in Ireland."

"What?"

"Your Majesty may recall that my uncle, Philip Cummings, went to Ireland with my lord of Essex last spring."

"Do not speak to me of that ill-fated expedition, I wish to forget it," Elizabeth snapped.

"It is not so much of the expedition I would speak, Your Majesty, but of how I came to be on it."

"On it? Explain yourself."

"My uncle wished to leave me with an order of nuns whilst he was gone. To avoid such a fate I stowed away on board the *Silver Swan* and landed in Ireland with the rest of the ship's company."

Alex had the queen's full attention now. The old

lady sat on a chair and gestured for Alex to do the same. "Go on," Elizabeth said.

Alex said a quick, silent prayer and then plunged into the story, telling as much as she could remember. They were interrupted midway by a knock from Lady Warwick, but the queen sent her away, telling her that she wished to be alone with Lady Selby until further notice.

"And so Burke came with me to London, intending to leave me here and then catch a ship back to Ireland," Alex concluded. "But when Your Majesty met us at the gate, he was compelled to stay, and then . . ." She hesitated.

"And then the encounter with Captain Markham."

"Yes, ma'am."

The queen rose, and Alex jumped up, too.

"Lady Selby," the queen said, pacing, "that is a most fantastical story."

"Yes, ma'am."

"So your son is not Lord Selby's, but Burke's."

Alex nodded, her heart in her throat, and then croaked, "Yes, Your Majesty."

The queen stopped walking and whirled to face Alex, clasping her hands together at her waist. "Something puzzles me, Lady Selby. What possible advantage do you hope to gain for your imprisoned lover by telling me this Byzantine tale?"

"No advantage, ma'am. I merely wished to tell the truth."

"A bit tardy about it, were you not?"

"Yes, ma'am."

"You hoped that I would dismiss the charge of desertion and so the rest of this sordid tale would never see the light of day."

"That is so, ma'am."

"Who else knows of this?"

"My uncle, and Lady Howard."

"Both of whom will keep it to themselves, for their own reasons. See you do the same. There are enough wagging tongues at court about this servant who turned out to be an Irish rebel. We can spare the idle gossipers the rest of it."

"Yes, Your Majesty."

"So, what's to be done? Captain Markham is pressing his suit most vigorously, and I must pay heed to his remarks. Amnesty for all the rebels in Ireland was a condition of the truce, so Burke cannot be prosecuted for his participation in that action." The queen paused. "But Markham seeks to turn my mind against your man on the desertion charge with this fresh evidence. I confess I am disposed to listen to a captain of my navy when his opposition is revealed to be a seditious scoundrel."

Alex could not control her change of expression.

"Your horsemaster, Lady Selby, is a knave who threatened my throne with unlawful rebellion and impregnated a gentlewoman of good family outside the sanctity of marriage!"

Alex inhaled sharply.

"All of this, however, is apart from your own actions, Lady Selby, which were, and are, inexcusable. I see that I have no recourse in the matter."

Elizabeth strode to the doors of her privy chamber and flung them wide. The guards standing outside snapped to attention.

"Lady Selby is to be confined to her room," she said to them. "She is not to be permitted to leave it and is to receive no visitors without my express command. Take her."

The guards lined up on either side of Alex. She was marched briskly down the corridor and through the warren of other halls leading to the quarters for the ladies-in-waiting. Courtiers froze in the middle of their conversations as the little procession passed. Alex could hear the buzz of their voices starting up again in her wake, animated, ravenous for gossip. As her door closed behind her she heard the guards bang their axes against the floor on either side of it.

She was under house arrest.

Alex sank onto her chair by the fire, in shock. It had happened so fast, and the queen's order had been issued so dispassionately, that she hadn't had time to absorb it.

She should not be surprised, after all; this was exactly how the queen had behaved under similar circumstances in the past. But Alex had counted on the bond of affection between them, counted on it to bridge an enormous gap and lead the old lady to understand a younger woman's actions.

She'd made a dreadful mistake. In thinking only of saving Burke, she had brought doom on both of them.

Alex bowed her head and put her face in her hands.

With both his parents under guard, what would become of her little son?

Several days passed, during which Alex jumped up and faced the door every time she heard footsteps in the corridor. When it swung open at long last, Lady Warwick appeared on the threshold and announced the queen.

Alex dropped into a curtsy, her pulses pounding, as Elizabeth swept into the room. Lady Warwick withdrew, and the door closed, leaving the two women alone.

"I have had a letter," the queen announced, withdrawing a missive from her capacious sleeve.

Alex was afraid to move.

"Oh, get up," the queen said.

Alex rose and waited.

"Madam," the old lady said, "your husband is dead."

13

Who will not mercy unto others show,
How can he mercy ever hope to have?
—Edmund Spenser,
The Faerie Queene

"*Burke?*" *Alex gasped, her* hand going to her throat.

"No, my lady," the queen snapped, "your official husband, your husband in law. I trust you remember who he is. This letter, which I received just this day, is from the Netherlands. Lord Selby has died there of the sweating sickness."

Alex tried to disguise the wave of relief that flowed over her, but the queen was not fooled.

"At least you have the good grace not to fall on your face and weep," Elizabeth said. "You have no comment on the matter? Pray, what say you to this news?"

"Lord Selby was a good and kind man, kind to me, anyway," Alex said quietly. "Beyond that I hardly knew him, as he was gone for most of our marriage."

"He was a good servant to me, and that's the very reason why I must punish *your* flagrant disregard of his person!" the queen bellowed, and stalked out of the room.

Alex fell back onto her chair, stunned. She looked up when Lady Warwick peeked around the doorway.

"Lady Howard sends greetings, try to be of good cheer," she whispered.

Alex nodded miserably.

"I will do what I can to calm Her Majesty down," Lady Warwick added, and then hurried away as they heard the queen calling her name from a distance.

Another day passed before the door opened again, this time to admit Mary Howard.

Alex rushed to embrace her. "How did you get permission to see me?" she said, looking over Mary's shoulder at the guards who were closing the door.

"I asked," Mary said.

They waited a moment longer, listening for sounds outside the door, then settled onto two chairs pulled close together.

"What did you say to cause your confinement?"

"I told the queen about Burke and me."

Mary closed her eyes.

"I know, you warned me. But there were no options left. Her whim might have favored me, as it has favored others in the past. I was desperate and had to try."

"You might have said nothing and saved yourself," Mary said.

"By speaking, I thought to save both of us."

"She seems fixed on the insult to Lord Selby. She talks to me of defending his honor or some such notion," Mary said.

"Lord Selby was aware of my circumstances when we married," Alex replied. "He accepted the situation, and gladly."

"That's not what has infuriated the queen," Mary said, as if Alex should know.

"What, then?"

"The insult to Lord Selby's indulgence. Your keeping your lover at Hampden Manor in the guise of a servant whilst Selby was away."

"But I never!" Alex gasped.

"What do you mean? He was there, was he not?"

"I never lay with Burke after I was married. Never!"

"The queen thinks you were conducting an illicit liaison while acting as Selby's wife, boldy keeping a roof over your fancy man's head with your absent husband's money, and right under the noses of his servants. You know how she feels about such furtive relationships. Nothing irritates her more."

"I didn't even know Burke was still in England until I walked into my stable and found him working there! There was no plan to keep him as my lover, you should know that, Mary. What was I supposed to do, throw him out onto the roads? He was going back to Ireland after he left me at Whitehall. It was a cruel misfortune that the queen saw him when we arrived, liked his looks, and told him to stay the night. Markham saw him the next day."

"I'm not the one who wants convincing," Mary said.

"I must explain it to her."

Mary shook her head. "She's not in a listening mood."

"But she's judging me unfairly! Mary, you must ask her to give me another interview. She must not be completely insensitive to my unhappy state, she let you come to see me."

"I think she is not pleased about keeping you confined like this, as she has always been fond of you. But her disappointment has no other outlet. She must show her disapproval of your conduct."

"Of my supposed conduct! I had no affair, on my oath. I wanted to, was often tempted, but never succumbed."

Mary sighed. "Do you think she will believe you?"

"I know not." Alex looked down at her hands and then up at her companion. "Mary, I must speak to you concerning a weighty matter."

"What?"

"Lord Selby is dead."

"Yes, I heard it."

"If both Burke and I . . . well . . . if fate is not kind to us, my son will have no one. My uncle will not recognize him, I know that."

Mary covered Alex's hands with her own. "Say no more. I will have Michael to live in my house and raise him as my own child. I promise you."

Alex lifted Mary's hand to her lips and kissed it. "I can't think what I've done for God to send me such a faithful friend," she said with tears in her eyes.

"He's sent you troubles enough to make up for it," Mary replied sympathetically.

Alex sighed, still retaining hold of Mary's hand. "Is there any news of Burke?"

Mary hesitated.

"Tell me," Alex said.

"A warrant is being drawn up for his execution."

"Has the queen seen it?"

"I think not yet."

"She's notoriously reluctant to put her name to any such document. Look you, Essex still lingers, and it took her ministers many tries to get her to sign away the life of the queen of Scots."

"That is true, but Markham presses his case very vigorously."

"Yes, I know."

"But too much pressure on a matter sometimes causes the queen to turn the other way," Mary added.

Alex nodded.

"It is impossible to say what will happen." Mary paused. "I've overstayed my time," she said, rising. "You have another visitor."

"Who is that?"

"Your uncle."

Alex shook her head.

"The queen has given him leave to see you, and it would not be wise to refuse the interview," Mary said.

"I suppose."

"Courage," Mary said as she left.

She had hardly passed through the doorway when Philip Cummings appeared in it. He was dressed in his usual sober color, a deep gray doublet and hose, and looked much the same as the last time Alex had seen him.

"Uncle," Alex said.

"Well, Alexandra, it seems you are in a pretty fix."

"No lecture, Uncle, I cannot abide one."

"So it seems," Cummings said, folding his arms. "All my lectures in the past were certainly to no avail."

Alex said nothing.

"I'm not surprised that your relationship with

that Irish blackguard has wound you up in such a case."

"Must we cover this old ground again?"

"He found you here, in England."

"Obviously."

"And you simply could not give him up."

"I gave him up, in the sense you mean, anyway. He was on his way back to Ireland when the queen saw him with me and asked him to stay to court. He was there spotted by Captain Markham, from whose ship he had deserted."

"Markham had no knowledge of Burke's rebellion in Ireland?"

"He does now."

"And why was Burke on Markham's ship?"

Alex sighed. "Burke was taken at sea. He was trying to get to England."

"And you."

"And me."

"So," Cummings said, unfolding his arms and putting them behind his back, "both of you are in this miserable circumstance because Burke pursued you here. If he had remained in Ireland, he would be free, having established his truce with the Crown, and you and your child would still be safe in Selby's house."

Alex looked away. "I cannot fault him because his love for me led him here," she said softly.

"A most determined man. Determined to have you, anyway."

The comment did not require a reply.

"I own I underestimated him."

Alex looked up at him. Her uncle rarely admitted a mistake of any kind.

"When he came to Inverary after you, and I told him you were married, I thought he would give you up. I should have borne in mind the long years he fought us in Ireland. Clearly, he is most tenacious about something, or someone, he wants."

"Yes."

"What about the child?"

"Pardon?"

Cummings eyed her judiciously. "Alexandra, you must show some responsibility in this matter. Selby is dead. A warrant is being prepared for Burke's condemnation and you are under house arrest, with a future that could be described as uncertain at best. Have you given no thought to your son?"

"I have. Mary Howard has promised to take him, and it is my heartfelt wish that he should go to her."

Cummings nodded. "I see. Well, I should not be surprised that you wouldn't want me to have him."

"You?" Alex said, shocked.

"Why not? He is my blood."

"And he is Burke's blood! As I recall, you came near to apoplexy when you heard of his impending arrival. Why are you interested in him now?"

"I am ready to do my duty by my brother's grandchild."

"Please," Alex said. "I have had enough of you doing your duty, Uncle."

"Very well," Cummings said briskly. "I will take my leave of you, wishing you the best."

"Is that so?"

"Certainly."

"You cannot be unhappy that all of your dire predictions concerning me have come true."

"I never wished you ill, Alexandra," he said in so sad a tone that she came near to believing it.

"I pray that is so," she said. She folded her hands and asked, "What is the news of your friend, Lord Essex?"

"His day has passed. His house has become a gathering place for grumblers and malcontents, it will come to no good in the end."

"But you, of course, are now allied with the other party."

"Of course."

"So you survive."

He smiled thinly. "Always."

"I admire your agility, Uncle."

He held out his arms. "Enough of this banter. Embrace me."

Alex went to him and endured the touch of his dry lips against her cheek.

"I will do what I can to procure your release," he said, stepping back from her.

"Really?"

"As much as I can without endangering my own position," he said, and Alex smiled. It was the most straightforward thing he had ever said to her.

"Good-bye, Uncle."

"Good-bye."

Cummings left the room. Alex sat once again on the deep chair that had become her roosting place since she had been under guard.

Burke sat up in his bed of straw and propped his back against the rude stone wall behind him. His manacled hands allowed him freedom of movement as long as he kept his wrists close together, as there was a foot-long chain linking them. He drew up his legs and rested his arms on his knees.

Something had happened to Alex. She had said she would come back, and he hadn't seen her since her first visit. He didn't believe that she had taken him at his word and abandoned him. Her vehemence on the subject was proof that she meant to return. So where was she?

Burke watched as the guard paused in front of the iron door and rattled the lock. The other men in the communal cell looked up and then away, their expressions as hopeless as his.

Burke spent all his time formulating an escape plan he was loath to use for fear that his flight would reflect badly on Alex. This was her country, and she would have to live here with their child long after his fate had been decided. He didn't want the mercurial queen to punish Alex for her servant's escape.

And so he sat and thought, wishing he were back in Ireland, free to bathe in the streams and wander among the trees.

Alex was trying to interest herself in a sampler when her door swung open and the guards in the hall snapped to attention.

"Lady Selby," the queen said briskly.

Alex curtsied. The queen was alone.

"I do not wish to be disturbed," Elizabeth said to the guards, who closed the door. This was followed by the sound of their axes banging on the floor.

"Rise," Elizabeth said.

Alex did so.

"I am here because your relatives have been plaguing me to converse with you again."

"My relatives, ma'am?"

"Your cousin, Mary Howard, and that unctuous uncle of yours, Lord Stockton."

Alex said nothing.

"Well? There is something you wish to say to me?" Elizabeth asked.

"I think Your Majesty may have . . . misunderstood something about my situation."

"Misunderstood?"

Alex lost her nerve and fell silent.

Elizabeth stared hard at her for a moment and

then looked around the room. Her dress, the same brilliant orange as her wig, stood out like a flaming sun against the background of the dark carpet.

"I mislike this, Lady Selby," she said softly. "I know very well what it is like to be a prisoner. During my late sister's reign I was under guard and in fear of my life many long and lonely days."

Alex said nothing, too wary of disturbing the queen's softening mood to speak.

"But what other am I to do when confronted with such blatant wickedness?" the queen demanded.

"What wickedness?" Alex asked.

"You kept your lover on your husband's estate whilst honest Selby, that good man, was away on *my* business!"

"Burke was never my lover after I was married!" Alex responded with equal heat, forgetting herself. "That was the subject I wished to broach with you . . . Your Majesty."

Elizabeth's eyes widened.

"I'm sorry, Your Majesty, for speaking so impetuously," Alex said hastily. "But I fear I have been misjudged and would set the matter right with you."

"Go on." The queen sat and gestured for Alex to follow suit.

Alex briefly explained Burke's presence at Hampden Manor and how he had come to be with her at Whitehall.

The queen listened without expression, and then finally said, "So this man Burke remained working in your stables for months after you had thought him gone."

"Yes, ma'am."

"And your only contact with him after your marriage was merely a friendly one."

"Well . . ."

"More than friendly?"

"I still loved him, ma'am, as I do now."

"So you wanted him."

"Yes, ma'am."

"And acted upon it?"

"To a degree."

"Oh, stop fencing, Lady Selby, and come out with it! Did you lie with him or no?"

"No."

"But you came close upon it."

"Yes, Your Majesty."

"Hmmph. The Bible says that lusting in the heart is the same sin as the act," the queen said.

"Oh, of course it isn't!" Alex replied. "Begging your pardon, ma'am, but if wanting to do something were the same as doing it, half the citizens of London would be locked up fast in the Tower this very minute."

The queen smiled. "I suppose there is truth in what you say. In my hot youth I wanted, and came close, several times, first with Thomas Seymour and later . . ." Elizabeth stopped, as if aware that she had revealed too much.

There was a silence. Then Alex said quietly, "I did not disregard Lord Selby's honor, ma'am, I swear it. I kept my vows, but I could not help my feelings."

"No, no one can," Elizabeth said softly. "And why is it, I wonder, that we always seem to want what we cannot have?"

Alex shook her head.

"Well," the queen said, rising, "I will think upon it."

Alex leaped to her feet. "Madam, I . . ." she began.

"What is it?"

"I should very much like to see my baby," Alex said, her voice breaking.

"You will see your child, Alexandra," the queen replied. "Very soon."

And with that, she was gone.

The next morning Alex was summoned to the presence chamber. As she walked along the halls between two tall, helmeted yeomen, she wondered if she were about to witness the signing of Burke's warrant or hear her own sentence pronounced. The guards were silent, and there was no way to tell what was about to happen.

Alex stopped short as she came into the room where the queen was seated on one of her elaborate portable thrones.

Burke was already there, his wrists manacled,

an armed guard at his side. He was wearing the same clothes Alex had last seen, and his face was darkened with a new beard.

These were the only people in the room.

"Come closer, Alexandra," the queen said, beckoning.

Burke's eyes never left Alex's face as she advanced toward the slightly raised dais where the queen sat.

"Lady Selby, here is Master Burke," the queen said with that self-satisfied look that always made Alex nervous.

"Yes, ma'am."

"It is my wish that he have his full say before sentence is pronounced upon him."

Alex saw then what the game was. The queen would have Burke lie himself right onto the scaffold.

Alex held her breath. There was nothing she could do.

"So, Master Burke," Elizabeth said, "tell us how you came to meet Lady Selby."

"I was hired to work in her stables at Hampden Manor," he said. "She knew nothing of my desertion from the navy."

Alex closed her eyes.

"Now, now, Lady Selby has already told me that she knew you in Ireland. It would behoove you to end this dissembling," the queen said genially.

Burke shot Alex a glance.

"I know about your rebel activity, Burke," the

queen said patiently, tapping a slender forefinger against the jeweled medallion she wore around her neck.

He coughed and looked at the ground. Alex could almost hear him thinking.

"I kidnapped Lady Selby to hold her for ransom in exchange for my brother, who was imprisoned at Inverary Castle," Burke then said. "She was an innocent party and remained so."

The queen sighed heavily and sat forward. "I know you are the father of Alexandra's son, Burke."

Burke's shoulders slumped, and then after a slight pause his head came up determinedly. Alex could see him searching for another way to extricate her from the situation.

"You seem determined to talk yourself into a hangman's noose as long as Lady Selby is spared," the queen said, voicing Alex's own thoughts.

"There is no reason she should suffer for my actions."

"What about her own?" the queen demanded. "She has admitted that she cohabited with you while in Ireland and later concealed the fact that her child was not her husband's."

"Many others have done the same," Burke said.

"Ah, I see you are familiar with court behavior. However, the commonality of disguising true parentage does not alter its iniquity."

"Her uncle left her no choice in the matter," Burke said.

"Her uncle! Pray tell."

"Alex wished to stay in Ireland with me, but while I was away Cummings forced her to marry Selby when he learned she was expecting a child."

"And what were you away doing?" the queen demanded. "Fighting my troops, the good Englishmen I sent to rout rebellion from your accursed country!"

"My people wish to be free," Burke said.

"Free from what? Free from good government, free to be barbarians?"

"If Your Majesty would like to hear a catalog of the abuses forced upon my people by your governors—"

"Oh, I'm sure," Elizabeth interrupted him. "People like you always have good reasons for your unlawful behavior. It never springs from the air, does it? I am well aware of the difficulty of ruling your land from such a distance. I have been plagued with its hazards for many years."

"Then why not give Ireland up?"

"I will not lose territory passed on to me through my father, and I will not see my empire evaporate before my eyes!" Elizabeth replied, the veins standing out on her forehead.

Alex shrank back, certain now that she and Burke were both doomed.

There was long silence while the monarch regained control of her temper.

"I assume you are not aware that Lord Selby is dead," Elizabeth said to Burke.

He started but carefully refrained from looking at Alex.

"I see that, like Lady Selby, you are not likely to fall into despair over this news."

Burke wisely said nothing.

"I have had a letter from Ireland," Elizabeth went on. "From Lord Carberry at Inverary Castle. It seems your master Tyrone has heard of your difficulties here, Burke. His news travels faster than mine, I must say, his spies surely have wings."

Alex saw the hope spring into Burke's eyes, and she felt a glimmer of it in her own heart.

"Tyrone has told Carberry that if I deal harshly with you, I will jeopardize the peace so lately made in your country."

Burke's expression didn't change, but Alex saw the fingers of his bound hands flex and relax.

"So, Master Burke, your friends at home have not forgotten you. You must have done O'Neill some stalwart services. I wish I inspired such loyalty. He wants you to live and prosper, perhaps to strike at my scepter another day."

"Your scepter was never our goal, ma'am. We wish only to be left alone to rule ourselves."

"This bog trotter dares to threaten me!" Elizabeth cried, lifting the letter from her lap and shaking it at them.

Burke fell silent again.

"Still," Elizabeth said, "I like a man who values a friend. Tyrone risks much to save your hide, my Irish friend, as you risked much to come here and claim your forbidden lady."

Alex bit her lip.

"And I am weary, weary, of sending my men across the water to die in your fens, Master Burke," Queen Elizabeth said. "I will do nothing, however minor, to disturb this truce, which was purchased with a full measure of English blood."

Alex and Burke remained frozen in place, hardly daring to draw breath. The queen held Burke's fate in the palm of her hand the way she'd held the golden globe in her coronation portrait, painted so many years earlier.

"Burke, your horse is ready and waiting for you at the royal stables. Take it and go. You have my full pardon and shall proceed unmolested from this court and this realm," the queen pronounced.

Alex was sure she could hear her thundering heart beating aloud. She looked at Burke. He went down on one knee and bowed his head.

"Thank you, ma'am," he said.

"You may approach me," the queen said, extending her hand.

Burke glanced uncertainly at Alex, who nodded.

Burke walked up to the throne and knelt again, taking the queen's hand in his manacled one and kissing the elegant fingers.

"Rise," the queen said to him. He did so.

"Take those chains off him," the queen said abruptly to Burke's guard, who bowed and then moved to Burke's side, releasing him from his shackles.

"And now Lady Selby, what shall we do with you?" the queen said, turning her gaze on Alexandra.

Alex swallowed nervously.

"You have been a most suitable lady's maid, but methinks you would prefer to leave my service and go off with this man. Is that so?"

"That is so," Alex said, finding her voice.

"So be it," the queen said, flinging her hands wide. "I shall miss you, but God shield I should be the occasion of keeping two such dedicated lovers apart."

Alex clasped her hands together, her eyes flooding with tears. "Your Majesty's clemency will be rewarded in heaven by the only Judge greater than yourself," she said.

"I pray that you are right," Elizabeth said, "as I may shortly determine for myself."

"Your Majesty surely has many years yet to live on this earth."

"Bah! You talk like Essex and Raleigh and all those flatterers. I had thought you a far more sensible creature. Come here."

Alex went up to the throne, taking her place next to Burke, and curtsied deeply. The queen leaned forward and took hold of her shoulders, helping her to rise and kissing her on both cheeks.

"My little Greek," Elizabeth said softly. "Keep up with your reading."

"I will, Your Majesty."

"My learning had always been a great comfort to me, as I trust yours will be to you."

"Yes, ma'am."

The queen sat back and observed the two young people, standing side by side.

"I own it is against my better judgment, but I verily wish you a long and happy life together," she said, her rheumy old eyes misting. "Now be gone before I rethink myself on the matter."

Alex curtsied and Burke bowed, then they backed out of the presence chamber as quickly as decency would permit.

In the corridor they turned and looked at each other.

"Let's run," Burke said.

"No!" Alex whispered.

Mary Howard came dashing around a corner and thrust a bag into Alex's arms.

"The queen told me what she was going to do, and I packed some things from your room," she said. "I'll send the rest on when you write and tell me where you are. Now go!"

Alex kissed her quickly.

"Good luck and Godspeed," Mary said.

"This way!" Alex said, taking Burke's hand and leading him in the direction of the stables. They wound their way through the palace corridors, not pausing until they stepped into the cobbled courtyard and saw the horse barn in the distance.

"Old Dealanach won't be half-glad to see me," Burke said.

"No more than I am," Alex replied, throwing her arms around his neck.

"We're free," Burke said, holding her close.

"I can't believe it."

"We should get right away from here," he said, his voice muffled against her hair.

"Yes, yes, time enough for this later," Alex said, breaking the embrace.

Burke released her reluctantly.

Alex looked over her shoulder. "Now we can run."

They rode hard and by nightfall had reached the inn where they'd stayed on the way in to London. The barmaid looked them over as they came through the door, travel-stained and road weary.

"Come back to us again, eh?" she greeted them knowingly. "Same room?"

Burke nodded.

"A shilling in advance," she said.

They looked at each other. The background noise from the bar echoed in their silence.

"These are solid silver," Alex said, ripping the buttons from her sleeves. They had been a gift from the queen.

"Is that so, dearie?" the barmaid said.

Alex handed them to her, and the maid put one in her mouth and bit it, hard.

"Seems all right to me," she said. She waved them toward the stairs. "Go on up with you. Will you be wanting food?"

"Later," Burke said.

"She thinks we're living in sin, that we're coming here to have assignations," Alex said as they ascended the stairs.

"Well?" He raised one brow and grinned up at her from the lower step.

"Oh, you're just as bad as she is," Alex said, unable to restrain a smile of her own.

Once in the room, Burke stretched out on the bed with a sigh and said, "Come here to me."

Alex lay down beside him and relaxed in the protective circle of his arm.

"I thought I'd be dead, hung or worse, by this evening, and here I am with you," he said.

"It's a miracle."

"I don't know if heaven had aught to do with it."

"When I was summoned this morning I was so afraid, I didn't know what to think," Alex said.

"Your queen was trying to trap me with her questions. She already knew exactly what had happened."

"I told her."

He looked down at her in surprise.

"In hope of saving you. Needless to say, it didn't work. She locked me up because she thought I was having an affair with you while I was married."

"I trust you lost no time in correcting that impression. Your virtue remained intact throughout that happy interval. I have the scars to prove it."

"Selby died alone in the Netherlands." Alex paused. "I feel so guilty."

"Why? You didn't kill him, Alexandra, and his death frees us to be together."

"I imagine that's why I feel guilty," Alex said, sighing.

"Will you have much to do for his estate?"

"No, his son is a solicitor. I'm sure he'll do what is necessary. I just want get to Hampden Manor, collect the baby, and then head for Ireland."

"You have no desire to stay here?"

"I have no wish to test the queen's patience with either one of us by remaining in England. She is wont to change her mind, and I will not give her an occasion to do so."

Burke stirred and kissed her hair. "She's an impressive old lady, and clearly feels an affectionate bond with you," he said. "I think that's what saved my rebel hide."

"That, and your handsome face." Alex sighed and snuggled closer to him. "The stories about her are famous. They say when she was young there was no one to touch her."

"There's few who could touch her now."

"I thought you hated her."

"I hated what her overlords did to my country,

but I have to admit that she cuts quite a figure. Her body may be aged and frail, but her mind is as keen as a Saracen blade."

Alex looked up at him and wiped a smudge of dust from his cheek with her sleeve. "Both of us are filthy from the road," she said.

"One of us is filthy from Ludgate." He fingered the stubble on his face, and sat up, swinging his legs over the edge of the bed. "I'll go and get some water from that tart downstairs. We can heat it over the fire."

"Do you suppose she'll have soap, or a length of flannel?" Alex asked.

"I'll try."

Alex undressed while he was gone and was sitting on the chair, wearing nothing but her chemise, when he returned. Burke took one look at her bare arms, the soft curve of her breasts discernible through the thin material covering them, and put aside the basin and ewer he was holding.

"The bath will do for later," he said softly. "Me first."

He scooped her up in his arms, carrying her to the bed. He took her remaining garments off in seconds and looked at her naked body, drinking in the sight.

"I thought never to have you again," he said huskily.

Alex put her arms around his neck and drew him down to her. "You were mistaken."

He lowered his body over hers and groaned

when he felt her yielding flesh beneath his.

"There's something I think you'd best do first," Alex whispered in his ear.

"What's that?" he asked as he devoured her neck with little nibbles.

"Take off your pants."

And so he did.

Epilogue

All's Well That Ends Well

—William Shakespeare

Dublin, Ireland
Autumn, 1600

"Rory, leave that alone!" Alex said, slapping his hand.

Rory dropped the apple he was stealing and said, "Alex, you are turning into a right frightful nag."

"Better that than have you eat up all my preparations before my guest arrives."

"Aye, everything must be grand for your English visitor," he said, rolling his eyes.

"This English visitor was a God-sent friend to me, and if you don't treat her with respect and courtesy, I'll know the reason why."

Rory feigned terror and dropped to the floor,

where little Michael was clinging tightly to a table leg, rocking unsteadily as he attempted to walk.

"Isn't he too young to be doing that?" Rory asked as the baby took a shaky step and then grabbed Rory's arm.

"Tell him about it," Alex said, shrugging. "If I confine him for fear that he may fall, he just screams until I turn him loose and let him tumble around again. That's why the floor is ankle deep in straw, my lad."

"Just like his da," Rory said with a grin.

"Heaven help me," Alex muttered, dropping her knife and scooping the apple peelings into a basket. "One is more than enough for me to handle."

"Where is Burke anyway?" Rory asked.

"Finishing a job with Aidan," she replied.

Burke and his brother were working as wheelwrights and stable hands in the city, repairing carriages and shoeing horses, saving money to buy land in their home district near Inverary. Rory, too, did what he could. Alex's inheritance from Selby would likely have been enough to get them started, but Alex had not wanted to take it and had only agreed when John Selby said he would give her portion to charity. Both of the Selby children seemed eager to be rid of her at such small cost to the estate, and she did not blame them.

"Are you sure your friend can find this place?" Rory asked, offering Michael an apple peeling. The child looked it over studiously and then went back to his wobbly gait, taking two steps and sitting down hard on the cushioned floor.

"I gave her directions in my last letter," Alex replied. She and Burke were renting the second-floor rooms above an apothecary shop in Dublin's Greene Street, not far from the docks. Rory and Aidan were staying in a boarding house a few doors away.

"When is her boat coming?" Rory asked.

"It's due this week, but who knows? Bad weather . . ."

"Or pirates, or sea monsters, maybe dragons," Rory concluded, making a gorgon face at the baby, who chortled delightedly as he tried to stand again.

"Rory, can't you make yourself useful?" Alex asked as the baby stood, waving his arms wildly for balance.

"What would you have me do, Your Ladyship?"

"You can bring in some wood from the back, for a start," Alex said. "I have some baking to do."

"Dishes fit for English royalty?"

Alex gave him a look.

"Settle yourself, I'm going." Rory slipped out the door. Alex heard him rattling around in the woodpile as she put the finishing touches on her tart. It was not exactly the fancy recipe she'd learned in England—several of the more exotic ingredients were missing—but she had already tried it out on Burke, and it had met with an enthusiastic reception.

She was setting aside the confection when Burke came through the door, whistling.

"Where's my boy?" he called, and Michael held out his arms, shrieking joyfully.

Burke dropped his pack of tools by the fireplace and scooped up the baby, kissing Alex on the back of her neck as he passed.

"Walking yet?" he said to Michael, who pumped his legs hard, giggling.

"Trying," Alex said. "Don't get him all excited, Kevin, I've been trying to put him down for a nap all afternoon."

Burke set the baby on the floor and bent over Alex's table. "What's for dinner?" he asked.

"Not that. I made it for Mary Howard's visit."

"Aye. Lady Mary on the Dublin docks, this I must see."

"Be nice. It's very sweet of her to come."

"I hope she's taking care of my Dealanach. He got used to the good life at Hampden."

"Don't joke about it. I'm worried that she won't make it here, many things can happen on the way."

"She's traveling with her husband, she'll be fine. She's as tough as you are underneath, I'm thinking." Burke took a spoon from the table and handed it to Michael, who proceeded to bang it on his foot.

"I hope so."

Rory came in with a bundle of wood and deposited it on the hearth. "I'm off to the pub," he said, winking at his cousin as he passed.

"Be back in an hour if you want to eat," Alex called after him. She waited until the door closed and then said to Burke, "What ails him? He's always at that pub. Is he turning into a drunk?"

Burke grinned. "Alexandra, you are sorely lacking in imagination. He's got a girl there."

The spoon went flying across the room and landed under a chair with a clang.

"Good shot," Burke said admiringly, fetching it.

"What, a barmaid?" Alex asked.

Burke shook his head. "She lives in back."

"Not that little waif with the dun-colored hair!"

"The same."

"Kevin, she's a child."

"She's sixteen. You were seventeen when I met you. You've a short memory."

"Wonderful." Alex reached for a potato and began slicing it. "Will Aidan be eating with us?" she asked.

Burke shook his head. "He got a job, exercising the lord mayor's horses a couple of hours in the afternoon, twice a week. The money is good, but he doesn't like the old boy much. More English than the English, you know."

"Please tell Aidan to hold his tongue. We don't need any more trouble."

"He'll behave, you have my word on it." Burke seized her around the waist from behind and murmured into her ear, "Did you say something about Michael taking a nap?"

"Does he look tired to you?"

They both glanced at the baby, who beamed up at them, drumming his heels on the floor.

"Let's put him in the cradle with some toys. Maybe he'll play for a while," Burke suggested.

Once the baby was settled in the crib at the foot of their bed he gurgled for a while and then fell silent. Alex peeked over the rail and saw that he was asleep, his thumb in his mouth.

She smiled at Burke, who began to unlace her bodice. As he removed her articles of clothing he tossed them on the floor.

"When will you learn to be neat?" she whispered, standing on tiptoe to kiss the side of his neck.

"When I no longer desire you, which will be never," he replied, lifting her onto the bed.

He kissed her, his tongue exploring her mouth, and she responded, turning her head when he moved his lips to her throat. He undressed her rapidly, his fingers nimble with practice. When they were both naked, he rolled onto his back and pulled her on top of him, running his hands up and down her satiny arms, burying his mouth in her flesh. Alex clutched him, closing her eyes and kissing his hair.

"Now," he said, and lifted her onto him.

Alex gasped as he entered her, his breath hot against her skin. He looked up at her, his eyes slitted, hers opening slowly. Then he pulled her tighter against him.

"Come with me," he said, and she did.

Alex wondered if such happiness could possibly last, then decided firmly that she would do her best to make sure it did.

Afterward Burke's hand claimed her breast casually, and she winced.

"What is it?" he asked, sitting up. "I saw that before, when I touched you there. Do you have a pain?"

"I think I am with child again."

He smiled. "Are you certain?"

"I felt the same with Michael."

He bent and embraced her. "A girl this time."

"Who can say? If it is a girl, I want to name her Elizabeth."

Burke groaned and collapsed next to her.

"We owe her our lives," she reminded him.

"I'll be tarred and feathered and run out of the bloody country."

"Then we'll call her the Gaelic equivalent. There must be something."

"Ealasaid."

"Good. I like it."

"That won't fool anybody. They'll know what it means."

"Mary for her middle name, I think. Mairi, right? And there's something else."

He covered his head, as if to protect it from a blow. "What, may I ask?"

"I want to get married."

"We are married."

"I do not consider Hugh O'Neill reciting a lot of

babble over us and cutting a loaf of bread in half a marriage."

"That was fine and noble ancient Gaelic, and it's not my fault you couldn't understand it."

"And what was that ceremony with the salt?"

"Good luck."

"And the wine?"

"A toast, for our health and fertility, like the fruit of the vine." He leaned over to kiss her belly. "It seems to be working."

"Kevin, I'm serious."

He rolled onto his back. "And what sort of a marriage would Her Ladyship like?"

"No more pagan rites, thank you. I want a legal marriage, one registered with the chancery, and I want a church ceremony to go along with it. We can do it when Mary comes. She and her husband will be the witnesses."

"Whatever you say, Alex. If it's that important to you, I'll go along with it."

"Don't you understand why it's important to me?"

He looked at her, his eyes wide and blue.

"I believe in God, and I want him to bless our union," she said.

"Still an English schoolgirl," he said affectionately, brushing a strand of auburn hair out of her eyes.

"I believe in God because he brought me to you and brought us through all of our troubles so that we could be together," she said, caressing his cheek.

"That's reason enough, sweetheart."

She bent and kissed him, and he pulled her down again, rolling her under him on the bed.

"Do we have time?" he murmured, glancing over at the cradle.

"Always," she replied.

And the baby slept on as his parents affirmed the love that had created him.

AVAILABLE NOW

TAPESTRY by Maura Seger

A spellbinding tale of love and intrigue in the Middle Ages. Renard is her enemy, but beautiful Aveline knows that beneath the exterior of this foe beats the heart of a caring man. As panic and fear engulf London, the passion between Renard and Aveline explodes. "Sweeping in concept, fascinating in scope, triumphant in its final achievement."—Kathryn Lynn Davis, author of *Too Deep For Tears*

UNFORGETTABLE by Leigh Riker

Recently divorced, Jessica Pearce Simon returns to her childhood home. Nick Granby, the love of her youth, has come home too. Now a successful architect and still single, Nick is just as intriguing as she remembers him to be. But can she trust him this time?

THE HIGHWAYMAN by Doreen Owens Malek

Love and adventure in seventeenth-century England. When Lady Alexandra Cummings stows away on a ship bound for Ireland, she doesn't consider the consequences of her actions. Once in Ireland, Alexandra is kidnapped by Kevin Burke, the Irish rebel her uncle considers his archenemy.

WILD ROSE by Sharon Ihle

A lively historical romance set in San Diego's rancho period. Maxine McCain thinks she's been through it all—until her father loses her in a bet. As a result, she becomes indentured to Dane del Cordobes, a handsome aristocrat betrothed to his brother's widow.

SOMETHING'S COOKING by Joanne Pence

When a bomb is delivered to her door, Angelina Amalfi can't imagine why anyone would want to hurt her, an innocent food columnist. But to tall, dark, and handsome police inspector Paavo Smith, Angelina is not so innocent.

BILLY BOB WALKER GOT MARRIED by Lisa G. Brown

A spicy contemporary romance. Shiloh Pennington knows that Billy Bob Walker is no good. But how can she ignore the fire that courses in her veins at the thought of Billy's kisses?

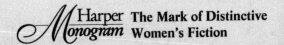

M Harper **The Mark of Distinctive**
Monogram **Women's Fiction**

COMING NEXT MONTH

MORNING COMES SOFTLY by Debbie Macomber

A sweet, heartwarming, contemporary mail-order bride story. Travis Thompson, a rough-and-tough rancher, and Mary Warner, a shy librarian, have nothing in common. But when Travis finds himself the guardian of his orphaned nephew and niece, only one solution comes to his mind—to place an ad for a wife. "I relished every word, lived every scene, and shared in the laughter and tears of the characters."—Linda Lael Miller, bestselling author of *Daniel's Bride*

ECHOES AND ILLUSIONS by Kathy Lynn Emerson

A time-travel romance to treasure. A young woman finds echoes of the past in her present life in this spellbinding story, of which Romantic Times says, "a heady blend of romance, suspense and drama . . . a real page turner."

PHANTOM LOVER by Millie Criswell

In the turbulent period of the Revolutionary War, beautiful Danielle Sheridan must choose between the love of two different yet brave men—her gentle husband or her elusive Phantom Lover. "A hilarious, sensual, fast-paced romp."—Elaine Barbieri, author of *More Precious Than Gold*

ANGEL OF PASSAGE by Joan Avery

A riveting and passionate romance set during the Civil War. Rebecca Cunningham, the belle of Detroit society, works for the Underground Railroad, ferrying escaped slaves across the river to Canada. Captain Bradford Taylor has been sent by the government to capture the "Angel of Passage," unaware that she is the very woman with whom he has fallen in love.

JACARANDA BEND by Charlotte Douglas

A spine-tingling historical set on a Florida plantation. A beautiful Scotswoman finds herself falling in love with a man who may be capable of murder.

HEART SOUNDS by Michele Johns

A poignant love story set in nineteenth-century America. Louisa Halloran, nearly deaf from a gunpowder explosion, marries the man of her dreams. But while he lavishes her with gifts, he withholds the one thing she treasures most—his love.

Harper Monogram **The Mark of Distinctive Women's Fiction**

ANALISE

Analise Caldwell was the reigning belle of New Orleans. Disguised as a Confederate soldier, Union major Mark Schaeffer captured the Rebel beauty's heart as part of his mission. Stunned by his deception, Analise swore never to yield to the caresses of this Yankee spy...until he delivered an ultimatum.

ROSEWOOD

Millicent Hayes had lived all her life amid the lush woodland of Emmetsville, Texas. Bound by her duty to her crippled brother, the dark-haired innocent had never known desire...until a handsome stranger moved in next door.

BONDS OF LOVE

Katherine Devereaux was a willful, defiant beauty who had yet to meet her match in any man—until the winds of war swept the Union innocent into the arms of Confederate Captain Matthew Hampton.

LIGHT AND SHADOW

The day nobleman Jason Somerville broke into her rooms and swept her away to his ancestral estate, Carolyn Mabry began living a dangerous charade. Posing as her twin sister, Jason's wife, Carolyn thought she was helping her gentle twin. Instead she found herself drawn to the man she had so seductively deceived.

CRYSTAL HEART

A seductive beauty, Lady Lettice Kenton swore never to give her heart to any man—until she met the rugged American rebel Charles Murdock. Together on a ship bound for America, they shared a perfect passion, but danger awaited them on the shores of Boston Harbor.

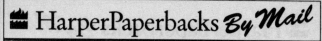